ALMOST PERFECT

ALMOST PERFECT

A NOVEL

DIANE DANIELS MANNING

ISBN-13: 978-0578136394

Dedicated to
the children, parents and staff of
The New School in the Heights
Houston, Texas 77007
www.newschoolheights.org

and

Arthur J. Farley, M.D.

Contents

CHAPTER ONE

Benny Neusner sat on the front porch of the New Hope School shivering in the cold December air. His shrink, Dr. Kate, would say he was angry because his mother was late again. The stupid divorce judge said he could see her every Wednesday after school and every other weekend, but what good was that when a mother was as busy as his? Sometimes he didn't see her for weeks at a stretch. The rest of the time he had to live with his dad and, worse yet, his stepmother Sonya. A boy who's fourteen is old enough to know whether a mom's a good mom or not, but the judge never asked him. Now his mother was poor, and his dad wouldn't give her any money ever again after the last time. At least, that's what his mother said, and she never lied. Sometimes she exaggerated a little, but that was different. At least, that's what his mother said.

He squirmed uncomfortably on the hard bench and tried to shake memories of the divorce out of his head. He had another worry today. More than anything in the world he wanted a dog. A dog would be someone to play with when his mother had to miss one of their visits. A dog would be company when his dad and Sonya left him home alone by himself. A dog would understand how he felt. But no matter how hard he begged, his dad always said no. They'd had the same old fight again this morning at breakfast.

"A boy who hides his homework in a pizza box isn't ready for a dog," Sonya had chirped with a satisfied smile.

"Your stepmother's right," his dad had agreed. "I expect a B in math, or at least a C, before I even think about getting you a dog."

He could never get grades like that. He was different from the other kids at New Hope School who were a bunch of brains. The teachers were kind and gave him special work to do, but school wasn't his thing. A dog was. Not that he wasn't awfully glad for the New Hope School. Dr. Kate had started it to help kids like him with a lot on their minds, and in a way it was his own special place. Look how she had built it practically next door to his dad's, even though it was on a street called Gallows Hill Road where a British spy got himself hung during the American Revolution, and no one could think that was lucky. Redding, Connecticut was full of historical stuff, not that he personally cared much about the old days. He was interested in how his life would turn out now.

The sky was dark by the time he gave up on his mom and started up the hill for home. At that hour he saw no one else. Not that many people used this winding country road any time of day. His dad's only neighbor for a quarter mile in each direction was an old woman who lived in a big Victorian mansion, and he wasn't in any hurry to meet her. He wasn't a baby who was afraid of witches, but there were a lot of mysteries in this world people couldn't be sure of, and he liked to keep an open mind. Just because it was the nineties didn't mean the old woman couldn't be a witch. Why else would she live in a huge house with a turret on top? He had spotted her there lots of nights through a small window, pacing up and down like she had a lot on her mind, maybe spells and stuff. He would have to have a really important reason before he would bother to meet her.

He adjusted the backpack straps digging into his shoulders and decided he would need an excuse for gym tomorrow from all the blisters he was probably getting. They were just doing boring pushups again so it wouldn't matter if he skipped. He shouldn't have tried to carry his whole collection of Spiderman comic books at once, but tomorrow was the last day of school before the Winter Holiday, and he didn't want to take a chance and leave such valuable possessions in his locker. Every few minutes he stopped for a little rest and tipped back his head, hoping to see the special star he and his mother used to watch together. He had learned in science class the star was really a planet, but he liked to imagine his mother was staring at it, too, thinking about him and all the good times they used to have together.

He had almost reached the bottom of his dad's driveway when a cloud moved, and his mother's star appeared. And at that very moment, he heard it: a puppy crying! At least it might be a puppy. He couldn't be sure. He wanted a dog so badly he was afraid he had only imagined it. Not that he heard voices in his head, human or animal. Dr. Kate had told him before that he wasn't nuts, just a little mixed up on account of the crazy life he had been living so far. Sometimes he acted young for his age, but like Dr. Kate said, a boy with so much on his mind burns up a lot of brain power.

He fished around the bottom of his backpack for a flashlight and an extra granola bar before he remembered he had polished it off with a box of Oreos and a carton of juice while waiting for his mother. He patted his little paunch and wished he had saved a couple of cookies, but at least he found the flashlight. He tossed the backpack into the bushes where his comics would be safe and picked up the pace. The weatherman had predicted a blizzard before Christmas. Too dangerous for a little fellow to be alone outside without his mother.

The crying seemed to be coming from the direction of the old woman's house. He would have to climb the stone fence that separated her property from his dad's and walk across a field to get there. If he did it now in the dark of night with only the moonlight and a flashlight to guide him, he could be putting himself in a lot of danger. Still, he wanted a dog really, really badly. He hopped the fence and zigzagged between the cedar trees commando style.

He was halfway across the field when his breath started coming in short gasps. He made a dive for a large cedar tree where he could rest up for a few minutes and his knee bumped on something hidden under a blanket of dead needles. He pointed the flashlight. The rectangular board must have been lying there a long time because it was covered with some awful looking green stuff. He fished around in the needles for a small branch and scraped away the slime. His eyes grew wide. Someone had painted the picture of a poodle with a fancy haircut and the words "Umpawaug Kennels, Elizabeth Rutledge, Breeder/Owner."

He slapped his head with his open palm. How he could have missed something as important as a kennel right next door? Even though he had only been living with his dad and Sonya for six months, he took a lot of pride in knowing what was happening around him. Whenever he relaxed and didn't pay attention, things boomeranged back on him. Elizabeth Rutledge, whoever she was, should be more careful and not leave her signs lying around where people could stumble over them. It made him mad, and when he got mad, he could lose his temper big time.

He checked the picture on the sign again. One thing for sure. The puppy had better not be a poodle. His dad wouldn't let him have a dog — period — but especially not a poodle. His dad said poodles were sissy dogs, and he was right. He had a book with pictures of every kind of dog in the world and he had already picked out his favorite: a brown and white beagle like Snoopy. He wouldn't mind a collie like Lassie, either. A collie might rescue someone from a terrible tragedy like falling through the ice and drowning. The same thing almost happened to him last winter, but it turned out to be a really deep pot hole. Even a dog from the pound would be fine with him, but not one time did he think a poodle with a goofy-looking hairdo was the dog for him.

The sound of crying came again and he pushed onward. He stepped through a hedge of overgrown privet and discovered he had mistaken the way. In the dark and thinking about the puppy, he had walked past the old woman's house and come out on a little rise to the west of it. Even further to west, he spotted three buildings he recognized as The New Hope School. Behind them, light was coming from a cottage at the edge of the school's property that he had seen from Dr. Kate's office window. So far, he hadn't gotten around to checking it out. His dad's house, the old woman's mansion, the cottage and the school were surrounded by stone walls that all looked the same, and he wondered if all that land had once belonged to a rich Yankee farmer a long time ago.

He fixed his eyes on the old woman's turret for a guidepost, and few minutes later he climbed over the stone wall onto her property. Rows and rows of kennels with empty dog runs were silhouetted in the moonlight like a city empty of life. Goosebumps rose on his flesh, and he started to back away when he heard crying again. The sound was coming from inside a small white building about fifty yards behind the old woman's house. The building looked like an oversized storage shed, but it was wood and way nicer than the one where his dad kept the dreaded lawnmower and a lot of old junk nobody used any more.

He gathered his courage. He had come this far; he

might as well finish. The shed had a window, and he shone his flashlight through it. The light bounced off the wall and revealed a room that was a mess even by teenage standards. Crates for carting dogs were scattered around the floor with their doors hanging open. A counter stacked with old magazines lined the far wall. A deep sink like a school janitor's stood at the end. On shelves above the counter dozens and dozens of silver trophies, some with statues of poodles, were stacked in neat rows like forgotten soldiers waiting for orders.

He moved the flashlight, and this time he noticed a door on the opposite side of the shed. It swung back and forth on its hinges, making an eerie, creaking noise he might have mistaken for a puppy. He listened again. No, the sound wasn't the door and it wasn't a puppy. A person was crying, maybe a boy even. Whoever it was, their heart was breaking.

Cautiously, he walked around the shed and stepped through the door. Now that he was inside, his flashlight illuminated a dark corner it couldn't reach through the window. He discovered a sort of stall, only shorter, that might have been meant for a pony. A pony wasn't a dog, but it wasn't bad. He tiptoed closer and pulled the latch. A ghastly squeak pierced the silence, and some awful tasting stuff lurched up from his stomach.

The crying stopped and a gravelly voice croaked from inside, "Whoever you are, you're trespassing on private property."

His heart pounded wildly. If he hadn't been gripping the flashlight for dear life, it would have dropped from his shaking hand. Scared as he was, he couldn't stand not knowing. He peered over the side of the stall. A battery operated lantern added to the dim light and illuminated an old woman hunched over on a three-legged stool. He was pretty sure she was the same one he had seen pacing the turret. Her bathrobe, if that's what it was, had ridden up over her knobby knees, and her curly gray hair stuck out every which way like she had been running her fingers through it. She couldn't weigh more than a hundred pounds. He was pretty sure she was the person crying, so she definitely wasn't a witch. Everyone knows witches don't cry. They hate water and, besides, she'd have shriveled up and died.

"You heard me, boy," she growled. "State your business."

His mouth was so dry he didn't think he could squeeze out a word, but he managed to say, "I heard a noise."

She gave her eyes a hasty wipe and stuffed a crumpled tissue in her pocket. "Noise?" she asked, her scratchy voice full of doubt.

"Sorry, ma'am, my mistake." He backed away slowly, hoping she wouldn't stop him, but she had already lost interest in him like she was used to strangers dropping in late at night. She turned and muttered a few words over her shoulder.

He pointed his flashlight. His jaw dropped. "A dog!" Not exactly the one he had been hoping for, but good enough. It was about three feet tall at the crown, with a chestnut coat, and looked up at Benny with kind, almond shaped eyes. No puffed out mane or pom-pom bracelets like the dog on the sign. Just a short bobbed tail and a fluffy topknot that practically made his fingers itch he wanted to touch it so badly. "I'm glad he's not a poodle," he said, stepping closer.

The old woman signaled the dog to her side and circled her arm around her neck protectively as if afraid Benny had come to steal her. Still, her words were calm enough. "Not he — she, and she's a poodle all right. About to become a mother any time now, maybe even Christmas Day. That's why she's in the whelping pen."

"You mean she's having puppies?"

She nodded, and for a moment he thought she might start crying again.

"I've been wanting a puppy," he said, his voice choked with longing. "Maybe they won't all be poodles."

"They'll be poodles. I made sure of that."

He wondered if the poodle on the sign was the father.

"It's Susie's first litter. That's why I'm out here in the puppy shed checking on her."

He peered into all the dark corners. "Any real dogs around here? I'll take anything that isn't a poodle, even a mutt."

Her thick eyebrows joined in a fierce frown. "Umpawaug Kennel Poodles are famous all over the world. People you see on TV every day insist on them — even politicians."

"You wouldn't be Elizabeth Rutledge by any chance?" he asked. "I saw the sign."

"That's me, but you can call me Bess. Everyone does. And you?"

He closed the middle button on his school shirt that had popped open again and straightened his jacket. "Benny, Benny Neusner. I live in the brick house over there." He pointed with his thumb in the direction of his dad's.

She squinted up at him like trying to decide if she'd met him before. "I've been there," she said without explaining. She gave Susie's topknot a friendly tousle and released her grip on the dog's neck, as if she had decided Benny was safe. She tucked her wrinkly chin against her neck and crossed her arms. "Say, shouldn't you be in school or something?"

He jerked back his head. Was she nuts? Even Sonya wouldn't make him go to school in the middle of the night. "You don't know much about kids, do you?"

She looked down. "No, not much. At least about boys."

"That's what I thought." Come to think of it, he didn't know a lot about old people, either. He'd never had a grandmother, at least not one he'd met in person, and he was kind of glad. A mother and a stepmother were plenty.

"For your information," she said, straightening her spine, "large poodles like Susie here are called Standard Poodles. They're hunting dogs, like a lab or a golden retriever, if you know what they are."

He nodded. "Oh, yes, ma'am. I have a book. No funny haircuts."

She sucked in a breath and spoke through her teeth like she had given this speech a hundred times. "The funny haircut, as you call it, is for show poodles. It's required by the judge."

He pointed at Susie resting her chin comfortably on the old woman's shoulder. "She doesn't look bad for a poodle. No pom poms."

"Susie's show days are behind her. Mine, too. I'm retiring. Selling off the dogs and closing the kennel."

"If you're retiring, why is Susie having puppies?"

She twitched like a flea had bitten her. "They're not mine. I sold Susie a while back. Her new owner tripped on a tennis ball one of the dogs left lying about and broke her wrist. I'm helping her out."

He decided this was as good time as any to leave, but before he could make his escape, the door squeaked open and a second large brown dog stuck his head inside. He had kind, intelligent eyes and a fuzzy coat the color of warm beach sand.

Bess pushed herself up off the stool, her knees cracking with the effort. The dog glanced at Benny with a wag of his tail and trotted over to her. She ruffled his topknot affectionately. "Champion Umpawaug McCreery," she introduced, "the world's top producer of champion Standard Poodles. He's the puppies' father."

McCreery raised his chin a little higher and held his tail in its full upright position.

Benny stuck out his lower lip and bobbed his head knowingly. He had read about stud dogs and was really impressed. He wasn't surprised the old woman was proud of the big guy, but he detected a note of sadness behind her bragging, like she had missed out on something important, or maybe McCreery had. Personally, he couldn't imagine a better honor than being the world's greatest stud.

"Producing great puppies isn't the only honor McCreery has behind him. In his day, he won every important dog show there is."

Benny thought McCreery probably liked the stud part better, but before he could say so, she lowered her voice and added in a whisper even a Jack Russell Terrier might miss, "Except the one."

Tears welled up in her eyes, and he was afraid she might start crying again. Nothing made him feel worse than an unhappy grownup. He knew better than to ask any questions, but he thought about offering her a tissue. Then he remembered the one in his pants pocket was kind of gunked up with melted chocolate, so he turned and held out his hand to McCreery instead.

The big dog ambled toward him, each step falling lightly in spite of his large size. He sat in front of Benny, studying the boy's face. He must have liked what he saw because he stuck out his paw. Benny grabbed it and shook up and down. McCreery jumped up on his hind legs, tail whirring, and tugged the boy's sleeve in an invitation to play. Benny laughed and hugged McCreery around the neck like he would never let go. The big dog pranced on hind feet, sweeping the boy along like they were partners at a fancy dress ball.

Benny turned to the old woman with an enormous grin. "I don't care if he's a poodle. I'll take him."

She signaled the dog to her side and drew him in close. "I'm sorry. McCreery's not for sale."

Benny flushed. "Not for sale? But you said you're getting rid of your dogs."

She stood. "Not McCreery. Never!"

McCreery, a worried frown between his eyes, nuzzled her hand. She stroked his head. It seemed to calm them both.

Benny felt sorry for the old woman, but what about him? He had been waiting all his life for a dog like McCreery. He didn't care what his father said or anyone else. He wouldn't give him up. He started to tell the old woman so when McCreery moved off silently. He and Susie stood nose to nose, sharing dog secrets. Susie yawned, circled in place, and lowered herself back onto the soft bedding.

In his mind's eye, Benny saw newborn puppies snuggling against Susie's belly, taking in their breakfast. One little brown fellow, pushing his legs against the others, was a miniature of his father. McCreery looked down on them all, guarding his little family: mother and father together with their children.

Benny balled up his fists. It wasn't fair. It really wasn't. No way he could break up a family, not even a dog's. He dropped to his knees in front of McCreery.

With a whimper, McCreery looked back and forth between the old woman and the boy. He nuzzled the boy's chin, then turned and leaned against Bess.

Benny wiped his nose on his sleeve and slowly got to his feet. "Good-bye, McCreery. I'll never forget you." He turned and ran into the night.

CHAPTER TWO

Bess hung up the phone and leaned heavily against the kitchen counter. She scowled at the cheerful sun streaming through the window and yanked down the shade. Thankfully, her sister Mona was still upstairs getting her beauty rest. She needed time to prepare herself for what lay ahead and didn't feel like answering a lot of questions that wouldn't change her mind.

Strange, with all she was facing today, she had fallen asleep thinking about the boy with the fine sandy hair and baby smooth cheeks in the puppy shed last night. His open honest face and crescent moon smile when he spotted McCreery didn't fit with his deep, sad eyes. She couldn't think where she had seen eyes like that before — besides in her own mirror this morning. He seemed familiar, like a memory she couldn't grab hold of, but of what?

Perhaps it was the way he had reacted to McCreery. She had observed the scene hundreds of times and knew what it meant. He had lost his heart to the big guy. More surprising was McCreery's reaction. McCreery was friendly, but he wasn't a golden retriever that never met a stranger.

She hated to disappoint the boy, but no way could she sell McCreery. Like she said, he was hers for life. She gladly would have let him have one of Susie's and McCreery's puppies instead. She was entitled to pick of the litter, so she could make it happen, but he wasn't interested. Even if he was, it would be another three months before they would be ready to go, and he didn't seem the type who could wait.

She sighed and pushed the image away. If she kept on like this, she would never get through what lay ahead today. She stuck her head in the refrigerator and discovered he plastic milk container was nearly empty. She tipped the dregs into her mouth and tossed the bottle into the trash. In the old days the milkman left glass bottles topped with thick, yellow cream conveniently on the doorstep. Now Burritt's Dairy had been turned into a farm museum so school children could learn what Redding was like fifty years ago before it got transformed into an ex-urban retreat for New York commuters.

She didn't feel like eating, but common sense told her she'd better have a little food in her stomach. She dropped a piece of homemade cinnamon bread into the toaster, expecting McCreery to come sniffing after the pungent aroma. When he didn't, she decided he'd let himself out the dog door. She placed her hand on the doorknob and automatically stuck out her foot to block a bunch of curious puppies bent on escaping. For a moment she had forgotten. For the first time in nearly a half century, there were no puppies. An unfamiliar tightness gripped her heart like an over-wound rubber band, but at least she had McCreery.

She opened the door and banged on a metal dog dish with a spoon. A moment passed, and she banged again. Still no McCreery. Her breath caught in her throat. Could the love-sick boy have snuck back and stolen him? It had happened more than once to valuable show dogs.

Before the terrible thought could take hold, a flash of grinning teeth and forty-eight pounds of curly brown coat trimmed in a lamb's cut rounded the corner with his lush ears flying. Even at ten years old, the last of the Umpawaug champions was everything a Standard Poodle ought to be:

alert, fun-loving, graceful.

McCreery rubbed his face against her leg in greeting and moved to check out his dinner bowl. Reassured, she poured his breakfast kibbles into a ceramic bowl decorated with poodles in various colors and poses, a Christmas gift from her son David years ago. The dry pellets hitting the bottom sounded overly loud in the oversized Victorian kitchen where a large staff once prepared enormous meals for a growing family. The cracked linoleum floor, the moss green cabinets with glass doors, and the wooden table with spindle legs were unchanged since the last century. Only the new, chef-quality stove and shiny copper pots belonged to the nineties. Mona had brought them with her last summer when she sold the house Benny lived in now and announced she was staying with her — temporarily — until her condo in Florida was ready. Two years later, she showed no sign of leaving. Thank goodness! The mere thought made her shudder even if she would rather die than admit it, especially to her sister. She rubbed her arms vigorously as if to erase the emotions her body had betrayed, but her twin was standing in the doorway and had seen.

"Are you all right?" Mona asked, permitting herself a rare frown. She had been avoiding wrinkles since her twenties. Even at this early hour she wore open-toed mules with two inch heels and an aubergine scarf that trailed behind her. Her artfully tinted hair was perfectly coiffed.

McCreery lifted his head, sniffing Mona's familiar aroma of vanilla and lilacs, and looked back and forth between the sisters, trying to decide if Mona's concern was more than the twins' usual sparring.

"Why wouldn't I be? In fact, I'm more than fine. I just finished phoning the man with the backhoe. He'll be here in a few minutes." For a moment, the shocked look on her sister's face almost made up for the knot in her chest.

Mona dropped into a chair, eyelashes fluttering. "You're

razing the kennel? Two days before Christmas?"

Bess dropped two pieces of bread into the toaster. "I told you I meant it this time," she said, eyelashes fluttering back.

Mona held up her palms as if to block her twin's disastrous choice. "You can't. Umpawaug is the top kennel for poodles in America. You've spent a lifetime building it, not that I would have chosen that life myself," she added with a tug at her scarf.

Bess crossed her arms over her chest. "Well, if that isn't just like you. For years you've been telling me ladies like us weren't brought up to raise a bunch of smelly dogs — not that poodles smell, mind you — and now that I'm retiring, you're first in line to criticize." McCreery padded over and pushed his nose under her elbow. For once, she ignored him.

Mona's artfully made-up face collapsed. She swallowed and forced out the difficult words. "I was wrong, Bessie. Of the two of us, you were the one who found what she wanted in life. I was too jealous to see it."

A smile flickered at the corners of Bess' mouth. "You, Mona? Jealous?"

Mona rose and tossed the end of her scarf over her shoulder. "Oh, for heaven's sake!" She lit the gas stove, cracked an egg into a frying pan and turned, face flushed with self-satisfaction. "It's a good thing you let Hannah Washington use McCreery with Susie. I admit I was against it at the time, but at least you'll have pick of the litter. You don't need a whole kennel for one little puppy." She raised her chin imperiously, signaling the grave sacrifice she was about to make. "You can keep it right here in the kitchen. I won't say a word."

Her twin's kind intentions finally penetrated Bess' carefully crafted armor, and the truth escaped. She dropped into a chair. "No more puppies, Mona," she said, her voice cracking in spite of herself. "I'm too old."

McCreery gave a faint whimper and placed his front paws on her lap. She wove her fingers through his curly brown top knot.

Mona stomped her foot. "Nonsense! If you're too old, then so am I, and that's ridiculous." She paused, studying her twin over the bridge of her nose. "Too old for what if I may ask?"

The answer came in a whisper. "To take a dog into the show ring myself. Standard Poodles are big dogs, or have you noticed? The handler has to be able to keep up so the dog can show off his stride." Mona flashed her loveliest smile, slid the egg onto a plate, and sat. "Is that all? You can hire one of those handler people. Isn't that what Hannah and the rest of them do?"

Bess waved the idea away like a pesky fly. Mona had never met Hannah and couldn't know the woman had no choice. Hannah's club foot, well disguised as it was by special shoes, would prevent her from showing a dog to its best advantage. "Sorry, that's not for me. I've never hired a handler before, and it's too late to start now."

Mona took a quick peek at her reflection in the toaster and pulled her scarf back around. "I'm sorry you feel that way. You don't hear me whining or letting myself go because of a few little inconveniences."

Bess swallowed a sigh. "What if I got in the ring and half-way through my asthma kicked in or my trick knee gave out, and I landed flat on my face? Would that be fair to the dog? To me? I'd rather Hannah gave the puppies the show careers they deserve."

Mona wrinkled her nose. "There's got to be more to it. Old age would never stop a person like you. Something must have happened you aren't admitting."

Bess bit the end of her toast point. A glob of strawberry jam fell unnoticed onto her lap. "Your egg is getting cold.

McCreery will be happy to eat it if you're not going to."

Mona sat and took a small bite, pushing a bit of the yolk to one side to slip to McCreery when Bess wasn't looking. "At least please explain why you're selling the puppies to Hannah of all people. You two were always at each other's throats, trying to one-up one another."

Bess sighed. Mona would never understand why she had picked her chief rival to carry on her kennel's line, but Hannah was the only sensible choice. A beautiful, trusting face was Umpawaug's signature contribution to the breed and the trait most easily lost through careless breeding. In spite of old wounds between them, Hannah was the one person on earth who would keep the distinctive expression alive.

"And what about a good home for the dogs — and love?" Mona added, pulling out all the stops.

"Hannah will love them," Bess said in a whisper. "Don't you think I considered that above everything?" She met her sister's eyes. "I'm finished, Mona. No more dogs."

McCreery rose on his hind legs and circled her face with curious sniffs, like a person reading Braille. "Don't worry, big fella. I didn't mean you." She gave him a quick hug and rose stiffly. She poured the remains of her cereal into his bowl and turned toward the door.

Mona knew without words what her twin intended to do. She stood. "I'll go with you."

Bess shook her head, unable to speak. She reached for the pea jacket hanging on a hook beside the back door and slipped her arms through the sleeves. A wool scarf with worn-down tassels stuck out one end. With a determined yank, Bess pulled it out and hung it around her neck. She took a deep breath and opened the door. McCreery grabbed his favorite toy, a pink and lime stuffed fish, and slipped through the opening ahead of her.

The cold, humid air seeped under her cuffs and down

her neck. She imagined the long, dreary winter ahead and wondered whether it might not be better to postpone the inevitable until spring. The whole world would seem more hopeful then.

Before she could change her mind, the wind caught the loose end of her scarf and whipped it across her cheek like a slap. Its sting snapped her back to reality. Why did she doubt the choice she had vehemently defended to Mona just moments ago? She knew the answer. Her argument was a child's popsicle stick fort held together with cheap glue. Now that her sister wasn't around to argue the opposite point of view, her locked-up fears threatened to escape. Yes, she probably could manage one new puppy. Yes, she was tempted. Yes, she could hire someone to help socialize him, maybe even that strange boy Benny. But no, she could never let a handler take her dog into the ring. Showing dogs wasn't a job; it was a passion. If she couldn't do it herself, her heart would go out of it. Now was the time to stop.

She shoved her hands in her pockets and frowned guiltily. She hadn't admitted the whole truth, not even to herself. Her twin had sensed as much. For a minute back there in the kitchen, she had even been afraid Mona had somehow tumbled onto her secret. But how could she? Only McCreery knew, and even Mona couldn't wheedle it out of him.

McCreery himself had no such gloomy thoughts. Oblivious to the destination and the task before them, he ran ahead in circles, raring to go wherever she took him. They passed rows of empty kennels, each with its own individual dog run, where as many as a dozen Standard Poodles once made up the Umpawaug Empire. Every few seconds he looked back, making sure he was heading in the right direction. Then he disappeared from sight behind a thick clump of laurel bushes.

A chill ran down her spine and it came to her in a flash,

like to someone drowning, how empty her life would be without him. What if she was giving up everything else she cared about today, and ended up losing him, too? She had Mona and her grown son David, but McCreery was different. He was the one creature on earth she felt completely safe with.

A moment later, he reappeared. She snapped her fingers, hiding her relief, and he followed her to the puppy shed. She opened the door, and he dashed in ahead, not even stopping to greet Susie in the whelping pen. He sniffed the room curiously, trying to figure out why they were there. The faint odor coming off his mistress told him heartache lay ahead. He dropped his stuffed fish and stood with his paws on the ledge, ears alert.

The sound of a powerful engine churning up gravel and road debris reached their ears moments before the backhoe appeared around the bend. McCreery pressed against her side, eyes dark with worry riveted on her face. Her hand dropped automatically and began stroking his head. He was the one she usually shared her feelings with, not that she was very good at it even with him, but today a different dog might have been nice. One who didn't share so many memories, one who didn't know her so well.

The backhoe was almost at the top of the driveway.

She tipped back her head and cleared her throat. McCreery recognized the sound and nuzzled his head under her hand. Together they watched the backhoe cut across the driveway toward the rows of silent kennels. She turned away before the first crunch of the blade against wood. Before the morning was over, all that was left of Umpawaug Kennels was a barren field and a puppy shed empty of life.

Chapter Three

Benny sat alone on the front porch. All the other kids had driven off with their parents right after the last note of the holiday concert had been sung, eager to begin the two-week vacation. Even Dr. Kate had left in a hurry for Bradley Field so she wouldn't miss her plane. He could have gotten a ride home with his dad and Sonya, but he was still hoping his mother might make it. She could've had a flat tire or gotten stuck behind a freight train at the railroad crossing in Bethel and think how disappointed she would be if he wasn't there waiting.

She would never disappoint him this close to Christmas by not showing up. His father might be Jewish, but his mother wasn't, and he was sure this year she would bring him something. Maybe even a puppy.

Thinking about a puppy made him remember meeting McCreery last night, and his mouth turned down at the corners. The old woman should have given him the dog like he asked. Big dogs need a lot of exercise. It said so in his dog book, and she was too old to run around and play. Not that he was that crazy about working up a sweat himself, but they could have had a great time curled up on his bed reading Spiderman comics together.

He polished off the last of the tree shaped cookies with red and green sprinkles he had hidden in his pocket and was about to leave when the sound of a car turning into the school driveway stopped him. It wasn't his mother. The engine was purring like a well-fed cat. A black stretch limo glided to a stop at the front steps. Before the liveried chauffeur could come around and open the rear door, a girl about his own age stepped out. Her mother, or whoever she was, waited inside. The girl hurried onto the porch, not stopping to admire the tall white columns, and rushed past him. She picked a window and pressed her nose against the cool glass as if her whole future was hidden inside.

He considered it his duty to know everything that happened at his school, and if the girl was a new student, it was big news. From the way she was dressed, she was probably an escapee from a British boarding school. He'd never actually seen anyone wear brown oxfords with flaps and knee-high wool stockings before except in the movies. On second thought she might be French. All those Frenchies wore berets with striped ribbons down the back. Or was it Scottish people? That would account for the short kilt she was wearing even though it was practically freezing outside.

He spit on his hand and slicked back the fine, sandy bangs that hung limply over his forehead and tried to remember if people from Scotland spoke English. He tapped the girl on the shoulder. "Can I help you?"

The girl whirled around and answered in perfect American, "Not really. My mother enrolled me here for next semester, and I wanted to check it out."

He hoisted his chinos back in place. "I'm Benny Neusner. School's closed for two weeks, but I can fill you in on everything you want to know. I'm kind of an expert."

The girl looked him up and down, not exactly curious but not indifferent, either. More like she was acting out what was expected. She stuck out her chin and locked eyes with him. "I'm Steffie and I have Asperger's. You know what that is, right?"

He felt the old anger rise up inside from all the kids who had called him stupid. Then he remembered it hadn't happened once at the New Hope School and unclenched his fists. "I think we studied it in Health class once, but I might not have been paying that much attention."

"That's understandable. In case you want to know, Asperger's kids are real smart, can't make friends and don't make eye contact. You can read all about it in the *DSM*. That's short for *Diagnostic and Statistical Manual*. It's practically my mother's Bible.

Benny nodded. He had seen one plenty of times in Dr. Kate's office. Once he even used the thick book to flatten out a homework paper he had dropped in the toilet by mistake. The print was real small and looked boring.

Steffie tossed her thick, black hair. "Say, you haven't told me what's wrong with you."

He wasn't sure how to take her question. Every student in New Hope School had a reason for being there, but no one went around bragging about it. He was about to tell her it was none of her business, but she was kind of cute, so he said, "I'm working on my temper."

"Well, don't forget I have Asperger's, so don't expect us to be friends or anything."

He blushed. Being friends was exactly what he had been hoping for, maybe more. Lately he'd been thinking he wouldn't mind having a girlfriend, especially since a dog seemed like a lost cause. "I overheard Dr. Kate telling one of the teachers half the students here diagnosed with Asperger's are really just anxious. I was resting up on the waiting room sofa, and they didn't know I was listening."

Her head jerked up, her brown eyes bright with interest. "Well, I have it. My mother heard about it on one of her programs. *Oprah*, I think. She dragged me to three different shrinks and every single one agreed with her I do. Two docs didn't even have to meet me to figure it out.

He didn't know what to say. Fortunately, he was saved when Steffie's mother summoned her with a flutter of fingers.

"See you next year," Steffie called as she climbed into the limo.

"Yeah, see ya." He hefted his backpack and headed for home wondering if Steffie would forget all about him when the other kids came back, or if this time he might have found a friend he could keep.

Chapter Four

Mona heard the dump truck heading down the long driveway and couldn't resist a peek out the kitchen window at the dregs of Umpawaug Kennels being carted away. Her heart ached for her sister, but when she heard Bess slip in the side door and ease it shut gently, she pretended not to notice. No words of comfort could reach the well of sorrow inside her twin.

She heard the click of McCreery's nails following Bess up the stairs, but when the bedroom door swung open, McCreery began a protesting whine. In her imagination, she saw Bess stick out her foot and block even him from witnessing her sorrow. She heard the door snap shut and the click of McCreery's nails circling the wood floor as he settled down outside the door. With the internal radar of a twin, her own energy plummeted as though she had experienced the end of a life's work, too. Too drained even for tears, she folded her arms for a pillow and dropped her head on the kitchen table. Her last thought before she fell asleep was how much worse it must be for her sister.

The sky was nearly dark when she awoke. She peered up at the kitchen clock, disoriented for a moment, not sure what had awakened her. An insistent tapping at the back door came again. McCreery hurried downstairs, ears cocked, eyes alert. He reached the door ahead of her, pushing his nose through the gap as she pulled it open. A stranger smiled in greeting, his white teeth accentuated by a two day-old beard. His eyes were hidden behind sunglasses although the sun had already dipped behind the horizon.

"Yes?" she said, glad for McCreery's protection in case it was needed, a thought she recalled later with painful irony.

The man took off his cap and held it respectfully against his chest. "Sorry to bother you, but I seem to have lost my bearings. I'm trying to find Route 53 and must have missed the sign." He put one foot on the bottom step, and McCreery let out a warning growl. He was a friendly dog, but Mona hadn't given him the signal to relax.

"You're pretty far afield," she said, keeping up her own guard. Redding's roads were a tangle of ancient cow paths, but Route 53 was clearly marked.

"I was pleased when I saw your light and the sign for Umpawaug Kennels," he said. "I'm a bit of an amateur breeder myself." His eyes traveled over McCreery's body with an almost professional air. "Nice looking dog — the famous Umpawaug Champion McCreery, I presume."

Mona wondered how he knew, but before she could ask, he slipped a large dog biscuit out of his pocket and held it up. McCreery quivered with excitement, his suspicions vanquished. He was only a pet after all, not a trained guard dog. McCreery snatched the biscuit out of the man's hand and slipped out the door into the night.

"McCreery, no!" she shouted, gathering her wits. Bess would never allow a stranger to feed anything to her dog. She rushed onto the back stoop, pushing the stranger aside and stared into the empty night.

"It's all right," the man said. "I have the biscuits made special. My bitch loves them."

Mona barely glanced at him. "Right at the dead end, right at the second stop sign," she said through a clenched jaw.

The man turned, now apparently as eager to leave as she was to be rid of him. Mona shut the door firmly and turned to see Bess staring after him.

"Who was that?" she asked, bending to pick up the toy fish McCreery had dropped by the door.

Mona colored, her anxiety rising. Perhaps her imagination was working overtime. Too many worries jarred loose by the backhoe and troubling thoughts of her sister's empty days ahead. "Some man looking for Route 53. He gave McCreery a biscuit. . . "

Bess didn't let her finish. A wood paneled station wagon, its engine turned off, was rolling silently down the driveway toward Gallows Hill Road. "Stop! Come back," she shouted, running toward the car. The driver switched on the lights, and the engine sputtered to life. Through the back window, she made out the wires of a dog crate. A pair of helpless eyes stared back at her.

McCreery!

She turned this way and that, arms flailing. She took a step forward and then a step back, as though trapped in indecision. A sharp wind cut across the lawn and rustled the branches of the fourteen foot pine tree beside the front door. A string of colored Christmas lights jangled like rusty blades in a tin can, flashing on and off. She sank to her knees, a wail rising from deep within her.

Watching from the doorway, Mona knew it was too late to hunt for the car keys. Even a minute's head start was too much. There were too many forks and side roads the driver could take. She stepped outside and draped her sweater over her sister's shoulders, but Bess shook it off and pushed herself up onto her feet. Without a word, she headed back into the house and slammed the door shut.

Mona slung the sweater over her arm and followed her inside. They stood and stared wordlessly at the toy fish lying limp and lifeless on the floor. They had too much to say to one another, so they said nothing.

Mona phoned the resident State Trooper. At first, he didn't think a missing dog was serious police business, but when she explained McCreery's credentials, he remembered other snatchings of well-known show dogs. The trooper asked for a description of the kidnapper, and she told him what she could. The man seemed ordinary enough, about forty, medium height, medium weight, medium everything. The only thing that stood out was the old fashioned station wagon with wood siding, but then again she could have been mistaken. She hadn't known that detail would be so important. All she knew for sure was it looked like a big car they had owned years ago.

The State Trooper promised to do what he could, but his voice told her he didn't hold out much hope. He suggested they contact fellow breeders and not just for the extra pairs of eyes. Unscrupulous people who ran puppy mills had stooped to thieving before, and the man might try again. Poodles weren't the only dogs that were vulnerable. Breeders of all types needed to be on guard.

Alone in the empty kitchen, Mona couldn't let go of what had happened. She turned everything she could remember about the man over and over in her mind, but nothing new came to her. She would never forgive herself that McCreery had been stolen on her watch, but more immediately she worried that Bess wouldn't survive the loss. Her sister had always put her dogs first. She would go through the motions as long as Susie's puppies needed her, but after that? Even a twin sister couldn't be sure.

CHAPTER FIVE

David Rutledge pulled down the bill of his red and black checkered cap and bent into the wind. The snow had begun falling a half hour earlier, and the steady pace of the tiny flakes promised an old fashioned white Christmas. He was heading for his mother's house with carefully wrapped presents tucked under his arms and planned to stay the day. His Aunt Mona always prepared a feast worthy of a second helping with plenty of leftovers for the next day.

In spite of his cap, the snow began caking his eyelashes, and he was glad he had chosen the shortcut through the empty field that used to house his mother's kennel. He climbed through a gap in the stone wall, taking care not to slip on the slick, wet rocks. If he hadn't sidestepped a rut the backhoe had left behind, he would have missed seeing the small dark mound buried under a half inch of snow. The object was too small for anything that had once been alive except maybe a rodent or a migrating bird left behind by its fellows.

Curious, he stepped forward for a better look, but a veneer of ice hidden under the snow caught him by surprise. His long legs slid out from under him, and he landed on his back. He lay still a moment, taking stock. He could wiggle all his fingers and toes, but his Aunt Mona's carefully wrapped present had been crushed at one corner.

Inside, a cashmere sweater in his mother's favorite cherry red would be safe; so would Mona's signature emerald green inside Bess' box. Every holiday and birthday since they were children, the twins had traded presents, each afraid the other's was better. After thirty-six years, he had found a solution.

He picked himself up, stomped his boots clean and brushed the snow off his backside. Up ahead, smoke spiraled out of the chimney of his mother's Victorian like a Currier & Ives greeting card. He knew the homey illusion was paper thin, but his throat grew tight wishing there would be more than the three of them at the Christmas dinner table this year. At least his divorce hadn't left any kids to divide in half over the holidays. He tucked the presents back under his arm and resumed his trek. Whatever the snow had claimed would have to wait.

He trudged on a few feet and turned. If he didn't satisfy his curiosity, the mysterious object would nag him all day. Swiping his eyes with the back of his glove, he gently brushed away the thin layer of snow. He stared for a long moment, uncertain what to do. Then, cupping his hands like a fisherman scooping his catch, he lifted the tiny object. Steadying it against his chest with one hand, he reached into his pocket for the rolled-up newspaper his mother had asked him to bring. He spread the paper out on the snow, gently dropped the object on top and rolled the newspaper up like a shroud. He stuck the little bundle in his jacket pocket and bent his head into the wind.

Looking through his bedroom window across the snow dusted fields Benny spotted a man in a red and black hunter's cap struggling to keep his footing. He was heading toward the old woman's house. The wind outside was howling like one of the lost souls left behind on Gallows Hill and bent the small cedar trees halfway to the ground. The man must be crazy to be out walking on a day like this. He even retraced his steps to pick something up.

Benny stepped away from the window and flung himself on his bed, rolling over at the last second to avoid scrunching the classic Spiderman comic his mother had sent him for Christmas. She must have bought it at the used-comics store in Danbury. They'd gone there together once, and the place was so cool — dark and dusty with boxes and boxes of old comics, and nobody saying you had to hurry and make up your mind.

He knew his dad had given his mom the money. He'd overheard them talking the last time she dropped him off. His dad came around to her side of the car and signaled her to roll down the window. He slipped her a bunch of bills and told her to get something for herself, too. Benny didn't care whose money it was. It was the thought that counted. Isn't that what people said, especially on Christmas Day?

He leaned on one elbow and sniffed, tilting his head back up at the ceiling. He couldn't help feeling disappointed there was no puppy even if he knew better. The old lady said he could have one of her poodles after they were born, but he'd never be that desperate. He wanted a real dog. His dad tried to make up for disappointing him with the super cool new game he'd been wanting for weeks. They'd even gone to buy a giant Christmas tree together like they did every year, except they laughingly called theirs a Chanukah Bush. It was almost like his dad knew how tough it was to be a half-Jewish boy at Christmas time.

He swung his feet over the side of the bed, wriggled his feet into his slippers and padded downstairs. He gave a quick glance at the blue box lying empty on the kitchen counter. His father had given the pin in the shape of a lightning bolt to Sonya over breakfast, but that was a couple of hours ago. He opened the fridge and pushed the low fat yoghurt to one side. He pulled out the red tin with the picture of old-fashioned people on a sleigh ride and cut off a big chunk of fruit cake. With his mouth full, he picked up the wall phone.

"Hello, Mom. It's me, Benny. Merry Christmas!"

He paused a minute, and then his face fell as he realized he was talking to the answering machine.

"Thanks for the cool Spiderman comic. Did you like the card I made you? The one with the secret money pouch?"

CHAPTER SIX

B ess couldn't remember a Christmas storm like this one in all her seventy years, a regular Nor'easter that would keep all but the most headstrong indoors. Not a pleasant day, but one that fitted her mood. For the hundredth time since the dreadful night when McCreery had disappeared, she tried to shake free the terrible image of him disappearing right in front of her like a magician's trick. From somewhere far off in her mind, she remembered a hand on her shoulder and from even farther away, the sound of Mona's voice saying over and over she was sorry, so sorry. A part of her the size of a baby hummingbird had wanted to reach up and cling to the hand patting her gently, but the feeling was too weak and the hurt too strong. If she had given in to the comfort Mona was offering, she would never forgive her sister for not calling her the minute the man arrived. It wasn't fair to think like that, but McCreery was gone and nothing was fair about that. The fact that his last litter of puppies was about to be born was poor consolation for maybe losing him forever.

She jerked herself upright, nearly toppling off the antique, three-legged milking stool. The puppy shed where generations of Umpawaug puppies had been born, waiting for Susie to whelp, was no place for negative thoughts.

As long as McCreery's puppies needed her, she could manage; but once she'd handed them over to Hannah, she was finished with dogs for good. She couldn't take the heartache one more time.

She reached over and gave Susie a brief pat on the head. Susie looked up with untroubled eyes. Bess didn't know how long it would be before the first puppy arrived, but decades of experience told her it would be soon.

She rose and walked to the window. Cold air sneaking under the window sill made her pull her sweater tighter around her chest. She lifted the blue gingham curtain, now faded with age, and wiped a circle in the mist that had formed in the over-heated room. Mona had sewn the curtain as kind of a house-warming present more than thirty years earlier. Jester had won Best in Show at Poodle Club of America and the Non-Sporting Group at Crufts in England. He would have won Westminster, too, if she had gone ahead and shown him. At the time, she had told herself she had refused the invitation for his health and almost believed it was true. He had developed Giardia by drinking water out of an empty flower pot after a big storm weeks before the big event. The vet said she had nothing to worry about; Jester was one hundred percent his old self again. Still, she demurred. She was young and so was her kennel. They both had years and years ahead to win the greatest dog show in the world.

Her cavalier decision hadn't seemed to hurt Jester's career. His picture still made the cover of every dog magazine, and *Life* did a feature article with photos of a smiling Bess and the champion himself. Better still, he sired his first litter. Three of the puppies finished their championships in puppy coat. The future of Umpawaug was secure, and she could risk financing the kennel of her dreams with clean, spacious spaces indoors and individual runs outside. The special, separate puppy shed came later.

Susie shifted on the bed of shredded newspaper, and Bess checked again. Still no puppy. She wondered how many there would be, and if they all would live. From what she could tell by palpating Susie's belly, it could be a good-sized litter. Hopefully, David would remember to bring more newspaper when he dropped by for Christmas dinner.

"You played in the snow a long time this morning," she told the young mother-to-be. "Even a lab would have whined to come inside. If I hadn't marked off the days since the breeding and taken your temperature, who knows where those puppies would've been born?"

The thought gave her a sudden jolt. She pushed Susie gently to one side. Just as she suspected, Susie had whelped her first puppy without the slightest fuss or bother: a robust black boy, wet and shiny. His mother needed to break open the sack so the puppy could breathe.

"Good girl, go on, lick," she urged, but Susie was already following nature's instincts. It had been that way with every whelping at Umpawaug Kennels, ever since her foundation bitch Hosannah. She shuddered, remembering how pathetically ignorant of the process she was, but mercifully Hosannah knew what to do. While she was flipping the pages of Birthing Puppies for Dummies, or some such guide, the new mother got the job done. Her belated awareness of the risks made her the first to volunteer whenever a neophyte breeder needed help. Hannah was only one of many. That's how they had met. Her chief rival had once been her protégé.

She waited another minute while mother and son finished their introductions. Then she picked up the puppy and held him in both hands up to the light. She counted twenty little pinpricks of toenails and nodded approvingly at the ripples where his black coat promised to grow in thick and strong. She placed him gently on the food scale and weighed and measured him, jotting down his vital statistics in a well-worn spiral notebook. She couldn't remember how many more were stored in file boxes. Every puppy born at Umpawaug Kennels had been recorded the same way. She imagined Hannah kept everything on computers these days, but she had no intention at this late date of changing a pattern that had worked for generations.

She lay the puppy down beside his mother. He latched onto a teat and began sucking greedily. With a pang, she realized she had been hoping for a brown boy like his father. Perhaps it was just as well. If he had been a miniature McCreery, she might have been tempted to keep him. Still, she had a good feeling about this fellow. First-borns often have a special something that makes them come alive in the show ring, and the way he thrust his little legs out at the world made her think he would be a strong competitor. Unbidden, the fantasy she had willed herself to forget rushed up from inside: the famous spotlight shining down on her dog, the gold and purple "W" under her feet.

She shivered, suddenly chilled. Perhaps the wind had crept under the door. She had rigged up a heat lamp to keep the newborns warm; perhaps it wasn't enough. Puppies can survive a while without food, but their biggest danger is the cold. They can't regulate their own temperatures. That's why she had pushed the ancient heater up as high as it would go. She grabbed a chunk of newspaper and rolled it into an impromptu draft catcher to slide under the door, but before she could lay it down, the door swung open with a bone-numbing blast of arctic air. A tall figure hurried inside, collar raised, a black and red checkered cap pulled down over his ears. Only his eyes, dark like her own, were visible.

"Oh, it's you," she said. "I thought you'd be supervising Mona's prime rib. How did you know I was here?"

"It was obvious," her son David answered, stomping snow off his boots.

"Was it?" She didn't know why. "The puppies have

started coming. They don't know it's Christmas." She glanced up at the window where the snow was piling up along the sill. "Good thing Susie waited to come inside to start delivering."

The room fell silent as if she had said the wrong thing.

He folded his scarf, placed it carefully on the counter and breathed a heavy sigh. She looked into his face and wondered if he was remembering another Christmas whelping thirty years earlier. Even a new Flying Ace bicycle with a silver horn under the tree didn't make up for her not being there when he woke up. Mona had tried her best to console him, but he had wanted his mother. She had thought back then that he would never forgive her. She still believed it today.

He pulled out a rusty folding metal chair and sat. "Every time puppies are born it feels like a miracle."

"Leave it to Hannah to spoil my Christmas." She hoped her grousing would disguise her pleasure at the birth of the puppies, but his expression said he wasn't fooled.

"I'm sure Hannah's grateful," he said. He stood and peered over her shoulders, keeping his hands tucked in his pockets. Only Bess was allowed to touch a newborn. "You're sure the puppies are McCreery's?"

"Of course, I'm sure," she snapped. The question of paternity was as important for show dogs as the royal family. "Hannah and I supervised the whole thing. In a way, I'm glad now that McCreery. . ."

He stretched out a comforting hand, but she pulled back unable to cope. She had almost resigned herself that McCreery would be lost forever — like the whippet that disappeared from Kennedy Airport after being shown at Westminster or the puppies of a champion bulldog that were stolen from their own living room. A wood paneled station wagon wasn't much of a clue, and it was the only one they had. The tattoo inside McCreery's ear would prevent him from being sold to a reputable breeder, but the thief probably wanted him for stud to pass off the puppies as some other dog's get.

She cleared the lump from her throat and attempted a triumphant smile. "Twelve weeks and the whole kit and caboodle will be Hannah's to deal with."

She turned her attention back to Susie. Another puppy arrived head first, curled in the fetal position. She urged Susie to break the sac and lick the puppy's nose and mouth clean. Susie dried the puppy and severed the umbilical cord. Moving blindly, the little girl staggered clumsily, seeking food and warmth. Bess weighed and measured her and then helped her to a teat beside her brother.

David smiled down at the scene. "It beats me how a first-time mother instinctively knows what to do. It's like Susie's done this a hundred times."

"Dogs are different than people," she observed wryly. If she hadn't been so preoccupied, she might have noticed the little catch in her son's voice.

Puppies sometimes arrive in pairs and a third puppy, another black boy, was already on his way. She scooped up the first two and lay them down in a small cardboard box. A heating pad underneath a layer of soft towels would help keep them warm.

David waited until she sat back and then reached inside his coat pocket. A frown deepened on his face. Slowly, he unwrapped the newspaper and held its contents out like a gift. "I'm sorry, Mother."

She was silent for a long moment. She always said there is no such thing as a dog without flaws, but her gut told her this brown boy would have been almost perfect. Maybe it was because he looked so much like McCreery the day he was born. She stroked its little head with one finger. "He must have slipped out when Susie was playing in the snow. I had to call her in twice."

His expression looked like he'd knocked the angel off the top of the Christmas tree. "What was I thinking, bringing a dead puppy here? Forgive me."

She waved a hand dismissively and turned back to Susie. Another puppy was on its way, and it was alive.

He rewrapped the tiny body in its newspaper shroud and laid it on the counter.

Before the morning was over, five healthy puppies — two black boys and three girls, two blacks and a brown — were lying together in a heap. Their eyes and ears were closed, but their noses worked fine, so they had no trouble searching out each other and their mother. Bess gave Susie a final pat on the head and struggled to her feet, joints cracking from sitting too long in one spot.

"All done then?"

She flinched. She had almost forgotten her son was there sitting quietly on a rusty folding chair. Her mind had been on the ice puppy. "A brown boy. So like his father," she whispered.

He hesitated, like a man braving the first swim of a long, cold season. "You're entitled to pick of the litter as the stud fee, and now Hannah owes you for the whelping, too. You could keep one or even two — maybe a boy and a girl."

Her face tightened. "Hold it right there," she snapped.

"But without McCreery. . ." He broke off in mid-sentence, the sound of hope draining away.

She stuck her hand out like a shield. "No puppies!"

Susie lifted her head, alarmed by the sharp voices. Bess saw it, too, and calmed the new mother with a touch.

He rose to leave.

"Wait! Did you hear something?"

He shook his head. Obviously, he thought her imagination was playing tricks on her.

Susie peered over the side of the whelping pen, sniffing anxiously.

Bess noticed and got to her feet. "There it is again."

"Maybe," he said, humoring her.

She walked to the counter. Hands trembling, she unrolled the newspaper. The puppy felt like a block of ice against her palms, but his little chest was moving up and down. He was breathing. Alive!

David's jaw dropped. "Hypothermia. The newspaper's saved him so far, but we've got to get more warmth into him."

She nodded. Her fingers were tingling with cold after holding the puppy only a few seconds. She glanced around the room for a solution. There was only one. She opened her flannel shirt and tucked the icy body inside.

"Should I call the vet?"

For answer, she slumped down on the floor, her back resting against the whelping box. The shallow rise and fall of the puppy's chest fell into rhythm with hers, taking in heat from her body, giving off cold from his. Peering down the neck of her shirt, she studied the sleeping puppy, so like the others that had come before him, yet different. Automatically, she rubbed her forefinger gently across the crown of his head.

David studied the scene with a gentle smile. "What will you name him?"

She thrust out her chin, her dark eyes flashing. "Hannah's. I'll call him Hannah's because that's whose he is."

The hope on his face faded like ink on an old letter. "You can't," he insisted, his voice too loud for the small room. "You need him, and he obviously needs you."

She waited a long minute before answering, gathering the strength to say what she must. "What I need is to be left alone. Go, your Christmas dinner's getting cold," she ordered, the hard words coming easier with practice. She pulled her shirt collar up higher around her neck and closed her eyes. The door clicked shut behind him.

She must have fallen asleep because when she awoke, she could feel no difference between her body temperature and the puppy's. He gawped and patted the air blindly as though feeling for her. The gesture was familiar, his father's. She leaned into him and breathed the warm puppy smell deep into her lungs. If he turned out to be half the dog his father was, there was no telling how far he could go. "You're going to be something special. Maybe even the one," she whispered.

Turning his head in the direction of her voice, the puppy opened its soft pink mouth and exhaled a long, contented yawn.

She yanked her hand back like she had seared it on a hot iron. She placed the puppy down beside Susie and watched him toddle his way blindly to his dinner. Using the edge of the whelping pen to push herself up, she rose and walked stiffly to the wall phone. If she didn't do it now, she might never find the courage. She studied the number she had written in pencil on the wall and dialed.

"Hannah?" she said when the voice on the other end answered. "The puppies have come. Three girls and three boys. No, I haven't changed my mind. Yes, all of them."

CHAPTER SEVEN

Benny flopped onto his bed and stared up at the ceiling certain he was the most miserable boy in Fairfield County. His mother was late picking him up for their weekend together, he hadn't seen his friend Steffie all week, and Sonya had taken away his game player just because he said he had emptied the dishwasher when what he meant was he was about to get around to it. Plenty of people exaggerate all the time and never get in trouble. Why did he?

He walked barefoot over to his desk, ruffled the pile of homework worksheets he'd meant to get started on right after the dishwasher and dropped them into the wastebasket. Life was bad enough without looking up a bunch of dumb vocabulary words he'd never use in real life. Besides, his eyes had been kind of itchy ever since Language Arts this morning. Whoever decided to make dictionaries with little tiny print must have been a sadist like that guy in the movie with Jodi Foster. He pressed his nose against the mirror over his dresser and pulled down his lower eyelid. The skin or whatever it was under the lid looked red and squishy, and he decided he'd better show his shrink Dr. Kate on Monday. All that school work could be damaging his eyes permanently.

He checked his watch. His mother said she'd be there a half hour ago. Something really important must have come up to make her late. *Scooby Doo* was coming on TV in a couple of minutes, and he was tempted. The other kids at school used to laugh over it together at lunch, but now they said it was for babies. If only he had a dog, they could watch together on the couch and share their laughs in private.

He went to the window and stared in the direction of the old woman's house. The turret was silhouetted against a gray sky like a castle's on the cover of a Gothic comic — the kind he and his mother loved to read out loud together and Dr. Kate hated. His stomach growled, and he remembered the frozen spinach tofu casserole Sonya had left on the kitchen counter for his dinner. Just the thought made him gag, and he wondered what pathetic supper the old woman was fixing for herself. He assumed it was what people even poorer than his mother ate like canned dog food. He hadn't talked to her for a couple of months, not since the night he thought he heard a puppy crying, but he had watched her from a distance. Odd as it seemed the happiest time of his day was spying on that decrepit old woman in her decrepit old house. At least then he knew for sure one person in the world was worse off than him.

What was that? He cupped one hand up to an ear. Maybe it was only the March wind playing tricks on him, but he thought he heard a noise. He threw open the window and listened again. The old woman said Susie would have her puppies by Christmas, and he was pretty sure that's what he'd heard. It wasn't like the time he'd been fooled. This time was for real, and he wasn't about to miss his chance to find out whether all the puppies were really poodles. If his mom did show up, he'd hear her car a mile away.

He hurried downstairs, climbed over the split rail fence and crossed the field to Bess' house. Dropping down on all fours, he crab-crawled to the picnic table someone had left out all winter and hid under it. The clouds had cleared and the afternoon sun felt warm on his back. A portable pen was set up on the lee side of the house. A graceful brown bitch he recognized as Susie hopped out. Five squealing puppies clawed at the sides and cried after her. The sixth, a round-bellied brown fellow, stared at him intently and wagged his bobbed tail. The puppy was too cute for a poodle, but he had seen all those trophies McCreery had won for being a famous poodle, and the puppy looked just like him. They both had curly brown coats and the amber eyes of the stuffed dog that used to sleep on his bed before his parents' divorce. When he squeezed its stomach, a music box inside played a lullaby.

The excitement of a new visitor was too much for the puppy, and the same eagerness for life that had turned him into a popsicle the day he was born grabbed hold of him again. He skittered back to the furthest corner of the pen and made a running leap. He just missed clearing the top and see-sawed back and forth on the rim, legs running in air. He heaved himself off and fell back into the pen, rolling onto his back. Unfazed, he shook his coat and leaped again. This time he landed in a heap on the ground outside. His eyes widened in delighted surprise. A shiny-coated black boy who was nearly his twin started to follow but thought better of it.

Benny started to laugh but choked it back and scrunched lower when a door creaked open. The old woman stepped out of the house with a stack of magazines in her arms. The puppy scrambled toward her with a cheerful grin unconcerned that he had escaped without parole.

Bess tried not to look, but she couldn't stop herself. The eyes of Umpawaug champions all the way back to Hosannah gazed up at her trustingly. A lifetime of feelings rose up in her lungs, threatening to suffocate her. She dropped the magazines on the picnic table and scooped up the truant, holding him out with both hands to ward off the warm puppy smell. The little fellow was six weeks old already. Four more and he'd be ready to leave. She'd be safe.

She lowered the puppy back into the pen, picked up her magazines and nearly stumbled over the foot sticking out from under the picnic table. She dropped her gaze, and Benny's open face, untouched as yet by teenage fuzz, stared back at her. Balancing her magazines on one arm, she wriggled an index finger to summon him out.

Benny turned his head from side to side, hoping she was signaling some other boy.

"Yes, you," she called in a croaky voice. "Who else could I mean?"

He scrambled out and brushed off his knees, smiling sheepishly. "I dropped by to say hello to McCreery. I didn't want him to think I'd forgotten him."

The old woman swallowed. Apparently the boy hadn't seen any of the Missing Dog signs posted all over town. "He's not here," she said, voice cracking. She couldn't trust herself to say more. She couldn't explain it rationally, but she was convinced McCreery was alive. She would know if he were dead. She understood the wives of soldiers felt the same when their husbands went missing in battle. Still, knowing McCreery was alive wasn't much comfort. Alive, but in what shape? He might be a great champion in the show ring and a prolific stud, but at the end of the day he was a pampered pet with no survival skills except the instincts he was born with. If he didn't find a way to escape and come home soon, he could be gone for good.

She looked more closely at the boy, staring at the puppy with hungry eyes. Shouldn't he have been more curious about McCreery's whereabouts? No one had ever fallen harder for McCreery. Could the boy have been the culprit, maybe convincing someone to kidnap the dog for him?

She shook the thought out of her mind. He was an

innocent if ever there was one. It gave her an idea. "How would you like to play with the puppies? They need someone who can run around with them and get them used to people."

He turned to find six eager faces and twelve over-sized paws scrabbling at the side of the pen, begging for attention. "No, thanks. I told you before. I'm not interested in poodles."

Her thick eyebrows flicked in surprise. What kind of a boy was he anyway? Most kids his age would give their eye teeth for an invitation like that. She shifted her magazines to her other arm. "If you don't want to help with the puppies, maybe you'd like to carry some of these magazines."

He pulled his mouth into a straight line. "No, thanks," he said again. "My stepmother says I'm lazy." He made it sound like a virtue.

She stifled a chortle and handed him half her magazines. The effort set off a coughing spell.

"You shouldn't smoke."

"I don't smoke. Well, only two a day now. Filthy habit." She signaled him to follow.

"My mother smokes," he said, hefting the magazines. He stuck out his chin, daring her to criticize. "You don't have cancer or anything, do you? You've got these dark circles under your eyes."

"No. Not yet, anyway. Your mother?"

"Hell, no! I'd never let that happen."

"I didn't know you could control something like that."

A couple of *Dog Worlds* slithered off the top of his pile. The dates went back to the sixties. He bent to retrieve them. "You know, this job'd go a lot faster with a wheelbarrow."

"Wish we had one," she said, not sounding sorry at all. "Mona said if I was serious about retiring, I'd get them out of the living room. She's my twin sister."

He slapped his thigh. "So there are two of you. I never

knew old people could be twins before."

She laughed her croupy laugh. It felt rusty, like she hadn't used it in a while. "We've been twins for seven decades now. We're nothing alike, though."

Susie heard Bess' voice and came running. She gave Benny a friendly sniff and rubbed her muzzle against Bess' pant leg. Bess ruffled the dog's topknot and signaled Benny to follow her inside the puppy shed. Dozens of magazines, all with champion dogs on their covers, spilled off the counter onto the floor. Bess dropped hers on top. She plucked a dead leaf from a geranium plant that had managed to survive the winter and twirled it nervously between her thumb and forefinger.

She nodded at the pile. "Drop yours there, too."

They landed with a thud. He bent over and rested his hands on his knees. "I'm not sure I should be doing all this heavy lifting. I'd hate to have to spend the night in the hot tub and skip my homework." He cleared a spot on the counter and hoisted himself up. "You got any kids?" he asked after a pause. As long as he kept her talking, she couldn't make him haul more magazines.

She sat on a rusty folding chair. "David's a grown man. Thirty-five, no six. He lives over there." She pointed vaguely in the direction of the stone wall that divided the school from the dregs of Umpawaug Kennels.

"I've seen his cottage from Dr. Kate's office window, but I haven't had time to introduce myself. Emptying the dishwasher and stuff. You know."

"David and I aren't on the best of terms," she said and blushed, puzzled by her own honesty.

"What'd he do? Steal money out of your wallet?"

"Nothing like that. He thinks he knows what's best for me."

"Maybe you should listen."

She tossed the dead leaf away. "Too late."

Susie caught the sorrow in Bess' voice and leaned against her thigh. Susie might belong to Hannah now, but she was Umpawaug through and through. Bess laced her fingers through Susie's coat the way a drowning sailor clings to the gunnels of a lifeboat.

Benny bounded to his feet and began pacing nervously. "I'm glad your son isn't trying to buy your house out from under you or anything. That's what happened to my mom. Well, not exactly, but she got kicked out for not paying the rent." He lowered his eyes. "I'm saving up in case it ever happens again."

The sound of a horn made them both jump. Benny popped up like his seat was on fire. "My mom!"

She watched him scurry down the hill, arms wind-milling. He reminded her of someone. She couldn't think who. It gave her an empty feeling inside, like an unfilled promise. In the distance, she could just make out a lone van hurrying down Gallows Hill Road. She recognized its ochre paint. Every holiday and birthday for almost thirty years it had arrived at her house with two sets of identical flowers. The flowers grew more elaborate with each passing year.

Benny must have seen it, too. He hung his head and walked slump-shouldered toward his dad's.

Bess raised herself off the bench and continued her work alone.

Chapter Eight

Benny stuck his hands in his pockets and swaggered out of Dr. Kate's office, chin tucked, chest out. She had just appointed him official school messenger which meant he was responsible for bringing the attendance sheet to the office every day. The job gave him the perfect excuse to stretch his legs and keep an eye on what was going on at the school.

Voices were coming from the playground where Ms. Kim's class was having recess, and he decided the attendance sheet could wait. He readjusted his waist band and ambled over to where a bunch of kids were shooting hoops. Other kids were hanging out together in small groups. Sitting cross-legged on the porch, off by herself, was Steffie. At least, he thought it was Steffie. The girl's hair was tied up in braids on top of her head, and where her coat was open he could see a dress with a bunch of little red and yellow flowers and a frilly white apron like a girl in a movie who loved Swiss cheese and goats. He thought she had painted freckles on her nose and cheeks, but he couldn't be sure. She was holding a thick book. Like he guessed, it was the *Diagnostic and Statistical Manual.*

Steffie pushed the bangs out of her eyes and looked up. "I'm studying up on Asperger's. There's plenty of good stuff in here that tells me all about my symptoms. I'm thinking about making a list and posting it on the refrigerator."

He gave her a doubtful look. "You're kidding, right?"

"My mother doesn't think so. For example, I shouldn't be talking to you. Asperger's kids don't know how to make friends, remember?"

He tossed the attendance sheet on the porch and plunked himself down beside her. "Maybe I can help. I've got lots of friends." He blushed. "Well, maybe not so many, but there's Adam. He's got Asperger's, too."

"Friends suck. As soon as I make one, my mother yanks me out of school. She'll do it again. Wait and see." She rose and pointed at the crumpled attendance sheet. "You need that?"

He shrugged and stood, too. "Not that much."

Steffie wrinkled her nose. It made her freckles pucker.

He decided she had used a brown magic marker. He nodded at her thick leather boots like mountain climbers wear. "You into goats or something?"

She stared at him for a second and her face cracked into a smile. "I never met a goat I didn't like," she said.

He felt his hands tighten into fists. Was she mocking him?

She held up a hand and waved her words away. "Sorry, it's a joke. I never met a goat in my life. You?"

He shook his head with an embarrassed grin. "Funny. Personally, I like dogs. Except for poodles. I'm into real dogs." He bent his head closer and looked hard. "Say, are you supposed to be staring at me like that? I thought you said Aspies don't make eye contact."

She brushed at her skirt and grinned sheepishly. "Good one. Not much gets past you, does it?"

Benny's heart swelled with pride. His heart soared. Maybe Steffie wouldn't turn out to be just another girl who thought he was a couple nickels short of a quarter.

His stomach gave a loud rumble and he remembered the cookies the school secretary kept in her desk drawer. He gave Steffie a sharp salute, ironed the attendance sheet with his hand and headed for the office.

He had only been back in class a few minutes when boredom began creeping in again. Ms. Jeanette was teaching about gerunds and participles and a lot of useless junk that was a complete waste of time. He'd been speaking English for years and nobody had ever complained they couldn't understand him. He was thinking about having a little nap when he spotted something suspicious out the classroom window. A stranger in a tweed jacket and a red and black checkered cap was peering under the deck of the main building the way he'd seen spies do on TV when they were hunting for secret messages.

"Gotta go, Ms. Jeanette," he called, holding his crotch and jiggling up and down like he couldn't hold it. He dashed out the door without bothering to hide the fact that he was heading in the opposite direction from the bathroom. At least he had the presence of mind to grab Volume A of the *Encyclopedia Britannica* in case he needed a weapon. Volume A was one of the thickest and the only one he'd had a chance to look at so far. Not to mention it was closest to the door. Ms. Jeanette probably thought he was planning to read it on the pot.

Fortunately, the stranger was so engrossed in looking behind the bushes he didn't notice him sneak up behind. "Stay where you are," he commanded. He'd been planning for his words to come out in a deep voice, but they eeked out in a squeak.

The stranger spun around. Even under his tweed jacket, the strength in his muscles showed. "Aren't you supposed to be in class?" he asked, like Benny was the one doing something wrong.

Benny wished he'd let someone know where he was

heading. Think of the irony — a word he'd learned from Ms. Jeanette one time when he'd been paying attention. A few minutes earlier he thought nothing exciting would ever happen to him and now here he was in terrible danger, maybe about to die. "If you know what's good for you, you'll beat it out of here. Dr. Kate's probably calling the cops this minute."

"You don't say," said the stranger, apparently unconcerned.

Benny considered telling him he'd been duck hunting with this dad before and was a good shot with a rifle, but he decided to memorize the man's face instead so he could give the cops a good description in case he was wanted for anything big. The stranger hadn't shaved, and the shadow around his mouth and chin heightened the kindness in his eyes. His thick eyebrows reminded Benny of someone. He couldn't think who. He was pretty sure the man's coat had a fancy label inside like his dad's. Still, there was such a thing as rich perverts, and he wasn't about to take a chance.

"This is a therapeutic school," he said, bouncing anxiously from one foot to the other. "My father says half the kids would end up in headlines if it weren't for Dr. Kate." He remembered a teenage boy hardly older than him had snuck into a Boy Scout camp with a gun last summer. All the teachers said things would have turned out differently if he had gone to The New Hope School. There was too much talk about gun control and not enough about mental health for kids and parents, they said.

The stranger reached into his pocket. Benny was sure he was a goner, but the man only pulled out a pipe. He tapped it on the bottom of his shoe before sticking it unlit in his mouth. "I'm David, David Rutledge."

Benny wrinkled his nose, considering. "Any relation to Bess Rutledge?"

David's eyes widened. "She's my mother. You know her?"

Benny shrugged. "Sure, she's a real nut about dogs, at least poodles."

David laughed. "That's her. At least, she used to be. Actually, I'm kind of worried about her."

Benny tipped his head. "Really, she seemed fine to me except old."

David picked up a stick and broke it into little pieces. "You know what depression is?"

"Sure. Plenty of kids at my school have it. Not me, though. I wouldn't be caught dead."

David covered a laugh with a cough. He scattered the broken sticks on the ground and studied them as though they could tell the future. "My mother's dreamed of winning Westminster her whole life. She's been invited dozens of times, but something always seems to get in the way."

"Weird!"

"Maybe. Anyway, now she's got this puppy that could keep her hopes alive, but she refuses to have anything to do with him."

Benny picked up a stick of his own. "She does seem kind of pig-headed, but I thought she liked poodles. What's so great about this Westminster, anyway?"

David tugged on the beak of his cap. "Sorry, I was brought up believing everyone knows Westminster. Actually, it's the biggest dog show in America, maybe the world. Twenty-five hundred dogs, two hundred sixty-five breeds. It's the oldest continuous sporting event in America except for the Kentucky Derby. They've held it every year since 1877, through blizzards, national depressions and two world wars."

Benny thought he'd probably go if someone gave him a ticket but watching a bunch of fancy dogs parading around a ring wasn't his idea of fun. His eyes lit up. "Say, I've got a great idea. If she doesn't like the puppy, why doesn't she take McCreery? He's a great-looking dog. He could win Westminster for sure."

"Good question. I've wondered myself for years." He narrowed his eyes. "You know McCreery?"

"Sure, I'm Benny Neusner. McCreery's practically my best friend."

David took off his cap and rubbed his hand across his head before replacing it. "McCreery's gone. Stolen. That's why I'm here. Someone said they thought they'd seen him at the school."

Benny gasped. "I went to visit him yesterday, and Bess didn't say a thing. We've got to get busy and find him." He turned on his heels and headed for the street.

"Wait!" David called. "You can't just leave school without permission. McCreery was stolen weeks ago."

Benny flung out his arms. "We've got to do something."

"Believe me, I've tried. People on the Lost Dog Grapevine have called from as far away as New Orleans, but so far no luck."

Benny squared his shoulders. Like Dr. Kate always said, anger felt better than sadness. "Bess should have sold me McCreery when I asked."

"We can't give up hope. He still might be found."

Benny spat. He knew all about hope. It led to broken hearts.

"For my mother's sake, I have to keep trying."

Mothers were something Benny understood. He looked up at the sky, his hands steepled together as if praying. "I'll find you, McCreery. That's a promise."

"You can't make a promise like that," David stammered.

Benny shrugged. "I just did."

"Really, we've tried everything. My mother even hired a private detective, but it hasn't done a bit of good."

Benny squared his jaw. "As soon as school's over, I'm on

the case."

"I don't want you to get hurt," David said, his voice softer.

"No sweat. I'm going to find him."

Benny broke up the stick he'd been holding and threw the pieces on the ground. When they didn't tell him anything special, he asked something else he was curious about. "You married?"

David shook his head. "Divorced, no kids."

Benny nodded knowledgably. "My mom's divorced. My dad, too, but he's married again. Maybe you should meet Dr. Kate. She's not bad looking for a meeting doctor." He pointed to a second floor window overhead. "That's her office up there."

David gave a hard look as though hoping for something. "A meeting doctor? What does a meeting doctor do exactly?"

Benny shrugged. "Nothing, just have meetings with kids all day. Parents have to pay her lots of money, and all she does is sit around and talk about feelings. I'm thinking about being one myself."

David stuck his unlit pipe in his mouth to stifle a laugh. "Sounds like a good deal."

Benny nodded. "Dr. Kate would probably like to meet you. She loves taking people around our school." He lowered his voice conspiratorially. "I think she's trying to get money to keep the school open." He gave David a piercing look. "Say, do you have a job?"

"Not as good as a meeting doctor. I'm what they call a CPA — certified public accountant. I help people manage their money."

"You have to know your times tables?"

"I'm afraid so."

"That's what I thought. Sounds boring."

The door of the old carriage house where Benny's class

met swung open. Benny's friend Adam waved at him. "Hey, Benny. Lunch."

"Gotta go," Benny said and hurried off.

CHAPTER NINE

David watched Benny disappear inside his classroom and turned to leave. He was startled to see a slight woman about his own age blocking his path. Her eyebrows were pulled into a slight frown, and he wondered how long she had been eavesdropping on his conversation with Benny. He thought she had chosen her severe navy blue suit so people would take her seriously, but her sling-back heels with criss-crossed straps revealed a lighter side. "Dr. Kate, I presume," he said, tipping his cap with an exaggerated old-fashioned bow.

She held back a smile, recognizing the literary allusion. "You presume correctly. You have an appointment?" she asked, suspicion clouding her tone.

"I was looking for my mother's dog, and Benny and I got to talking. He's been telling me about you. I was curious." She frowned again, and he added quickly, "Ooops, that didn't come out right. What I meant is I've been meaning to introduce myself. I'm your neighbor, David Rutledge."

She hesitated, then held out her hand. "Kate Kumar. You're the man who lives in the cottage behind us?"

"That's me," he admitted, holding on to her hand a moment longer than necessary. He checked her fingers. No rings but a gold bracelet dangled off one wrist. A little dirt shown beneath her clear nail polish. He had noticed her earlier with some children in the garden. Maybe Benny was right. Dr. Kate might be worth taking a chance on. She was intelligent and kind, at least to troubled children like Benny, not to mention beautiful with her café au lait skin and surprising green eyes.

She tucked her hand behind her back, blushing. "I was helping the children plant zinnias. I hadn't planned to get involved. It just happened."

Something in her manner made him think she wasn't spontaneous very often. "Sounds like fun."

Her ankle turned in for no apparent reason, and she teetered a little. The movement was so slight he almost missed it. It must be an effort to chase after a bunch of kids like Benny all day in high heels.

"A lot of the neighbors weren't too happy when they heard we were opening a therapeutic school. Afraid the kids would wear Mohawks and tattoos, but we're nothing like that."

"Most people probably think your school's an improvement over a bunch of barking dogs," he said. "I guess you know the school is on land that used to be part of a famous kennel. My mother's actually."

The tension around her mouth eased. "I hope I didn't insult you, but I can't have strangers hanging around my students. Benny spends too much time wandering the campus when he's supposed to be in class. Fortunately, I can keep an eye on him from my office window."

He wondered whether she had ever watched for him. She had known where his cottage was. "Benny seems like a good kid but maybe not too sure of himself."

She looked down, the tension reappearing in her shoulders. "I don't want to be rude, but I can't talk about my students."

He stepped back, waving a hand and smiling. "I didn't

mean to pry."

She pushed back her bangs, revealing a smooth broad forehead, but the dark circles under her eyes told him she'd been losing sleep over something. "No offense taken. I can say that my job is to help parents better understand and accept their children's strength and weaknesses."

"Sounds like a challenge."

"Some special children can have a brilliant understanding of a complicated emotion one minute and the next throw a pencil against the wall because they can't solve a simple math problem like 2x3. It can be confusing."

He lowered his eyes. "I hope I haven't added to your difficulties. I had to give Benny some bad news"

Her face fell. "Oh?"

"A dog of my mother's was stolen. Apparently, Benny was fond of him."

"How terrible. Your mother must be heart-broken."

He nodded. "That's putting it mildly. She still has a whole litter of puppies — one that's extremely promising, but she's refused to keep any of them. I suspect she's afraid she'll get her heart broken."

She nodded.

The thoughtful look on her face reminded him she was a shrink. Some men might feel intimated, but he took her agreement as a compliment. "Actually, Benny's given me an idea," he said.

She fingered her chin. "Really?"

"I was thinking I could hire him to help me with the promising puppy, maybe even take him to a couple of dog shows. Just small ones, nothing big."

"Benny? He owns a pet gerbil and a couple of garter snakes, but no dog."

He leaned forward. He wanted to please her more than anyone for a very long time. "It might help him get over McCreery."

She drew herself upright. "Help? Or lead to more heartbreak? Not to mention Benny's father would never allow it."

"Lots of kids get over losing one dog by getting another."

Her jaw tightened. "Benny's a student in this school for a reason. No offense, but better leave him in the hands of the professionals."

One side of his mouth slid into a half-smile. "It's just a puppy, not rocket science."

"I'm talking about his heart, not his brain," she shot back. "Your intentions may be good, but Benny's had enough disappointments in his life already. I can't let you build up his hopes for nothing." She looked at her watch. "If there's nothing else?"

He pulled down the beak of his cap, camouflaging his face. "No, nothing."

Banging the gate behind him, he wondered what in the world ever gave Benny the idea Dr. Kumar would be his type.

⚜ ⚜ ⚜

"Benny's been off his game lately, have you noticed?" Benny's Dad asked his wife Sonya.

"Noticed? I'll say. I left a tray of chocolate chip cookies cooling on the counter while I went to change my shoes, and when I got back Benny hadn't snitched a single one. You could have knocked me over with a feather."

"Think he's worried about something?"

"Could be he's still pining over that dog he wants. I wouldn't worry. Kids are always upset about something."

"Maybe, but he'll never get into law school with his grades."

"Law school? He hasn't even made it to high school yet.

Remember what Dr. Kate told you: Benny's not you."

"Shrinks don't know everything. Benny's just like me. I needed someone to keep my nose to the grindstone when I was his age. Now it's my job."

CHAPTER TEN

Fun House Friday was an incentive the teachers used to motivate their students. The children earned this special time to relax with their friends if they finished their class work, did their homework, and stayed in charge all week.

This Friday Benny had earned the privilege easily mostly because it was standardized testing week and homework was cancelled. Hands in his pockets, he sauntered around the converted carriage house hoping to find Steffie. He didn't see her right away, but he did notice his friend Adam Sarkejian. Adam was thirteen and tall for his age. People said he looked like a young Abe Lincoln with dark skin because he had loose arms, loose legs, a bent spine and sad, sad eyes. Adam was plenty smart and already doing calculus, but he was shy and didn't hang out much. Mostly he was crazy about Prince Valiant, his favorite cartoon character, and drew him every chance he got. He even kept a pile of old comic strips from the Sunday paper in his locker, so he could study them when he finished his schoolwork early. His greatest regret was he was born ten years too late to meet Hal Foster in person, the man who created Prince Valiant, but at least he got to pass by the house where Hal used to live every day on his way to school.

For once Adam didn't have a colored pencil in his hand.

He was playing chess with a girl Benny didn't recognize. That was a surprise. The only new student this semester was Steffie, and this girl looked nothing like her. No British boarding school uniform; no Swiss goatherd outfit. This girl's hair was blond and hung down in corkscrew curls. Red ribbons were tied at the top of every one of them. It must have taken hours to fix. Her frilly white blouse had a matching red bow at the neck and topped a short red skirt with white polka dots. Black patent leather shoes and white socks with lace rims finished off her outfit. He had never seen anyone look so out of it except some goofball little kid who sang about lollipops in a black and white movie. Not exactly girlfriend material.

Benny sat at the far end of the long table and pulled his geography book out of his backpack. He had chosen it because it was the thickest. He didn't want the girl to think he was a dummy or anything. He gave the chess players another look over the top of the page, and that's when he realized his mistake. The girl *was* Steffie and from what he could tell from her body language, she wasn't enjoying herself. She stood and arched her back like a cat.

"I'm tired of sitting," she announced to the room. "The List says Aspies can concentrate for long periods of time, but so what?" She nodded at a small girl reading a book by herself. Even though the day was warm, the girl was huddled inside a wooly white coat that looked like polar bear fur. "Taylor will finish my game."

Silently, Taylor stuck a finger between the pages to mark her place and joined Adam at the table. Neither of them said a word while she studied the board. She chose a pawn and made her move.

Steffie picked a chair opposite Benny and helped herself to popcorn. He was glad she had decided to give up the chess game. He didn't want her to find out he couldn't remember all those crazy moves. Besides, this was as good a time as any to tell her about McCreery, but her eyes were focused on something over his shoulder. He turned. Dr. Kate was opening the carriage house door for a man he recognized. She had a smile on her face like she had just won the lottery.

"Is that man Dr. Kate's husband?" Steffie asked, twirling a corkscrew curl around her index finger.

"Naw, he's my friend David. She's not married. All she does is work. I'm trying to help her with that."

"You must be getting through. She's really putting the moves on him."

"Dr. Kate always looks like that when she's trying to get money for the school. To tell the truth, the first time they met things didn't go so great. He thought she was a control freak, and she said he was sticking his nose in where it didn't belong. I've been working on it. I told her David is crazy about the school, and I convinced him she'd love to show him around." He hooked his thumbs under his armpits and grinned. He was convinced the new braces on his teeth made him look more mature, especially with the cool blue rubber bands.

Steffie jutted out her head like a turtle. "Jeez, don't you think they're kind of old for dating?"

He looked again. David's smile was as big as Dr. Kate's. If he didn't know better, he'd think they were flirting. "Dr. Kate says you're never too old, but she might have been trying to convince me I have plenty of time for sex." He clapped his hand over his mouth. Too late he realized he shouldn't mention the "S" word to a girl with a head full of ribbons. "Sorry, I've got a lot on my mind."

"Can I help?"

He shrugged, his happy mood sliding away like custard on a fork. "Someone stole McCreery. "He's my best friend — for a dog," he added tactfully. "He's been gone for weeks. I'm afraid if we don't find him soon..."

His voice trailed off, unable to finish. He wanted to find McCreery so badly he even dreamed about it. In fact, he'd had the same dream practically every night since he had learned McCreery was missing. Dr. Kate warned him that dreams show us our wishes and don't always come true, but he was sure this dream was real.

Steffie reached out her hand and for a minute Benny thought she might touch his arm. "I'm really sorry," she said instead. "There must be something we can do." She fussed with the lace tatting around the rim of her sock and then tilted her head up. "I've got it. We can make posters and spread them around town in the limo after school."

He dropped his chin. David had already tried that, but Steffie was being awfully nice. She had never even met McCreery, and Aspies aren't supposed to be that interested in other people's problems. "It won't hurt to try. We can't give up."

She smiled. "True. Now, we need a description."

He straightened his shoulders. "That's easy. McCreery's the most famous poodle in the world, but he doesn't look like one. You should see all the trophies he's won."

She nodded. "That's probably why he was stolen." She rose and grabbed her backpack from the back of her chair. "Come on. You tell me what to say and I'll type."

He scooped a last handful of popcorn and followed her to the Art Supply shelf. They had to find McCreery soon. They just had to.

CHAPTER ELEVEN

Benny shivered at the end of the school driveway with his hands stuffed in his pockets. He and Steffie had tacked up posters about a missing dog near every school in Fairfield County, and the weather hadn't bothered him a bit. Now, waiting for his mother, the sharp March wind cut through his jacket straight to his bones. He would have punched anybody in the face who said they felt sorry for him. That wasn't exactly what he'd done to get kicked out of his old school, but a girl said the wrong thing at the right time, and her desk sort of got knocked over. The principal told his dad it was one meltdown too many, and he would have to go. No one figured out he actually had a crush on the girl.

He stepped out into the middle of the road and peered ahead as far as he could see. No car yet, but at least his mother was coming. Not like last weekend when she had a really good excuse. A sales clerk at the mall had insisted on checking her credit card and made her so late getting started they wouldn't have gotten home in time to find out whether the lady on TV would win all that money — something she and Benny were both really excited about. Saturday there was always too much traffic, and besides, they would just have to turn around and face more cars on Sunday.

He pushed up his sleeve and checked his watch. Realizing how long he had been standing in the cold made him notice how tired his legs were of holding him up. It was Ms. Jeanette's fault. She was on a kick that everyone should pass the President Clinton's Physical Fitness Program. Personally, he didn't see how it would help America if every kid his age could do a bunch of squats. Maybe that would be useful for people living in a one of those foreign countries where people ate dinner sitting on rugs and had to get up and down a lot, but personally he preferred a table and chair.

If he had known his mother would be this late he could have spent a little extra time hunting for McCreery. With every fiber of his being, he longed to find him. Each afternoon on his way home from school, he checked under all the trees and bushes by the side of the road. Every night, he snuck food from the kitchen and left it in a bowl where McCreery could find it. Sometimes he could only manage a leftover broccoli casserole or Tofu Lemongrass Surprise, but he figured it was better than nothing. He was even planning to take a morning off from school to look for him at the top of Gallows Hill where a revolutionary spy had been hung. He didn't believe in ghosts or anything, but McCreery was too smart to hang out at a place like that after dark, and the sun went down early these days. In fact, right this minute he could barely see his own hand when he held it in front of him.

He wrapped his arms around himself and shuddered. Too many thoughts crowded his brain at once. The worst was the dream — nightmare really — he'd had over and over ever since McCreery was missing. The details grew more gruesome each night. A fat man with pointy teeth and a scar like lightning was holding McCreery prisoner in a cave somewhere. He had kidnapped McCreery because he was the most famous stud dog in the world, and he wanted him to be the father of his bitch's puppies so he could sell them for a ton of money. He kept McCreery locked up in a cage with a lot of bars with spikes on the end, only when the man opened the door so McCreery and the lady dog could do their thing, McCreery bit the man's rear and ran. He ran so fast he made it back to Redding in practically no time, only by then he was hungry and tired and his poor paws were all bloody and sore from all that running. He lay down in some leaves under a tree and fell asleep, and that was the part where Benny always woke up crying because right now McCreery was out there waiting for him to bring him home. The colors in his dream were getting brighter all the time, so he knew McCreery would be coming home soon. Maybe even tonight.

He wiped his eyes and snuffed as the cough and sputter of his mother's '86 Chevy reached his ears. He didn't want her to think he was crying. She loved him so much she couldn't bear to see him unhappy, especially over a dog. He dashed down the stairs and slid into the passenger's seat.

His mother blew him an air kiss and began rummaging in her purse. She held up the prize lipstick and craned her neck toward the rear view mirror. "It's only the Golden Arches tonight, Benny. I had a lot of expenses this month," she said through tight lips.

He turned his jacket pocket inside out. Crisp dollar bills fell onto the seat. "Surprise!"

His mother pulled her half-painted mouth down in fake disapproval. "Benny Neusner," she sing-songed. "Have you been 'borrowing' money off your father's dresser again?"

He hung his head. "Gee, Mom. He doesn't even miss it."

She slapped his thigh playfully. "You bad boy," she giggled.

He laughed, too, a bit nervously. "You're not mad?"

She flipped her fine, straight hair over her shoulder.

"Honey, that money's as much mine as that witch Sonya's. If it was up to her, you'd be living in poverty like me. No nice clothes, no fancy restaurants. I lost my child support the minute I let you live with your dad, but I gladly made the sacrifice so you could live in that huge mansion." She waved up the hill at the handsome brick house and sighed.

Benny winced guiltily. "But Sonya says…"

She cut him off. "Are you going to listen to that woman or your own mother? You don't see Sonya eating at the Golden Arches, do you?"

Benny didn't think the Golden Arches sounded so bad. He remembered the garlic spinach and cold boiled eggs his stepmother had sent in his lunch box today. He'd wanted to punch her one for saying he was getting fat like his mother. If they went to the Golden Arches, maybe he could sneak out a cheeseburger for McCreery. Dogs have a terrific sense of smell, and the aroma would tell him he was on the trail home — especially if it had lots of onions and extra cheese.

"I'm practically starving for a double bacon cheeseburger. I've got enough for the extra large fries and a drink, too," he said, beaming conspiratorially.

Instead of the approval he expected, his mother exhaled a heart-piercing sigh. "Maybe someday I'll get to go to The Spinning Wheel. That's where your father takes Sonya. He loves the Caesar salad, the double stuffed potatoes, those thick, juicy steaks."

Benny squirmed. He could hardly stand it when his mother was upset. "I'll take you."

She peeked at him, her smile encouraging. "How much you got?"

He told her.

She wrinkled her nose. "Too little."

His chin dropped like a popped balloon. He wished he'd taken a bill or two from Sonya's purse, too. She deserved it the way she lied about his mom.

They rode in silence for a couple of miles, past the old Burritt's Farm and Redding Elementary School. As they approached the intersection for Bethel, his mother perked up. "We've got enough for Buffy's Buffet," she said, veering left.

"Do they have double bacon cheeseburgers?" He was thinking how much McCreery would love one hot off the grill. His dog book said all dogs love cheese, and McCreery deserved a big chunk after what he'd been through.

His mother shook her head and started to giggle. "No, sweetie. Buffy's is a real restaurant. All you can eat."

He rubbed his little paunch and hung his head. "You won't tell Sonya? I'm supposed to be watching my diet."

She took his hand and squeezed. "No way, darling. Eat your heart out."

CHAPTER TWELVE

Benny's mom dropped him off at the end of the driveway and tooted the horn good-bye. He had stuffed his pockets with treats for McCreery — the crust off a macaroni and cheese casserole, two buffalo wings without the bones, a beef taco with the shell mostly in one piece and the crust off an apple pie, but he was so worried about what Sonya would say if she smelled pepperoni pizza on his breath that he was two thirds up the hill before he remembered to check for McCreery. Tired as he was from all those squats President Clinton loved kids to do, he trudged back down the hill and started over. McCreery was close by; he was sure of it. He'd practically felt McCreery's breath on his face last night. He had woken up in a sweat and had to drink a quart of milk to calm himself before he could fall asleep again.

He stood back and took a hard look at the scene in front of him. He had studied it dozens of times before, but tonight something new caught his attention. He tipped his head way back, so he was staring straight up at his mother's star when he noticed a pattern that was oddly familiar in the way the tops of the pine trees fit together. He half closed his eyes and squinted. Yes, that was it! The very same pattern he had seen in his dream. McCreery was so close he could practically smell him.

His heart started pounding, and all that oxygen getting to his brain must have been the reason he suddenly got a terrific idea. He had seen a program on late night television where the good guys were trying to find a chest with lots of gold and valuable stuff hidden in a cave. He couldn't remember where exactly, but the place had a bunch of coconuts. The hero did what they call a "triangulation" which isn't that hard. All you do is pick three spots, and that's where you'll find what you're looking for. It could work for McCreery.

He found the flashlight and snapped it on. Taking the star as point one and the tops of the trees as point two, he moved his arm until the flashlight formed the third point of a triangle with the star and the trees. He hustled to the spot where the flashlight pointed. He pushed against a branch and looked. Nothing. How could that be?

His legs collapsed like wet spaghetti. The ground underneath him was cold, but he felt peaceful lying there in the quiet night. Even the birds were silent. He closed his eyes.

And then he heard it: the sound of tiny puppies like he imagined hearing the night he met Bess and the cries of McCreery and Susie's puppies after they were born. It was the beckoning call of the dog he had dreamed of all his life, and this time it was real. He jumped to his feet and raced to a spot only a few yards away. He shone his flashlight. The wobbling light illuminated a long ear, and then a shoulder, and then a bobbed tail that flicked once or twice before giving up the effort. An eyeball blinked back at him.

McCreery!

Benny dropped to his knees. Just like in the dream, McCreery's coat was shaggy and full of burrs. Bloody sores caked his foot pads. His dull eyes were pleading for help.

Benny held out his hand. "Come on, boy, get up."

McCreery made a brave effort to rise, whimpered softly

71

and rolled over onto his side.

"Up, boy," Benny begged, snapping his fingers for encouragement. McCreery tried his best, feet running in air, but he was too weak to gain purchase.

What to do? McCreery couldn't lie there forever. Benny reached under his belly and tried lifting the dog up on his feet, but he jerked away with a sharp yelp. Now what? Benny remembered the dog book said a person could tell a sick dog by touching his nose. He stuck a finger out tentatively. Hot, crusty leather met his touch.

He needed to think. He wasn't sure he could cure a sick dog. Bess was the only one he knew who could help, but she was the last person he'd ask. It was her fault McCreery was in this terrible state. If she had sold him McCreery when he asked, this never would have happened. He wouldn't have let McCreery out of his sight for a single minute. Besides, she'd probably want him back.

He rose and gave McCreery a gentle pat on the head. "Stay, boy," he ordered, as if the poor dog was able to go anywhere. "I'll be right back."

He raced up the driveway, his lungs wheezing like a broken accordian, but he didn't care if the effort took his last breath. McCreery was meant to be his dog, and Fate was giving him another chance. So what if McCreery would never win another prize at a dog show? It wasn't McCreery's fault he was a little the worse for wear. He wasn't dead or anything, and he wasn't going to die, either, not if he could help it. Who cared if McCreery used to belong to Bess? She didn't deserve such a nice dog, a dog that looked up at him so trustingly with those sad eyes. He and McCreery were meant to be together. It was Destiny. Why else would his mother have dawdled a few extra minutes over that second piece of cherry cheesecake? If she'd dropped him off at his dad's a few minutes earlier, McCreery might not have gotten there yet; a few minutes later, and he might have crawled on. Like the dog book said, man and dog have special powers of communication, and that's how it was with him and McCreery. They were a team, a boy and his dog forever. Just let his dad or anyone else try to come between them now.

He let himself in the back door and tiptoed upstairs. It was early for his dad and Sonya to be locked up in their bedroom, but that's where they were. For once he was glad. He grabbed the dog book from where he kept it handy on the top of the toilet and tiptoed back downstairs to the kitchen. Flipping through the pages, he didn't find a lot of helpful information about a dog who wouldn't get up. Then he remembered his mother always gave him chicken soup when he was sick. He pulled a red and white can off the shelf and emptied it into a bowl. McCreery wouldn't care if it was hot, and he didn't have time to waste. Cradling the bowl carefully in both hands, he hurried back down the hill.

He found McCreery lying on his side, panting heavily. He held the bowl under the dog's nose and moved it back and forth so he could get a good whiff. McCreery didn't move. Benny tried again to lift him to his feet, but McCreery flopped in his arms like an empty sack. Hot tears ran down Benny's cheeks. Even his dog book wasn't a help. He had run out of ideas. Then he remembered a favorite saying of his mother's: "Time heals all wounds." He'd wait a little longer, and let time do the healing.

Bess' arm throbbed from lying in bed too long in one spot. She could change her position, but what was the point? Some other part would start to hurt instead. Besides, pain was a good thing. It kept her mind off the hurt inside.

Just to be contrary, she rolled over anyway. Her toes

bumped against something at the foot of the bed, and her heart gave a little leap. "McCreery!" she breathed, and then she remembered. It was only the tray Mona had left for dinner, still untouched. Homemade chicken soup, to judge from the aroma, as if chicken soup could fix what ailed her.

A knock came and the door opened a crack. Bess lay still, imitating sleep. She hoped it wasn't David again trying to persuade her to keep the brown puppy. The puppies were almost old enough to leave for Hannah's, and her son was growing more insistent. The scent of hyacinths reached her, and she knew it was her twin sister.

Mona walked to the window and threw open the curtains. She glanced at the untouched bowl on the tray. She sat on the side of the bed and yanked back the duvet, slopping some soup onto the bed. "This has got to stop," she insisted, shaking Bess' shoulder. "Sit up! I'm talking to you."

Bess rose up on one elbow as though roused from deep sleep. "What is it? What's happened?"

Mona jabbed Bess' sore arm, making her wince. "Nothing's happened, and nothing's going to improve until you get another dog. McCreery's gone. There are six perfectly good puppies in the whelping shed. Pick one."

Bess hung her head. "I can't…"

"Don't start that 'I can't' business with me, young lady. You can and you will. Our doctor says we could live to be a hundred, and I don't intend to go on like this for another three decades."

Bess couldn't help a small smile. It was so like her sister to take her pain and transform it into a burden for herself. Still, in a way, Mona was right. They had been carrying each other's emotional baggage all their lives.

Mona rose, chest thrust out triumphantly. "That's better. Now, which one will it be? The brown boy? He looks the most like his father."

Bess rolled back onto her pillows, a small moan escaping. She didn't want a puppy that looked like McCreery. She wanted McCreery, but there was no getting past Mona this time. She would have to choose. Better make it one of the females. The brown girl with the charming smile was pet quality. That's what she wanted, wasn't it? A good companion dog?

Mona tapped her foot impatiently. "Well?"

Before Bess could answer, someone banged on the front door. Mona looked out the window. The gas lamps gave off enough light to see. She turned to her sister with a puzzled look. "It's that strange boy."

Bess bolted upright. "McCreery!" she breathed. This time she was certain. Her dog had come home to her.

Bess drove her car because that would be the fastest. McCreery must have recognized the sound of the engine because when they got to the spot where Benny had left him, he struggled to his feet. He managed a soft, "Woof," and slipped back down on the ground, too weak to stand.

Benny rushed to McCreery's side and slid his hands underneath. Once again he tried lifting the big dog, but as before McCreery whimpered and jerked away.

"Wait, let me see," Bess said, pushing Benny aside. Tenderly, with expert movements, she felt along McCreery's spine and joints. She drew a deep breath. "Thank goodness. Nothing's broken."

"Maybe if we try lifting him together," Benny suggested. "You take one end, and I'll take the other."

She shook her head. "We might hurt him. Let him do it himself if he can."

Benny dropped down on his haunches and stuck out his hand. Bess stood beside him, her hand out, too. "Here, McCreery. Come, boy," they called.

The dog tried and failed and tried again. Benny and Bess held their breaths. McCreery made one last scramble and rose on tottering legs like a newborn colt.

"Don't feel bad if he comes to me," Benny said. "I'm the one who found him when everyone else gave up."

"Except me," Bess said, "but thank you."

"Here, boy."

"Here, McCreery."

The dog looked from one to the other. First Benny, then Bess.

"You can visit him every day if you want," Benny promised.

Bess said nothing and didn't move.

"He can still love you. I won't mind," Benny said, his voice growing louder as if to make his words come true.

Slowly, slowly the dog moved forward, his head down. He turned his head toward Benny and gently licked his cheek.

"See, he picked me," Benny shouted one last time, and then watched tearfully as McCreery slid his head under Bess' hand and closed his eyes.

Benny got to his feet and ran.

"You can have one of the puppies, any one you want," Bess called after him. Just as she expected, Benny kept running. She supported McCreery onto the back seat of her car one end at a time and took him home.

Chapter Thirteen

Slowly, Bess became aware that someone was in the room with her. The intruder, whoever it was, tiptoed so as not to be heard. Her heart jumped into her throat, and she willed herself to breathe. She eased back a fraction of an inch. Yes, it wasn't her imagination. McCreery was still pressed up against her like he had been before she fell asleep beside him on the kitchen floor last night. If the person moving toward them like a cat on the hunt intended to steal him again, she would die first.

She opened one eye and exhaled a sigh of relief. Mona, dressed in a pink negligee with a frothy scarf around her head was peering down at them, a large wooden spoon in her hand. Bess rose up on one elbow. Her arm creaked, reminding her she wasn't a young girl any more camping out on the ground. McCreery was too weak to climb upstairs to their bedroom last night, and she couldn't have carried him herself. A pillow for her head and a soft blanket had been added during the night. Mona must have done it.

"You're up early," Bess observed. The sun was barely over the top of the pine trees, an hour Mona hadn't witnessed for years.

Mona flounced the hem of her negligee. "Never mind that. What did Dr. Hammer say?"

McCreery stretched his legs and shifted in his sleep. Bess held a finger up to her lips and lowered her voice. "He'll be fine. He has some superficial injuries and has lost a lot of weight, but he'll be back to his old self in no time. Mostly he needs a lot of TLC."

"No problem," Mona promised with the certainty of a spokesperson on a TV infomercial. She opened a cabinet and shook the ingredients of her sister's secret recipe into McCreery's dog bowl one by one. She seemed to know exactly how much of each was needed, like she had been doing it all her life.

Bess watched wide-eyed as Mona even remembered to sprinkle wheat germ on top. "I had no idea."

Mona pulled her hem out of the way and placed the bowl beside the sleeping dog. "You think I've been watching you all these years for nothing?" She stood back, hands on hips, to admire her creation. "There, that's what he needs. Some good home cooking."

Both women waited, sure the familiar aromas would rouse the sleeping dog. McCreery slept on.

Mona leaned in for a better look. "Is he all right?"

"Of course, he's all right," Bess snapped. "Give me a hand up. My leg's asleep or I could manage myself." She limped to the other side of the sleeping dog. She held her hand under his nose, feeling for breath. The dog opened one eye, as if winking, and gave a soft, playful "Rrrrr."

She jerked back her hand. "You!" she scolded with a laugh. She turned to Mona. "He's fine. He's playing with me."

Mona leaned in closer. "Are you sure? Shouldn't he be diving into that food?"

Bess' smile faded. "He's low on energy, but the dog we knew is still inside. It's just going to take a little time."

Mona pointed at the dog dish. "Here, give me that." She held out a handful of the gooey mess and made encouraging, yummy noises. "Mmm, good," she said, pretending to eat a bit herself.

Bess made a sour face. "Oh, for heaven's sake. If you keep that up, he'll expect to be hand fed every day."

"I suppose you wouldn't."

McCreery lapped a handful and then stuck his nose in the bowl.

Happy tears formed in Mona's eyes. "See it's working. Your dog is back."

The emotion was too much for Bess. "If you're not heading back to bed with some of those cucumber thingies on your eyes, I don't suppose you'd like to make some of your famous blueberry sweet potato pancakes."

Mona reached for a well-used frying pan. "Actually, it's seaweed wrap with jojoba, and it wouldn't hurt you any to try some."

Bess examined the bags under her eyes in the metal toaster, shrugged indifferently and sat. She unrolled the morning newspaper Mona had left at her place.

Mona mixed the batter and poured. "Any clue who took him?"

There had been enough heartache. Bess wanted it to end. "Let it go, Mona. McCreery's back. It's over."

Mona drew herself up, a small ladle raised like a scepter. "I disagree. Stealing McCreery wasn't a one-time thing. Whoever took him is going to slip up, and then we'll grab the culprit."

"You've been watching too much television," Bess scoffed, but Mona had her attention. "Exactly how and when do you think he'll 'slip up,' as you call it?"

Mona slid a steaming stack of pancakes in front of her sister. "He wanted something he didn't get, and he'll keep trying. You'd better warn Hannah and the rest of your poodle friends." She gave her sister a hard look. "And keep an eye on McCreery at those dog shows of yours."

"Now I know you're nuts. McCreery's not going to any dog shows, and neither am I." The words came out harsher than she had intended.

Mona gave her sister a curious look. Years of experience told her Bess had more on her mind. She sat in the chair opposite and pushed the maple syrup aside to see her sister's face more clearly. "Something's still bothering you. What haven't you told me?"

Bess waited a long moment before answering. When she did, the bravado was gone. "Benny, the boy who found McCreery."

Mona's eyebrows flew up. "You mean he's a suspect?"

Bess grunted like Mona had just told her the world was flat. "Of course, not. I've broken his heart."

Mona pulled the ends of her head scarf tighter. "For a minute there, I thought you were serious."

Bess pushed away her plate. "I am. You didn't see the look in his eyes. He's wanted McCreery from the first day he saw him. He thought this was his chance."

Mona rose and dropped the frying pan into the sink with a thud. "I don't see why everything has to be so complicated. He can't be that attached. He barely knows McCreery."

Bess shook her head, remembering Benny and McCreery the night they'd met. She hadn't forgotten that the dog was nearly as smitten as the boy. "It only takes a minute," she said. "I told him he could have any puppy he wanted instead, but he said he wanted his dog. *His* dog." She picked up a napkin and blew.

Mona turned on the faucet and scrubbed the breakfast plates like they needed to be taught a lesson. "He'll get over it," she announced over the running water. "His parents can buy him another one."

For once Bess didn't argue, but she had been in Benny's shoes before. He would always want McCreery. No matter what.

CHAPTER FOURTEEN

Kate was in a rush. If she didn't hurry she would be late for the professional seminar required for her license. She shoved the stack of unread reports into her briefcase and peeked under the desk. Her white, mixed breed dog named Lotus looked back at her, eyes bright, tail thumping. About the size of a cocker spaniel with a long fringed tail, Lotus' most distinctive feature was her over-sized pointy ears with soft, white tufts that stuck out every which way like dandelion seeds. As more than one student had let Kate know, Lotus looked a lot like one of the friendly creatures in a Japanese card game. With her dog for company, she would never be alone. It was enough, wasn't it?

"Time for home," she announced. Lotus was already sitting by the door. Kate slipped into her coat and had her hand on the doorknob when she heard the knock. She glanced at her watch and sighed. Clients didn't just drop in without an appointment. Who could it be, at this late hour?

She signaled the reluctant Lotus back into her hidey hole and swung open the door. A short woman with curly gray hair stood before her with her arms crossed. Kate knew the gesture was defensive and not aggressive as most people thought.

Kate smiled, hoping to ease the older woman's discomfort. "You're Bess Rutledge, aren't you? How can I help you?"

Bess stepped back. "I'm not here to get my head screwed on straight, if that's what you think. It's about Benny." She peered past Kate into the office as if checking his whereabouts. "You know him, I believe."

Kate glanced at her watch and gestured for Bess to come in and sit in one of the facing chairs. It must have taken courage for Bess to come, and Kate couldn't help being curious. Still professional ethics compelled her to say, "I can't discuss the children I work with."

Bess tucked in her chin protectively. "I know." She moved one hand over the other as if applying an expensive lotion and looked around the room. "I've never been in a mental health professional's office before. I hope you'll be patient with me."

"I'm happy you came," Kate said and was surprised to find she meant it.

Beth took a deep breath as if about to plunge off the high diving board. "I didn't know how to be a good mother to my son. I'm trying to do better with the boy." She stared at her feet apparently unaware she was wearing one white and one blue sock.

Until that minute, Kate's impression of David's mother was that her only interest was dogs, yet here she was worried about Benny. Kate decided to make up the seminar another time and leaned in closer.

"You may know Benny found a lost dog of mine named McCreery," Bess continued. She posed it as a half-question and didn't wait for an answer. "The boy was counting on keeping the dog for himself, but that can't happen. I'm afraid his heart is broken, and I was hoping you could help."

Kate started so speak, but Bess interrupted as if eager to

get it all out.

"Benny thinks it was some kind of miracle that he found McCreery — a sign they are meant to be together, but McCreery has let him know he prefers to stay with me." She lowered her voice confidentially. "McCreery and I have been together ever since he was a puppy, you understand. I delivered him into the world with my own hands, been practically his mother." Her voice choked. "He means everything to me, but that doesn't mean I want to break the boy's heart. I've done that enough in my life, and I want it to stop, believe me."

"I do believe you."

She could see in Kate's eyes it was true. She suspected Kate's understanding of her pain went beyond her professional training. If she had to guess, she would say she and Kate had more in common than their backgrounds suggested, maybe even more than she and Mona in some ways. It helped her continue.

"I offered him one of McCreery's puppies, but he refused. I couldn't come up with a better idea, and then I thought of you." She stared pointedly at the diplomas lining the wall behind Kate's desk and said, "Maybe you can think of a way to fix it."

Kate waited a moment, but the woman seemed to have finished. Now that it was her turn to speak, she didn't know what to say. "I'm sorry," was all she could think of.

Bess stared at her a long minute, hoping for more. When it was obvious nothing was forthcoming, she rose. "Well, if that's all..."

Kate waved her back down with a weak hand. It fell onto her lap like a dropped fly ball. "I wish I could help, but there are some outcomes therapy can't change, and this is one of them. Benny will have to get over his hurt in the usual way. He will have to find another dog to love."

Bess sat again. She looked around the room for a long

moment, her eye scanning the bookshelves, the spot on Kate's desk where family photos might have been, the Oriental rug. Finally, she looked directly at Kate and said, "I think my son David is growing fond of you."

Kate blinked in surprise. She didn't think David would have discussed his feelings about her with his mother. Still, Benny had said more than once that David was just like him, always thinking of his mother first. Some men never grew out of it. That was a highway to disappointment she didn't need to travel.

As if reading her concern Bess added, "Of course, he wouldn't say anything directly, but lately I've noticed a lot of 'Kate this' and 'Kate that.' My sister Mona pointed it out first. Now that I've met you, I can see why."

Kate squirmed in her chair. She didn't enjoy people analyzing her and hoped Bess would interpret her discomfort as professional caution. "Really?"

Bess wasn't prepared to tell her the whole truth. "My kennel, your school. The kind of women people think don't have real lives."

Kate felt something loosen inside and surprised herself by laughing. "You mean a man in her life?"

Bess laughed, too. "Exactly." Her eyes dropped to her feet, and she noticed her socks didn't match. She shrugged.

Both women stood at once. "Thank you for coming," Kate said.

Bess held out her hand, then jerked it back like she had touched a hot stove. "Is there a charge?"

Kate reddened, disappointed Bess hadn't understood she wanted to be friends. She spent all day talking to people she needed to keep at a professional distance. She had let herself hope for something different this time. "Not at all."

Bess nodded. "I wasn't sure. I wanted to do the right thing."

The two women eyed each other shyly as if calculating the value of an unclaimed pawn ticket. There was an unsettled feeling in the room like something unplanned might happen.

Bess made a decision. "Maybe it's none of my business, but David is my son and I love him. Don't be like me, always guarding your heart. Be like Benny. Take a chance." She turned quickly before Kate could speak and hurried out the door.

David found Bess standing over the kitchen sink, a carrot in one hand and a vegetable peeler in the other. He leaned in to buss her cheek. A mouth watering aroma rose from a Dutch oven on the stove. Mona's pot roast, he thought. "Carrots?" he teased, raising an eyebrow. Mona didn't think carrots belonged in pot roast, so if Bess wanted them she had to fix them herself. He had heard the argument a hundred times.

"Humph," she replied, rubbing where his lips had touched. "I heard you offered Benny one of the puppies for finding McCreery. That was kind."

"Not really. He wants McCreery."

"If he keeps the puppy that looks like McCreery, the two of you could take him to a couple of dog shows, find out what the puppy's made of." He tried sounding indifferent and failed.

"Not going to happen. I'm perfectly happy being retired." She dropped the carrot into the Dutch oven and wiped her hands on a towel. Signaling him to follow, she led the way into the living room. She slid into her favorite Queen Anne's chair beside the fireplace.

He lifted a magazine off the matching chair opposite hers and flapped it at her. "Dog World?"

She dropped her eyes. "I've been meaning to cancel my subscription. Been so busy I haven't gotten around to it."

He sat and crossed his legs as if he intended to stay a while. He ran his eyes over his mother's uncombed hair and carelessly buttoned shirt, but kept his observations to himself.

His mother broke the silence. "I'm beginning to think your Aunt Mona's not moving to Florida after all."

"Really?" he asked, skepticism plain in his voice. He had predicted many times the two sisters would never be able to live apart.

"She claims one thing after another's not finished in her condo, but I can tell she's making excuses." She tapped the side of her nose with her forefinger. "The woman's on a mission. Maybe to get you married again."

"Really," he said again, sitting forward.

His mother grinned like she had just snatched the last chocolate-covered cherry in the box. "She saw you talking to the director of that school Benny attends. She was full of questions."

He rolled his eyes. "I might have known Mona would jump to conclusions. Dr. Kate's no more interested in Benny helping me with the brown puppy than you are." He leaned across the empty space and picked a strip of carrot off her shirt sleeve. "Really, Mother. How are you getting along?"

"Fine, thank you very much. Not a single dog in sight." She swept her arm past several unwashed coffee mugs, a stack of unopened bills and a couple of old Christmas catalogs crowding the coffee table. Her hand halted in mid-arc. McCreery had chosen that moment to come padding through the door with his toy fish in his mouth.

David raised his eyebrows.

"Oh, for heaven's sake! McCreery doesn't count. He's a member of the family."

McCreery pushed his fish into David's hand and stared

up hopefully. David gave it a toss, and McCreery ran to retrieve it. Apparently once was enough because the dog settled down beside Bess, his chin resting on her foot.

"McCreery's still got a lot of life left in him," David said, giving him the once over. "He still might be good for a few more trophies."

She pulled her thick eyebrows into a warning frown.

He held up his hands in mock surrender. "Okay, okay, I give." He sat back and so did she.

"So, why are you here?"

His face softened. "I've been thinking about you, Mother. How special you are."

She studied a stain on the Oriental rug. When she spoke, her gravelly voice was almost a whisper, "I wasn't cut out to be a mother. It's a wonder I didn't ruin you all together. I have to give Mona credit for that."

He leaned closer. "Mona helped, but you were my mother. Talking to the boy has made me remember."

He held out a hand, but she hoisted herself out of her chair as if she hadn't seen, coughing something back. She snapped her fingers. "Come, McCreery," she ordered, perhaps not noticing he was stretched out at her feet. "That dog's so spoiled he has to be reminded to pee." She glanced at her son. "You can stay for supper if you want. Pot roast — with carrots!"

CHAPTER FIFTEEN

The Danbury Kiwanis had set up a treasure hunt for this week's Funhouse Friday, and Benny and Steffie were a team. In honor of the occasion she had dressed like a pirate in a long black skirt, a white blouse with puffy sleeves and a red bandana around her neck. Two gold hoop earrings hung down nearly to her chin. Benny had tied a neon blue scarf borrowed from Sonya's underwear drawer around his head and stuck a black patch over one eye. The two of them had been first to find all the clues because he knew every inch of the school and she was good at finding the hidden meaning in the words. They were sitting outside on the picnic bench waiting for the others to catch up. She shoved the popcorn bowl closer to him, but he shook his head.

"You feeling all right?" she asked with a worried frown.

He shrugged, but a small smile twitched at the corners of his mouth. He lowered his voice dramatically and dropped his head so he had to look over the tops of his eyes. "I took a personal holiday yesterday and went to the top of Gallows Hill Road." He reached into his pocket and took out a tattered piece of something that might once have been rope. With a fiendish grin, he tossed it at her like a snake.

"Gotcha!"

She jumped back, nearly tipping over her chair. When

the snake didn't move, she straightened her bandana and gave him a withering look. "So puerile."

He rolled his bottom lip and hung his head. "Sorry, Steffie. That was dumb. I found McCreery, but not on Gallows Hill."

Her angry look vanished. "Really, you found him just like in the dream

He dropped his chin. "Yes, but it didn't turn out the way I thought. He picked Bess."

Her face grew serious. "Gee, Benny. I'm sorry."

"And that's not all. Bess was so guilty she tried to give me a puppy that looks exactly like McCreery. He's practically a famous champion. At least he will be soon."

"So what's the problem?"

"He's a poodle, and besides my dad won't let me have a dog."

"Poodles are the world's smartest dogs." She winced, apparently remembering he could be sensitive about the topic of brains.

This time he didn't mind. "You're right. The puppy is pretty smart, and he doesn't look that much like a poodle."

"A puppy's a big decision, but you'll figure it out. Isn't that what your meetings with Dr. Kate are for? To solve big problems?"

"Good idea. I'll bring it up at our meeting Monday."

Her cherry lips parted in a radiant smile. "Whatever you decide, I'm proud of you for finding McCreery."

Benny's insides melted like butter on a hot scone. His toes and fingers tingled as if waking from a hundred years' sleep. No one had ever had so much confidence in him before, at least not a girl.

From the other end of the field, Adam signaled and pointed to where the other students had gathered. The treasure hunt was over. Benny grabbed his backpack and slung it over his shoulder. Something fell out and clattered to the floor. It rolled under the table.

He and Steffie reached at the same time. She grabbed it first. She held up a prescription bottle full of bright blue pills. "What are you doing with these?" she gasped.

His face turned red. He grabbed the bottle from her hand. "Mind your own business." He stuffed the bottle in his pocket and ran before she could ask any more questions.

CHAPTER SIXTEEN

Benny's oversized feet hung off the end of the couch. A big toe stuck out of one sock. His appointment was for ten thirty, but Dr. Kate wouldn't mind if he was a little early. Ms. Jeanette was just going over a bunch of boring spelling rules, and he had been using Spelling Checklist since fourth grade. He was worried Steffie might have said something to Dr. Kate about the pills. It was hard to know what a girl dressed like a lollipop might do, but today Steffie wasn't his biggest worry.

As long as Dr. Kate wasn't there yet, he decided he might as well look around for some clues about her life. He didn't bother getting off the couch. He could see the whole office just fine where he was. Besides, she got mad the last time she had caught him poking around in her things.

As usual, she hadn't left out anything personal. No family photos, no souvenirs of past vacations, no greeting cards from long-lost friends. A china tea pot in the shape of an elephant with long, painted eyelashes was the only interesting thing in a shelf full of boring books by some guy named Freud that he'd seen a hundred times before. He knew the elephant was Indian by the ears. He had studied the difference in science, and because it was about animals, he had no trouble remembering. In a rare slip, Dr. Kate had mentioned her grandfather had sent it from Bangalore. Her green eyes came from her Irish mother.

He checked the clock on the mantle and saw he still had a few minutes to wait. He heard a rustling under the desk. It was only Lotus repositioning herself in her dog nest. She scratched at the pillow and circled in a tight ball before heaving herself back down with an explosion of breath. He considered tossing her a wadded up homework paper to kill time, but she was already snoring. He decided to catch up on his own rest instead. He was still a growing boy and had spent most of the night tossing and turning, trying to decide about the brown puppy. Bess said it would turn out like his father McCreery, but what if he didn't? Besides, why didn't Bess keep him herself like David wanted?

Benny's eyes widened. He tapped his head with a finger. He had an idea. A true inspiration. He heard light footsteps hurrying up the stairs. He checked his watch. Ten thirty-one. It was about time she got there.

Kate hesitated in the doorway to her office. When upset, Benny had been known to shred his homework over the Oriental rug or bury a tiny china doll head first in the philodendron. The doll wore a dress that had once been yellow and said things that sounded a lot like Kate. Coming from Benny's voice, they helped her know what he was thinking but couldn't say directly.

Today the office seemed in order. An oblong table with eight padded blue chairs where the teachers and therapists held their meetings took up one end of the room. The other end was decorated home-style with a fireplace, two wing-back chairs and a three-cushioned couch where Benny was sprawled. A comfortable leather chair with ottoman was tucked in one corner. She had decorated the office herself with her first pay check after paying off her student loans. Official class photos of past students, children's art work and a few softening pillows added a feminine touch, but the navy, tan and mustard color scheme was all business.

"Hello, Benny," she said, taking her usual spot. "Ms. Jeanette has your spelling words waiting for you when we're finished." She stuck a stray lock of hair back into the ornate gold clip holding her French twist in place and waited. She should have locked it away with the ring and her crushed hopes, but it had meant too much once to put aside all together.

He opened one eye but said nothing. After a few moments, he squirmed uncomfortably, like the princess and the pea, and held up the offending plastic cup. Traces of chocolate pudding that matched the rim around his mouth were stuck to the sides. It was the gesture of a much younger child and Kate was reminded once again how different Benny was from most kids at The New Hope School who were extra smart. Even physically he seemed a little behind the other boys his age whose faint mustaches were announcing their arrival into puberty.

Before he came to New Hope School, several doctors had misdiagnosed him with ADHD because he fidgeted a lot. One even labeled him as Tourette's. It was easy to miss the symptoms for anxiety without a good history, and psychotropic drugs can't cure a broken heart. That's why she and the teachers paid attention to the way each child interacted with the world, not what a paper and pencil test said about them. If a child had a meltdown, they tried to figure out what had triggered it instead of just writing contracts or passing out stickers.

She nodded at the plastic cup. "I think that was meant for your lunch."

He rolled down his lower lip. "Sonya has me on a diet. I

only had a half a granola bar for breakfast."

She sighed. The boy was hungry for so much more than chocolate pudding. It made him stretch the truth.

"Maybe you're upset at someone else, like Bess for instance."

He rolled over so she couldn't see his face. He said nothing.

"I'm sorry about McCreery. I know how much you wanted him to pick you."

He sat up and pulled a Spiderman comic book out of his backpack, withdrawing from her and the possibility of comfort.

A feeling of helplessness threatened to overwhelm her. She decided to follow his lead. "Sometimes you act like make-believe comic book characters are more important than real people. For instance, you haven't mentioned your new friend David lately."

"Daa-vid, Daa-vid," he sing-songed. "Dr. Kate has a crush on David."

She felt herself blushing. Benny had a vivid imagination and a hunger for family that included the fantasy that she and David would get together. She was sorry he'd be disappointed again.

Benny thumbed through his comic for a minute, jiggling his foot like he did when he was worried. She realized he had something important to say.

"My dad says I might not be having meetings much longer. He thinks I'm doing great," he said without looking up.

A shiver ran down her spine. Parents often pulled their children out of treatment at the first sign of progress. It was one of the heartbreaks of her work. She might love the children she worked with and be privy to their feelings, but their futures and their hearts belonged elsewhere. In the end she always had to say goodbye. Sometimes it happened at the worst possible time, like now.

"I'll give him a call, but your dad's the boss. We only have meetings if he says so." she said, trying to keep the worry out of her voice. Children experienced a loyalty conflict any time they brought up a concern about their parents. Benny had taken a risk by giving her a heads up.

He wriggled in his seat and tugged at a wedgie. "Actually, I've been thinking."

"Really?" she asked absently, wondering how to approach Benny's dad. He wasn't really a bad father, just more caught up in his own wishes than his son's. Maybe someday he'd be proud of Benny for what he could do instead of focusing on what he couldn't.

"Yeah, I might be getting a puppy." He paused, waiting for her reaction.

She tried to keep her voice neutral. "A puppy? That's interesting. You used to say McCreery was the only dog you'd ever love. What changed your mind?"

He flipped his hands out at his sides. "McCreery, of course. He loves both me and Bess, and I figured if a dog could love two people, a boy could love two dogs."

Kate smiled to herself. Benny had taken a big step. The solution she had mentioned to Bess was already happening. Benny could learn to love a dog of his own and love McCreery, too. Maybe someday he would even let go of his mom the same way. Someday.

Benny stood and began pacing. "Everyone says McCreery used to be the greatest show dog in the world. He even could've won Westminster if Bess had given him the chance." He shot a hard look at Kate.

She leaned forward in her chair, afraid she could guess where he was heading. "Go on."

"There's this puppy that looks a lot like him. Bess won't admit it, but he does. For example, they're both brown. I'm thinking about taking him to Westminster. My mother would really be impressed."

She shifted uncomfortably. For a minute, she had hoped Benny might actually be thinking about himself, but no. It was his mother, always his mother. "So you want the puppy to impress your mother, not because you like him?"

He stuck his fingers in his ears. "I'm not listening. La, la, la, la."

She suppressed an angry sigh. Benny's mother loved him in her own self-absorbed way, but she would always put herself first. As Benny's psychoanalyst, her job was to help him accept that and move on, but so far she hadn't succeeded. The boy was an endless fount of schemes to win his mother's attention that inevitably ended in failure. There was the black belt in karate that ended when he took a swing at someone, the skate board championship that collapsed when he tripped and bloodied elbows and knees, and the basketball trophy that shattered when a well-aimed ball knocked the wind out of him. And now this! Benny had no idea how much work it would take to qualify for a world-class show like Westminster, let alone win it. He could never manage without Bess' help. Still, crazy as it sounded, this particular idea seemed to have extra sizzle behind it.

"'Maybes' don't always come true, Benny. We've talked about that before."

He sat up, locking his fingers behind his head. "It can't be that hard. I just have to play with the puppy and teach him stuff."

"I think teaching is the important part. Besides, I thought your dad said you can't have a dog."

He rolled over so she couldn't see his face. "He's small. I'm thinking about hiding him someplace."

"I don't think that would work," she said, drumming her fingers. "A puppy needs a lot of care. Besides, you'll need help with the training"

"David will help me. He promised."

She hadn't expected that. "Are you sure?"

"David is like me. He loves making his mother happy. He thinks taking me and the puppy to Westminster would be the perfect hobby for her old age. She's wanted to win her whole life but never took a dog before, not even McCreery. Nobody knows why."

Kate glanced at the clock. With Benny's limited attention span, it was helpful to meet frequently in shorter sessions. "Our meeting is almost over. We'll talk more about this next time."

He clasped his hands together prayer-like. "Five extra minutes?"

It would be easy to give in, but children with complicated attachments to their mothers needed help with separating. She had to stay firm. "Is it good-bye forever or just until tomorrow?"

"Tomorrow," he muttered under his breath. He picked up his back pack and shuffled to the door. She came around and stood in front of him. Last fall, they had stood eye to eye. Now he was half a foot taller.

He looked at the floor. "Do you think my mother's proud of me?" His voice was so small she almost didn't hear.

She struggled to keep her voice even. "What do you think?"

His bottom lip trembled and he didn't answer.

She stood quietly, waiting, not wanting to undermine him when he was trying to act manfully.

He hoisted his backpack and started downstairs. Halfway down he began whistling one of those tunes from a band with a funny name she never could remember. All the kids loved it.

He turned to see if she was watching.

She was there, looking down. She whispered something softly to herself, like a blessing.

He smiled and gave a thumbs up. "Don't worry, Dr.

Kate. Everything will work out. You'll see. Everything will be super fine."

"A dog?" Sonya squeaked, wriggling her nose like a weasel. "A boy who can't remember to empty the dishwasher can't take care of a dog."

Benny's dad looked up over the top of his reading glasses long enough to tell his son, "Listen to your stepmother."

CHAPTER SEVENTEEN

Bess turned the page on her desk calendar and scratched an "X" through the date with the big red circle. Today the puppies were a full three months old, and she could let them go. Some breeders separated the puppies from their mothers at six weeks, but eager as she was to have this job behind her, she could never let a puppy go that young. The extra time with the mother made a better dog for life: calmer, more trusting, ready to learn. It was the same for both show dogs and pets.

She pulled back the curtain and peeked through the gap into the breaking dawn. Just as she thought, Hannah was pacing in front of the puppy shed. A white van with "Hannah's Own Kennels" written in black letters was parked to one side. Six puppy-size crates were stacked and waiting by the tailgate. Hannah's hands twisted nervously in front of her, and Bess concluded there was no lingering pain from the wrist she had broken three months earlier. At six feet tall with steel-colored braids tied across the top of her head, she was one of Redding's few African Americans and bent her neck to no one. Her family had arrived by the Underground Railroad generations ago at the home of a Quaker family, making her more of a native than most of the so-called swamp Yankees who wore their heritage like a badge of honor.

Bess checked the bedside clock. Five minutes to six in the morning. She didn't intend to be one minute early or one minute late, either. At age fifty, Hannah had been waiting twenty years to become the top poodle breeder in the country. She could wait another five minutes.

Bess patted her hair into place and examined her face in the mirror. No tell-tale dark circles from a sleepless night, no red swollen eyes. The ice-packs had done their job, not to mention Mona's expensive creams. Even so, just to be sure, she had rubbed on some borrowed concealer. She couldn't bear for Hannah to know what today was costing her. In building the kennel of her dreams, she had constructed herself along with it. The eighteen hour days, the ledgers that balanced by a wing and a prayer, even the puppies whose promise fizzled when they hit adolescence were as much a part of herself as her own flesh, blood, and bone. Letting go of Umpawaug Kennels was letting go of herself.

Not that she had ever thought the task would be easy. She had read somewhere that one could inoculate oneself against something unpleasant, even traumatic, by rehearsing it over and over, and she embraced the idea whole heartedly. For almost a decade she had been picturing today in her mind's eye. She had let her imagination run over the empty puppy shed, the barren field where the kennels once stood, the silence that would greet her when she opened the front door, but now that the actual day had arrived, her rehearsals seemed pitifully naive. Was it possible she had mistaken the problem all along? Maybe the challenge wasn't letting go of the past but facing up to what came next. For that she was utterly unprepared.

It was the brown puppy's fault. Until he had come along, she had resigned herself to the inevitable. Nothing could stop Hannah's Own from becoming the new top kennel in the country for Standard Poodles, and that was just fine. But now, unexpectedly, the old ambition she had tucked away so neatly was stirring again. If only the puppy weren't so very like his father. Still, this was no time to waver. She couldn't handle a dog in the ring herself any more and hiring a handler wasn't for her. She had never done it before, and she wasn't about to start now. Besides, no matter how tempting the little fellow was, until he passed through adolescence no one could be sure how he would look in maturity.

Still, one question circled round and round in her brain. Why had she agreed to that last breeding with McCreery? Surely, she wasn't hoping for one final try at Best in Show at Westminster. No, that was ridiculous.

She picked up the envelopes containing the AKC registration forms filled out in her flowery script. "Umpawaug" was recorded as the kennel name like she and Hannah had agreed when she had sold Susie. That way McCreery's last litter of puppies would be tied to her kennel forever. The space for the owner's name was left blank, so Hannah could sell the puppies or keep them herself. She shuffled the envelopes and counted them again to be sure. Yes, six. It was all right. She was safe.

She stepped through the back door, hands on hips, as though she had been the one kept waiting. She walked briskly, shoulders straight, as if she didn't have a care in the world. When she reached Hannah, she tipped her hand toward the puppy shed door. "You know where they are. It's not like you haven't been here before."

Hannah hesitated. Bess ought to lead the way. It was almost like she was forcing her into the position of usurper. Still, there was no point in arguing. She stepped inside. The puppies scratched eagerly at the sides of the whelping pen, barely large enough to hold them all now, and set off an excited chorus. To her ears, it sounded like a welcoming cheer.

Bess had a different explanation. "They're hungry. I didn't feed them yet this morning. I figured you wouldn't want a bunch of puppies yerping all over your nice, clean van."

Hannah knew Bess was hiding her hurt behind gruff words. She regretted that her windfall came from Bess' loss, but the prospect of the future ahead lightened her guilt. She began to feel almost giddy. Her eye rested on the brown boy who looked so much like his father. Instinctively, she knew he would be Bess' favorite. His father McCreery had had the most spectacular show career of any dog in Umpawaug history, and this puppy resembled him closely. To this day, no one understood why Bess hadn't entered him in Westminster. For that matter, why had she never entered any of her champion dogs?

Hannah didn't need to choose among the six puppies, but if she had to pick just one, it would be the robust black fellow staring up at her with hungry eyes. He seemed to say he could hardly wait to start winning. As if to underscore the point, he gave his brown brother a solid bump, hind end to hind end, and dislodged him from the front of the pack. She leaned into the whelping pen and scooped him up. She tucked him under her arm and reached for his brown brother. The little fellow scooted backwards, just beyond her fingertips. His bobbed tail was wagging, so he was playing with her. Still, it made her think. Perhaps she should try one more time to convince Bess to keep him. She hoped someone would do the same for her when her time came. She decided to leave him for last.

As if seeing through Hannah's plan, Bess busied herself by gathering up the last of the puppy paraphernalia. The other four puppies bunched together, paws scratching excitedly at the side of the box.

Hannah sighed, uncertain what words would suffice for

such a poignant occasion. Still, it wasn't in her nature to let the moment pass unremarked. "My heart goes out…" she began in a choked voice, but before she could finish, the door flung open and Benny burst in like the king's messenger.

"I've changed my mind. I'll take him!" He tugged at his waist band with a pleased grin and looked at the two women for approval.

Hannah gripped the black puppy tighter and glared at Bess. What kind of stunt was she trying to pull? "Whom does the boy think he's taking exactly?" she asked in a thin voice.

Benny's eyes shot to the black puppy in her arms, the temper that had brought him to The New Hope School threatening to explode. He turned to Bess. "You said I could have any puppy I wanted for saving McCreery's life. Don't tell me you forgot?"

Bess paled. She remembered all right. She had made the promise precipitously in the heat of the moment and regretted it almost instantly, but he had steadfastly refused her offer, so it hadn't seemed to matter. And now this, at the last possible moment. A puppy was an awesome responsibility, one Benny wasn't ready for. Still, if he hadn't found McCreery. . .

She couldn't bear to think of it. She studied Benny's face carefully. The hunger in his eyes reminded her of another boy and promises made, and broken, thirty odd years ago. Whatever his reason for changing his mind, the puppy was important to him.

She turned to Hannah. "It's true. I promised. I'm entitled to pick of the litter, and the boy can choose for me. Go ahead, Benny, pick the puppy you want." She leaned against the counter, and crossed her ankles nonchalantly, as if his decision was of no greater significance than what she would have for dinner tonight. Meryl Streep would have envied the performance.

Hannah pulled the black boy closer and told Bess in a firm voice, "If even one of these puppies turns out like his father, the Umpawaug legacy will continue another generation. At their age, even you can't be sure which one it will be. Surely you're not going to give a puppy of such immense potential to an inexperienced child."

Benny puffed out his cheeks, but Bess silenced him with a glare. Hannah was correct, but Benny would soon tire of the work involved in caring for a puppy, and then she could send the puppy to Hannah like she had planned. She would still be safe. She turned to Hannah. "Not that it's any of your business, but no, not exactly. The boy and I will co-own the dog. The puppy will stay here with me until Benny is ready to take care of him himself. We'll work out the financial details later. Who pays for what, et cetera."

Benny jerked up his head. Finances were an aspect he hadn't considered, but he pushed his doubts aside in the desire of the moment. As long as Bess kept the puppy at her place, Sonya and his dad couldn't say a word. It was the perfect solution. He made an "I told you so" face at Hannah. "That's more like it," he said.

He leaned back for a better view of the puppies and rubbed his chin the way his Dad did when he had to make a tough choice. The puppies were thrilled by this exciting new person's attention and squirmed and bumped their little butts against each other to get closer. He took his time, enjoying the drama too much to be rushed. He seemed about to choose, then hesitated. "What if I decide to enter the puppy in dog shows and stuff?"

Bess jerked back her head. She thought the boy wanted a pet, not a show dog. She had tried to avoid the pain of not handling McCreery's puppy herself, and instead she was faced with the prospect of watching a clumsy boy make a mess of his career. Worse, she had no one to blame but herself.

She forced herself to take a calming breath. She had nothing to worry about. The boy would never be able to manage on his own, and it would be cruel to encourage him. She folded her arms. "That's up to you. Just don't expect me to help."

Hannah's mouth opened and a mocking laugh rumbled out. She nodded at Benny who had collapsed in the only chair while his elders stood. "That boy? Turn an obstreperous puppy into a show dog?"

A hush fell over the room. Benny's face flushed red, but before he could react, Bess pointed at the puppies jostling together at the edge of the pen. "Go ahead. Choose."

He gave Hannah another dirty look and leaned into the whelping box. This time the brown boy pushed to the front of the pack, scratching and whimpering to be chosen, but Benny wasn't about to be rushed. The tip of his tongue showed between his teeth as he studied them one by one.

He turned to Bess, avoiding Hannah's eye. "Which one do you like?"

Bess stepped back, waving her hand. "Oh, no, you don't. It's your call."

He didn't know it, but she was giving him good advice. If he were to have a prayer of beating the odds and turning the puppy into a champion, he and the dog would need a strong bond connecting them.

Hannah gave a little gasp when Benny started to reach for the black boy in her arms, but then he remembered the brown boy was the one who had jumped out of the box and run toward him the day he'd first seen the puppies. The black one had held back. Maybe the brown boy was best.

As if reading Benny's mind, the brown boy scratched harder at the sides of the box, his nails making a rat-a-tat sound against the wood. He opened his soft, pink mouth. His sharp baby teeth were clean and white. He squeezed the space between his eyes into a small frown, and gave a high-pitched, sharp whine. He was begging Benny to choose him.

No way Benny could resist love like that. Every blue rubber band on his braces showed in his crescent moon smile. "If I can't have McCreery, I'll take this one," he announced, hefting the puppy onto his shoulder.

The puppy seemed pleased and licked Benny's chin excitedly. So far, the puppy seemed to like everything Benny did. Every time he moved, the puppy wagged his tail.

Hannah exhaled slowly but kept her arms wrapped tightly around her favorite.

Now that Benny had made his choice, his temper cooled toward Hannah. "I'm naming mine Breaker because he'll be a record breaker. What about you?"

"His call name will be Chicory," she replied without hesitation, as if she had been thinking about it for a while.

Benny lost his concentration trying to remember if chicory was something good to eat, and Breaker wriggled out of his arms. The puppy slid to the floor and began running in circles between the three pairs of human legs, tail whirring like a fan on a hot summer's day.

"That one's going to be a handful," Hannah predicted.

An affectionate smile twitched at the corners of Bess' mouth. "Just like his father," she said. Then she remembered herself. "Catch that puppy, Benny, and put him back where he belongs."

Grabbing the squirming puppy under his front legs, Benny dropped him into the box. With a heavy sigh, the boy fell onto the rusty metal chair with his legs outstretched. "Puppies sure are a lot of work."

Hannah and Bess exchanged knowing smiles. "It'll be like old times being back the ring together," Hannah said, still grinning.

Bess scowled and held up her hands. "Why can't people get it through their heads? I'm finished, finito, done. The boy and I will be co-owners. That's all. The puppy can stay here in the puppy shed, and Benny can visit whenever he wants. It'll be his job to take care of him after school." She pulled the AKC registrations from her pocket and counted out five. She held back the sixth and handed the others to Hannah.

Benny watched silently from his chair as Hannah and Bess left with four squirming puppies tucked under their arms. The fifth followed closely behind, not wanting to be forgotten. Breaker remained alone in the whelping pen like the last patron in an empty theater. The thump of his tail hitting the sides was the only sound in the room.

Benny leaned into the box and pulled out his new puppy with one hand. Gently, he placed him down on the floor. The little fellow stood on his hind legs and scratched excitedly at Benny's leg, wriggling with unrestrained happiness. Benny had never felt so important in his life. He clasped his hands over his stomach and nodded slowly, as if he'd worked out a thorny problem. "I've thought a lot about it, Breaker, and I've decided we can be best friends even if you are a poodle. McCreery's my first best friend because I saved his life, and you can be my second best friend."

Breaker grabbed Benny's shoe lace and gave it a good yank, as if he understood he had been given second place to his father and didn't intend to remain there. Benny lifted the squirming mass of muscle and warm puppy smell and held him close against his chest. Delighted, Breaker slurped Benny's face and neck with a tongue that seemed as long as he was. Benny's eyes closed in dreamy happiness. He was on his way to Westminster. So what if Bess wouldn't help him. How hard could it be? He'd get right on it — first thing tomorrow.

Chapter Eighteen

The first of May ushered in a picture perfect spring day. The sun was warm, the daffodils were in bloom, and two robins pecked for treats in the tender grass. After months of heavy wool coats and gray skies, Kate couldn't resist. She shoved the notes from her last session into the file drawer and draped a light sweater over her shoulders. Lotus heard the hopeful sounds and scrambled out from beneath the desk. They headed for the wooden swing hanging off the maple tree and Kate sat, dragging her feet along the spot the students had worn down in the grass. The sun was warm on her face, urging her to close her eyes and rest for a minute.

She must have nodded off because Lotus' sharp barks jerked her awake. She opened her eyes to find David standing over her. Maybe her guard was down because it was springtime and she was still half-asleep, but she felt magnanimous and willing to overlook the way their last meeting had ended. She didn't know many accountants, but it was hard to picture him hunched over a thick ledger like Scrooge, not with that cleft chin, well-tanned face and hands, and dimples at the tips of a welcoming smile.

Lotus was even more smitten. Her feathered tail swept back and forth, eyes fixed on the handsome brown puppy at the end of David's lead. Breaker was fascinated himself. His bobbed tail whirred back and forth, and his nose quivered with excitement.

Kate smiled at the love-sick dogs. "That handsome fellow must be Breaker."

"That's him," David agreed with an easy laugh. "He's taken quite a fancy to your little dog."

"Lotus," she said, shielding her eyes from the sun with her hand. "With the long days I keep, I couldn't keep her locked up at home. Besides, the children love having her here."

He took a long, quiet look at the campus. "I've never heard of a school before that helps children with their feelings. It's got to be rough on your own emotions sometimes."

She tried to hide her surprise. It wasn't often someone thought about her work from her point of view. "It can be. We've been known to keep children with serious emotional problems out of mental hospitals."

"Really? Little kids get admitted to mental hospitals?"

"Unfortunately. More often they're put on a bunch of psychotropic drugs that nobody ever tested on children."

He nodded at a garden chair lying on its side. Scattered branches were piled up behind it. One of the younger kids must have been making a fort. "Mind if I sit? I'd like to know more."

She waved permission and watched him pull the chair closer. She suspected he was trying to keep her talking by focusing on the school, but he seemed genuinely interested. "Generally, our students follow what we call 'the two to six rule,'" she said. "Two to six psychiatric labels, two to six previous mental health professionals, two to six previous schools and two to six medicines."

His mouth dropped open. "I had no idea. The classrooms seem like any other school's. Calmer, even."

She smiled, pleased at the compliment she knew to be true. "Just shows what the right kind of care can do. You'd be amazed how many children are labeled with the wrong diagnosis and given prescription drugs. A lot are highly addictive."

David shuddered. "I'm glad Benny's not on any pills. He was boasting about it the other day."

Kate's eyes knitted in a little frown. "Really, I wonder what brought that on?"

"He said he was on two different medicines before he came to your school, but you got him off them."

Kate couldn't comment on Benny's treatment, so she studied her shoe.

David seemed to understand. "You have so much passion for what you do. You remind me of my mother when she talks about her dogs, or at least the way she used to." He clapped his hand over his mouth. "Ooops, I guess I shouldn't mention my mother to a Freudian."

She laughed, and he laughed, too. Then she added seriously, "It's not easy helping children like Benny. I'm sorry I didn't trust you before about Benny and Breaker, but Benny wanted the puppy for all the wrong reasons. I was afraid he'd get hurt."

David met her gaze. "I'm more of an expert on kids getting hurt than you can imagine."

The emotion in his voice went straight to her heart, but Benny was her responsibility. "Then you understand my concern. I only hope he doesn't get his heart broken again. Her voice was sharp as the last winter wind.

He straightened his cap. "Believe me, I'll try to keep that from happening."

She did believe him, but that wasn't the problem. "Sometimes one's best efforts aren't enough. I'm more of an expert on *that* than you can imagine."

They stood staring at each other for a moment, the

silence separating and connecting them at the same time. He started to say something, but the dogs charged around the corner, barreling toward them, and the frail link snapped.

Was that regret in his eyes? She couldn't tell.

"I'll walk you back to your office," he offered.

If she agreed, another invitation would follow. "Thanks anyway," she said and turned away. Lotus gave Breaker a lingering look and followed.

CHAPTER NINETEEN

Benny had something important to ask Steffie and was hoping to catch her before she left, but when he reached the bench, she was nowhere in sight. A stranger was seated where he expected her to be, and from what he had seen in the movies, she looked exactly like a sixties flower child right down to the daisy behind her ear. Only this girl didn't seem all full of peace and love. Her stringy dark hair hung down around her face like a shield, and she was worrying a hangnail. She gave him a quick look. The flower child was Steffie.

His heart sank to the pit of his stomach. What had happened to his little lollipop girl? His dad was right. It's hard to find a woman a guy can depend on. Still, he needed to find out if she had told anyone about the bottle of pills.

He cleared his throat and asked, "Mom late?"

Steffie's hair swung back and forth in a "No," but she didn't speak. Maybe she thought it was none of his business. She crossed her legs, and he noticed a pair of cool red and silver high tops that didn't exactly go with the rest of her outfit. He'd been begging Sonya for a pair just like them for months, only for boys.

"Mine, neither," he said, glad it was true for once. He stood and stuck his hands in his pockets, legs apart like the cool cat his mother liked on her show. "Say, you didn't mention anything about that bottle to anyone, did you?" His voice quavered a little and he hoped she wouldn't notice.

She met his eyes. "Duh."

She hadn't exactly said no, but he decided his secret was safe for now. "Thanks."

"You shouldn't be fooling around with drugs."

"It's not what you think. They're medicine, not drugs. Besides, someone dressed like a flower child shouldn't talk."

She stood and began swinging her arms in wide circles. "This school is for babies. No gym or cafeteria like Hamilton Middle. That was the best school my mom ever pulled me out of."

"Sounds cool," he said, but silently he liked New Hope School best. "Personally, I'm going to Joel Barlow when I get to high school. The softball coach is a famous rock star. You've heard of him, right?"

"Duh."

"I'm glad you're here now. How many schools have you been to anyway?"

"Seven. It's sort of a hobby for my mom. She yanks me out before I can get expelled."

"You won't get kicked out here. This place is different."

"You can say that again. Kids here get away with a ton of stuff they never would at a real school. Eric Huffstudler kept his head on his desk the entire math period today, and Ms. Kim didn't do a thing just because he's supposed to be upset over a cat dying or something. It wasn't even a real cat, just something he saw on TV."

Benny knew Eric wasn't upset about a cat. His little brother had some awful disease and was bald as a hard-boiled egg. No one knew if he would get better. "Ms. Kim isn't as dumb as you think. I'm not crazy about regular teachers myself, but the teachers here are different. They

like kids like us. Otherwise, they'd be nuts to work here."
He smiled sheepishly. "Face it. They have to put up with
me."

She looked at him harder. He was teetering forward and
back on his heels like the empty rocking chair in Psycho.
"You don't look so hot. Something bothering you?"

"My mom, my dad. You know, the usual." He hung his
head. "And that's not all. I sort of forgot to mention you-
know-what to Dr. Kate. We promised each other to always
tell the truth, so even if I wanted to, I can't tell her now.
She'd kill me if she knew I lied."

Steffie sighed, like she'd been imagining something
worse than the pills. She returned to her hangnail. "Tell
her now. How mad can she be?"

"You don't know meeting doctors. Dr. Kate says honesty's
more important than anything."

"Tell her you're sorry. That's honest."

"I am. Real sorry." He was, but he still couldn't tell Dr.
Kate about the pills.

The stretch limo glided to a stop in front of them, and
he watched Steffie slide into the back seat. He had trusted
her with his secret, and she had kept it. They were partners,
secret agents on special assignment. His whole body
tingled; his chest swelled with pride. He could hardly wait
for tomorrow to see her again.

He was so busy enjoying the sweet feeling that he didn't
hear David until he was practically on top of him. David
wiped a bunch of potato chip crumbs off the bench and sat.
Breaker bounded up and nosed in between his two buddies.
Benny felt something pushed into his hand and looked
down to see a slimy, yellow tennis ball. Breaker thumped
his tail against the wood and grinned. Benny gave the ball a
half-hearted toss. Breaker rushed to retrieve it, but when he
asked for seconds, Benny dropped the ball on the bench.

David picked it up, hid it behind his back and slipped

Breaker a dog biscuit. He gave Benny a hard look. "Something bothering you?"

Benny felt his happiness fizzle like shaken soda pop. He stuck out his chin. "Why do people keep asking me that?"

Breaker caught the harsh tone and wormed his head under Benny's arm.

Benny ruffled the puppy's topknot. It was all the encouragement Breaker needed. He stretched his front paws out in front of him, grabbed the toe of Benny's shoe and tugged. His tail whirred like a hummingbird's wings.

"Cut it out, Breaker," Benny ordered, louder than he had intended. Breaker slid down on his belly and hid his eyes behind his paws. The puppy waited a couple of seconds, feigning contrition, and opened one eye to peek at Benny.

He ruffled Breaker's topknot. "Sorry, boy," he said, patting the bench. The dog jumped up and leaned up against him. Benny turned to David. "If you're hoping to see Dr. Kate you can forget it. One of the mothers just went upstairs for her meeting, so she'll be forty-five minutes at least."

David rubbed his arm like someone had hit him with a sucker punch. "Not today."

Benny thrust out his chin. "She's not supposed to tell you secret stuff about me. It's illegal."

"People have other things on their minds besides you. You think it's easy running a school like this?"

"For a bunch of weirdoes, you mean?"

David thought a minute. "Did you see your mother yesterday?"

Benny wriggled his shoulders like he had an itch he couldn't reach. "None of your business, but for your information I'll probably never get to see her again."

David raised a skeptical eyebrow.

"It's true. My dad said he'll call the cops if she ever comes around again."

David tried a smile that didn't quite work. "Your dad didn't mean it. He couldn't."

"He meant it. Sonya had to pour him a triple." He hesitated. "If I tell you something, promise you'll keep it to yourself?"

David considered. "Promise, but its sounds like something you need to share with Dr. Kate."

"She knows. My dad caught me taking a couple of twenties out of his wallet, and when I said it was for my mother, he nearly split a gut. And that's not all. Sonya said that's what they get for wasting a ton of money they could spend on a lot better stuff, and that's probably where I learned to be a little thief."

David took off his cap and rubbed his hand over his head. What if Benny's mother weren't the real reason he needed money? Sometimes kids his age needed money for stuff they thought was cool but wasn't, like illegal drugs. He watched the evening news and knew what could happen. He could talk to Kate, but she might accuse him of sticking his nose in again. Besides, he hated to add to her worries when there might be no need. If Benny was taking drugs, the boy wouldn't be able to hide it for long. For now, he would wait and watch. He pulled his cap down snug on his head. "Your dad's not so bad. There are lots worse."

Benny stood, his fists tight, his chin thrust out. "How would you know?"

Breaker jumped off the bench and looked back and forth between the two of them, a frown wrinkling his handsome brow.

David opened his mouth with a ready answer, then closed it again. He rose, too, and turned to leave. "You're right. How would I know?"

Benny stretched out a hand to stop him. "Sorry, David, sorry. I was angry at my dad, so I picked on you. Dr. Kate says I do that a lot. It's just that I had a really great plan, and now it's all ruined."

David waited.

"I've been saving up for a special birthday dinner for my mom at the Spinning Wheel. It's her favorite restaurant. Maybe then she'll. . ."

David felt the blood rush to his head. All the times he would have given anything to feel as important to his mother as her dogs came flooding back: the mornings he had eaten a cold breakfast alone; the afternoons he had rushed home to an empty house to show her what he had made in school; the nights he had lain awake listening for her footstep on the stairs. Every rational thought in his head told him Benny was setting himself up for more hurt, but, like Benny, he couldn't stop wishing. "Maybe Dr. Kate can convince your dad to change his mind. Would you like me to talk to her?"

Benny's whole body relaxed. "Would you? She always says I need to speak for myself, but it never does any good."

Too late, David realized that he had stepped into deep waters without his boots on. "Dr. Kate's right," he hurried to say. "Besides, I'm not sure she'd listen to me."

"Sure she would. She likes you. She probably thinks you'll give the school money."

David laughed. "If that's what she thinks, she's hiding it well."

Benny was undeterred. "So you'll talk to her?"

David hesitated, but his heart was too strong for his head. He nodded.

Benny popped a wide grin. "Thanks, David. You're the best."

Sonya thrust an arm through the Corvette window. A piece of paper dangled from the tips of two fingers. "Look at this. Fifty-seven on a spelling test. I found it crumpled up in an empty potato chip bag in his lunch box — as if stealing from your wallet wasn't bad enough."

Benny's dad cut the engine and loosened his tie. "I thought he was supposed to be in his room doing homework every afternoon." He grabbed his briefcase from the back seat and headed toward the door. "Fix me a Scotch and get that doctor of his on the phone. I intend to get to the bottom of this."

CHAPTER TWENTY

Benny dangled a bit of glazed donut left over from breakfast above Breaker's head. "No, sit," he shouted like people do when they're trying to make foreigners understand English. It didn't work any better on the puppy. Breaker leapt for the donut and grazed it with the end of his tongue. Benny studied the donut carefully for dog germs and ate it himself.

David groaned. It was the first week of June. The Housatonic dog show was three weeks away. Breaker could just slip under the six months age requirement, but at this rate he wouldn't be prepared. The boy was as much of a problem as the dog. Kate had phoned using an "I told you so" voice and let him know Benny's dad had threatened to ban the boy from dog shows unless his math grades improved. He had thanked Kate for the heads up and promised to turn Benny's math grade around. It was a promise he hoped he could keep.

"Shall we try that again?" he asked with a weary sigh.

Benny glared at him. "*We're* finished, but you can try if you want."

David silently warned himself to be patient. Teaching Breaker a few basic manners was harder than he ever imagined it would be. Good thing help was on its way. Jim and Holly Wren had trained almost as many poodles as Bess. Hopefully, he could keep Benny on board until they arrived.

"You almost had it that time," David encouraged. "One more try."

Benny dropped down onto the grass. "Bess has the right idea. I'm thinking of retiring myself." Now that he thought of it, he hadn't paid Bess a visit lately. Old people needed cheering up, and he was good at that. He had caught her sneaking out of the puppy shed a couple of times when he was early picking up Breaker, but she had hurried away without speaking. Maybe she was sick. Old people were always getting sick. She said she didn't have cancer or anything, but a person never knew. He wasn't feeling so great himself. A greenish-purple bruise had formed on his shin when he bumped into Ms. Jeanette's desk on his way out to recess, and it could be serious. Practically the same thing happened to a guy on TV. The wound got infected, and they had to cut off his leg! He'd better show it to Dr. Kate at their meeting tomorrow — just in case.

David was afraid he was losing the boy. He sat beside him and asked calmly, "If you give up now, what'll happen to Breaker? You can't just say you want a puppy one minute and throw him out the next."

Benny lifted his eyes in a cool stare. "Why not? People do it to kids all the time."

David took a deep breath. "Breaker loves you. Doesn't that mean anything?"

Benny hadn't expected that. He shifted his gaze to Breaker. The puppy was shaking a chew toy back and forth like a dead rat and making pleased puppy growls. Breaker felt Benny's eyes on him and hurried over, his tail whirring with pleasure at being noticed.

Benny's shoulders dropped. He wrapped his arm around the puppy's neck. "Don't worry, big guy. You're safe with me."

David nodded, satisfied the crisis had passed. "See if you can get Breaker to heel," he said, but the boy's attention had wandered to a different dog. McCreery had slipped quietly into their little group. He made a wide circle, came to a stop, stood at attention and circled again. His stuffed pink and lime fish stuck out of both sides of his mouth. Obviously, he thought he looked rather fetching.

Benny wrinkled his nose. "What's McCreery doing?" He pointed at his own head and drew a corkscrew in the air. "Do you think he has mental problems or something? You can tell me. Some of the kids at my school do, so I'm used to it."

David smothered a laugh and studied the dog more closely. McCreery still wasn't back to one hundred percent of his old self, but his coat was thick, his almond shaped eyes were bright with a lively intelligence, and his gait was elegant as a gazelle's. "If you ask me, he's practicing for the show ring."

Benny gripped his waist and spat out an exaggerated guffaw. "Good one."

"No, really," David insisted. "I've been watching him do it for years. If I didn't know better, I'd say he's staying in shape in case his time ever comes."

Benny's eyes grew wide as twin moons. "You mean for Westminster?" He gave the dog a second look and frowned. McCreery's close-cropped coat looked nothing like the photos taken back in the day when he was a famous champion. "I'm not sure."

McCreery tossed his head, nose in air as if highly insulted, and made the circle again. He seemed to be enjoying himself, perhaps remembering the applause when the judge handed Bess a silver trophy.

"He could use a haircut but if ever a dog deserved a chance at Westminster, it was McCreery," David explained.

"Even my Aunt Mona doesn't understand why my mother never entered him. He was a finished champion, so she could have."

Breaker had listened to enough talk about his father and gave an impatient, sharp puppy bark. At five months old, he had almost reached his full size and looked more like his sire than ever. The proud thrust of his chest and his regal head — when he was quiet long enough to show them off — were qualities that had made his father a champion when he was almost the same age.

McCreery sat, scratching an errant itch behind his ear, and dropped his toy fish on the ground. Seeing his chance, Breaker dashed in and snatched it away. He made fast circles around McCreery, tossing his head with a wide grin that said, "Come get me."

"Oh, oh," Benny said, leaping to his feet. "This isn't going to be pretty."

McCreery let out a low growl and stayed put where he was. That's all it took. Breaker dropped the fish like it was made of hot chili peppers and huddled behind Benny, tail tucked under his tummy. McCreery gave a disdainful look at the cowering puppy and picked up the prize in his mouth.

David smiled. "McCreery's still top dog. Now, let's see if you can get this puppy back on track."

Benny slipped a couple of dog biscuits out of his pocket, tossed one to McCreery, and shouted, "Sit!" at Breaker. The puppy dropped like a stone, quivering with excitement. He took the biscuit gently from Benny's hand, but his good behavior lasted only as long as the flavor. He gave a shrill bark, tail vibrating with anticipation. Clearly, he thought he deserved another. McCreery gave a disgusted snort, or maybe it was only a sneeze, and padded off.

"Looks like the puppy's winning," boomed a man's voice.

David looked up with a smile. A man and a woman in

their forties were heading toward them. They were both thin and of medium height. The man had salt and pepper hair; hers was dark and hung in a neat page boy. Her silk scarf sporting a famous signature hung loosely around her neck and matched the aubergine and navy in her husband's tie.

David waved his hand toward Benny like the maitre d' at a fancy restaurant showing a good tipper to his favorite table. "Holly, Jim, this is Benny Neusner, the young man I've been telling you about. Benny, meet Holly Wren and Dr. Jim Wren. They've bred a kennel full of champion Standard Poodles themselves and have offered to give us a few tips."

Benny remembered his manners and shook hands with them both. He gave Jim a careful look. "Don't tell me you're another meeting doctor?"

Jim smiled. "No such luck. Head colds and flu, mostly." He turned to David. "We saw McCreery heading back home just now. Did you ever find out who stole him?"

David shook his head. "The only clue was a wood paneled station wagon, and that's not much to go on."

Jealous that he wasn't in the spotlight, Breaker wriggled and pulled on his lead, eager to meet the company.

"It's okay, you can let him go, Benny," David said.

"You sure? He's got his ADHD really bad this morning."

Breaker ran back and forth between Holly and Jim, tail hidden, butt wriggling. He was so beside himself he piddled on the tooled leather flap decorating the top of Jim's shoe. Benny was sure some cuss words even his mother hadn't heard of before would follow, but Jim just took out the handkerchief folded in his breast pocket and wiped it dry. Before Jim could put the handkerchief away, the wind lifted a corner, catching Breaker's eye. Wouldn't a game of capture the flag be fun?

"No!" Benny hollered.

The puppy pressed his belly against the grass and covered his eyes with his paws in a passable imitation of regret. He lay quietly for a moment, then removed one paw and peeked at Benny impishly.

Benny grinned back.

David stuck his unlit pipe in his mouth the way he did when he was worried. He turned to the Wrens. "Do you think he'll settle down enough for the show ring?"

"The boy or the dog?" Jim asked in a stage whisper.

Holly frowned at Jim, but she was smiling, too. She turned to David and Benny. "Poodles are supposed to be lively. It's in the standard." Her musical voice might have belonged to an opera star.

Benny puffed out his chest. "Yeah, lively. You could say that."

Jim scrunched down and held his hand out to the puppy. "Come, boy," he called firmly. Breaker approached slowly, head down. Jim reached for the lead, and Breaker sprung back, grinning and wagging his tail. He ducked under Jim's arm, ran around Holly like a goal post and snagged David's khaki pants cuff.

"He's usually not this bad," David apologized, trying to keep his dignity as he grappled with tenacious puppy teeth.

Holly bent down. "Let me try. Come, Breaker. Good boy," she called in a soothing whisper.

Lo and behold, the puppy came and sat at Holly's feet like he was planning to do it all along if only someone would ask nicely. She reached into her pocket for a training treat and let Breaker get a whiff. Then she straightened up and jiggled the lead. "Heel!"

"Yeah, sure," Benny said under his breath. He had tried it a hundred times, and it had worked maybe twice.

Without missing a beat, Holly said in a voice that melted

like whipped cream on cocoa, "Benny, watch what I'm doing. See how I never take my eyes off him." The puppy heeled perfectly like he had been doing it all his life.

"No way!" Benny exclaimed. "A miracle."

Holly held up another treat and made Breaker sit prettily before getting his reward. "It's called baiting," she explained. "Breaker must learn to stand on his own looking handsome. No judge wants to watch a handler constantly moving a dog's legs into position."

Jim leaned back with his arms folded, taking in every move as Holly and Breaker completed a circle. "Beautiful," Jim pronounced when Holly came to a halt in front of him like he was the judge at an important show. He took the lead. "Now you watch," he told his wife.

For the most part, Breaker walked politely around the imaginary ring, even if he did try to pounce on Jim's stomach when Jim told him to stay. Jim corrected him immediately with a quick jerk down on the lead. When Breaker got back in control of himself, Jim slipped him another training treat.

"That's a good trick," Benny said to no one in particular. An almost imperceptible nod passed between husband and wife, and he wondered if he'd be the next to be tested.

Jim handed Benny the lead and a couple of liver treats. "Your turn."

Benny shrugged and took the lead. "What the heck? Let's go, big fella," he boomed.

The three adults groaned at once. "Calm voice," Holly coached, but it was too late. Breaker landed with his front paws on a tender spot between Benny's legs.

Ignoring Benny's pained expression, Jim ordered, "Pull straight down on the lead and tell him, 'No,' like you mean it." Benny managed to pull on the lead, but his "no" fell short of a masterful command. Breaker jumped into the air, yanking Benny's arm skywards. The boy tumbled onto his back and lay there while Breaker licked his face.

"Is Benny all right?" Holly asked with a pretty frown.

"He's fine, just playing it for all it's worth," David reassured her.

Jim lowered his voice. "I'm not sure about the boy. Couldn't you handle Breaker yourself, David, or maybe hire a professional?"

David held a warning finger to his lips. "The boy can hear like a Chihuahua." David stepped closer to the Wrens. "Bess has a soft spot for Benny. He's the only reason she kept the puppy at all. I know it sounds crazy, but I'm convinced that if she gets back in the game, it'll be because of him."

"Breaker shows all the promise of his father," Holly said. "I don't see how she can resist."

"Once she sees him in the ring, she'll be hooked," David said confidently.

Jim shifted like he had a burr in his sock. "But she knows? You're not training Breaker in secret?"

David shrugged. "Not exactly. She gave Benny permission to show him, but naturally she never thought he could. She didn't count on me helping him."

Jim and Holly exchanged worried glances. "Legally Breaker's her dog. You can't enter him in a dog show unless she registers him." Holly said.

An ominous silence fell. No one spoke. Even Breaker froze in place.

David turned and discovered Bess standing behind him. She looked like she had just gotten out of bed, right down to her scruffy slippers. McCreery was at her side. She gave Jim and Holly a cool look and circled Breaker slowly, hands clasped rigidly behind her. Anger and pleasure struggled for dominance in her face, or perhaps it was fear. Breaker seemed to know something momentous was happening and stood like a statue until she completed her circle. Then she turned and headed back towards her house.

For once, McCreery didn't follow. He walked purposefully up to the younger dog, head erect like a champion. It was almost like he was trying to let his son know he was still the superior dog.

Breaker lowered his head, tail swaying slowly, and waited.

CHAPTER TWENTY-ONE

Standing on the front stoop of Bess' house, David spied his mother through the living room window. She was alone, so she must have sent the Wrens packing. She paced back and forth between the matching Queen Anne chairs on either side of the fireplace. Each time she made a turn, she grabbed onto their backs for support.

He rang the front doorbell.

She hesitated and began pacing again.

"I know you're in there, Mother. I'm not leaving."

She waited a minute and then swung the door open. She peered behind him. "Any more surprise visitors?"

"Only McCreery." Oddly, the old dog was waiting patiently at David's heel as if he were a guest who needed an invitation himself. "May we come in?"

She waved them inside. "Go ahead and say your piece, but it won't do any good. Holly and Jim already gave it their best shot." She sat in one of the Queen Anne chairs.

David moved to the chair opposite. He plucked a current issue of *Dog World* off the seat. He looked back and forth between the photo of Picture Perfect Pete on the cover and the headshot of McCreery occupying pride of place on top of the mantle. If he didn't know better, he would think the photo was Breaker.

McCreery bounded up on the good sofa and circled around for the right spot. Bess threw him a warning look but let him stay. "If you're using McCreery to soften me up, think again."

He felt like a chunk of suet was stuck in his throat. "Sorry, this isn't easy."

She snorted. "Glad to hear it." She squeezed her thick eyebrows together and glared at her son. "How could you encourage the boy like that, getting his hopes up for nothing? Anyone can see he'll never be able to handle a spirited dog like Breaker. The poor child can barely manage himself. And to do it behind my back. With Jim and Holly, no less!"

He leaned forward, hands folded prayer-like. "Mother, your life is a mess. You don't go out, you don't talk to people, the house is a wreck, and the way you dress? Anyone who didn't know better would think you're a bag lady."

"It's my life. What's it to you?"

He rose, his arms stuck out like a battered scarecrow's. "You don't get it, do you? You haven't the faintest idea?"

"Not really."

"I'm your son. I love you." Maybe if he said it loud enough, she would hear him.

She stared at him, face blank.

He waited, but she said nothing. He spun on his heel. He had almost reached the door when she spoke.

"Wait, what do you want from me?"

He turned. Her mask was gone, leaving only a defeated old woman behind. In a flood, the bitterness drained out of him. "It's not what I want from you, mother. It's what I want *for* you." He stared at her for a long moment, the silence encasing them like a sprung trap. All of her muscles strained to keep her body in check and betrayed how much she wanted to give in and accept what he was offering.

"The puppy?" she asked finally, choking.

He exhaled a long sigh. He hadn't realized he'd been holding his breath. He nodded. "Breaker's as good as his father. Maybe better."

Hope flickered in her eyes, danced there for a moment, and fizzled like a candle with a wet wick.

Hot blood rose in his cheeks. "Why?"

She had no answer.

He turned and closed the door with quiet finality.

She moved to the sofa and pulled McCreery in close. She lifted his chin and looked in his eyes. McCreery was the only one who knew her secret. He had been there.

It was true she only wanted to show her dogs if she could take them into the ring herself, but there was more. Even after she had first made up her mind to raze Umpawaug Kennels, she still planned to keep one puppy from Susie's breeding with McCreery. She told herself she needed a younger dog for company now that McCreery was getting up in years, but in her heart of hearts, she wasn't ready to give up on her dream of Westminster if a special puppy like Breaker should come along.

All that changed one morning last fall when she was in the kitchen fixing breakfast. McCreery was with her, as usual, nosing around underfoot. She reached for something in the top cabinet and her trick knee gave out. She collapsed onto the floor, her leg twisted painfully underneath her. The slightest movement was excruciating, too agonizing even for tears. Of course, McCreery thought it was a wonderful joke. They had fooled around on the floor like this hundreds of times. He pounced on her with his paws on her shoulders, grinning widely, tail wagging excitedly. Off-balance and in pain as she was, the weight of him knocked her over the rest of the way. Instinctively, she shot her hand out and slapped him. Hard. McCreery cringed and crept back into a corner. His eyes were full of pain and confusion. She never wanted a dog to look at her like that again.

Nobody had seen her. No one else knew, but she could never trust herself again. Poodles love to fool around, and when McCreery only did what was in his nature to do, she struck him. She had done it out of fear, the fear of an old woman who was only now learning what it would be like to feel helpless, too weak to get up from a fall using her own muscles. The future had risen up to meet her. She wasn't ready, but she had no choice. Puppies are all play; they follow no rules. One minute they are loose skin and big feet curled up on a chair looking good enough to eat, and the next they are crawling between one's feet. She must have tripped over hundreds in her time. She couldn't take the chance again, not any more.

As if he were remembering along with her, McCreery stared at her in mute silence, eyes dark with worry. He shifted restlessly, dropping his chin lightly onto her shoulder.

"Sometimes, when you disappeared that time, I thought you had run away on purpose," she confessed in a choked voice. "My brain knew it wasn't true, but I worried you thought I might give you away, too, like the puppies. As if I could ever do that, darling, darling McCreery." She wrapped her arms around his neck. She knew her misery was making him miserable, too, but she couldn't get herself under control. The guilt had been held inside too long and streamed forth in the tears running down her face.

McCreery wriggled his head back and forth, freeing himself from her grasp. He hopped off the sofa and placed his front paws on her shoulders, sniffing her face, his touch as light as a friendly kiss. If he could have spoken, he would have told her all was forgiven the moment it happened. Instead, he lowered his head onto her lap and waited quietly until she wove her fingers through his topknot and held on for dear life.

CHAPTER TWENTY-TWO

Benny was seated at the computer station chasing sharks on the screen. Every time he answered a multiplication fact correctly, one of the sharp-toothed creatures got blasted to smithereens.

"Splat! Gotcha!" he announced, looking around the room for approval. No one paid any attention. Unperturbed, he returned to the screen. He hadn't seen Kate waiting, or pretended not to.

"Can you save that for later?" she asked. She noticed he had lost a bit of baby fat in the past few weeks. Maybe he was taking his work with Breaker seriously and getting some much needed exercise.

"Sure. Ms. Jeanette's just going to tell us about the dairies they used to have in Redding a long time ago. I like milk and everything, but I'm not interested in seeing it squirt out of a cow, if you know what I mean."

He put the game on "pause" and waved good-bye to the other kids with a flourish. Joel gave a half-hearted salute back without looking up from his book.

She led them to the lawn chairs on the deck of the main building. The chairs were the old-fashioned metal kind that populated the front of motels in the nineteen-fifties, only these were moss green and fresh from Millie's Plant and Garden. She got them for half-price at the end of last season when she said they were for the New Hope School. She sat and Benny sat beside her.

"Summer's here," he pronounced with a big smile. He threw out his arms and sucked fresh air deep into his lungs.

She wasn't there to discuss the weather. "Something has come to my attention that we need to discuss, Benny."

He rolled his eyes. "You need to get a life, Dr. Kate. All you do is work. Can't you smell the flowers? Hear the birds?"

She flushed. The boy felt responsible for every grown-up he met, not to mention everything that went on in the school. It was one of the things they were working on in their meetings. "Thank you, but I can take care of myself."

He rapped his knuckles on the arm of his chair. "I haven't seen David over here lately. You don't have a new boyfriend or anything, do you?" His eyes flashed to her ringless fingers.

Suddenly, she felt naked. She donned her most serious shrink face. "We're not here to talk about me, Benny."

He leaned back in his chair, surveying the grounds like they were his own particular kingdom. "Hey, where's Lotus?"

"Napping. She wore herself out playing Four Square with Miss Kim's class."

He drew his mouth into a frown. "That's not good. Lotus could be pregnant. Women get tired all the time when they're having babies."

Her head jerked up. Usually when kids started talking about pregnancies, they had overheard something at home. The last thing Benny needed was a new baby in his life.

He made a face. "You can breathe. Sonya's on the pill. I heard them talking."

"I see. Well, Lotus was fixed before I found her, at least

I think she was, so there won't be any new puppies, either."
Kate hoped it was true. Someone had dropped her off
at the school or maybe the little dog had found her own
way there. Kate had looked everywhere for an owner and
failed.

"You think?" Benny asked, lurching forward dramatically.
"You'd better know for sure unless you want a little surprise.
That's what my dad says anyway."

"Your Dad's right. We don't want any surprise puppies."

"Or kids!" He puffed out his chest. "My dad says I'm more
than enough."

She hid a smile. They needed to discuss what was
bothering her. "David stopped by to see me. He said you
want me to talk your Dad into letting you see your mother
again."

He beamed innocently. "It was David's idea. He's nuts
about you."

"Next time, please tell your friend David I'll handle the
therapy," she snapped, regretting it instantly. "It's nice that
he's helping you with your math, but it's your job to talk to
your dad. We've discussed that before."

He pouted, obviously unconvinced.

She struggled to keep her temper. Benny needed to
learn how to speak up for himself, and now weeks of work
were down the drain because of David's naive interference.
Benny's father wasn't the only parent who had a hard time
accepting that his son hadn't turned out the way he had
planned in the birthing room. No high school track star,
no ivy league graduate, no partner to take over his law firm
in time. In short, no one to walk in his footsteps. He loved
Benny, but he had trouble accepting his son's strengths for
what they were. They were working on that in their weekly
Parent Helper meetings. Benny's dad, and his mom, would
be his parents forever. If she could help them now, Benny
would succeed better in life after he moved on from New

Hope School.

When she felt composed again, she asked, "How's the dog training coming along? You and Breaker making any progress?"

Benny laced his fingers together and stretched his arms in front of his chest. "To tell the truth, me and Breaker aren't doing so hot. Housatonic's less than three weeks away, and that puppy would rather fool around than work. Sometimes he tries to outsmart me." His eyes started to fill. "I was fine when Jim Wren was showing me what to do. David's tried, but he's not that good." He gasped, afraid he'd undone his sales pitch. "About dogs, I mean. About other stuff, he's real smart."

She suppressed a sigh. Just as she had feared, Benny's hopes had outstripped his ability. "Breaker's a very energetic puppy, and you're just learning. It sounds like you could use some help."

His eyes lit up. "What about you? Lotus is a real obedient dog."

"Lotus was born with a different temperament, and she was pretty much trained when I found her. I'm afraid I don't know much about dogs. Not like Bess. If Housatonic's important to you, you know what you need to do."

"Yeah, yeah, I know. Talk to Bess."

She nodded. Maybe she was getting through to him after all.

"It won't do any good. Even David can't convince her, and he's tried, believe me."

"You're not David. They have their own issues."

"No kidding. All he thinks about is making his mother happy."

Kate let that one pass. Instead she said, "Even if Bess agrees, you'll be going up against some very experienced handlers. You can't let your heart get broken if you don't win. You've got to be prepared."

Benny held up both hands, palms up, like a man spinning pizza dough. "Don't worry, Dr. Kate. I'm prepared. No problem at all."

Chapter Twenty-Three

Now that Benny was standing on Bess' doorstep his stomach was twisted in knots. It didn't help that the house was dark and lonely-looking, the sort of place where a person could get swallowed up and disappear forever. He bent his neck back as far as it would go so he could see the turret rising into the night sky. It had a small window with diamond-shaped panes, and he thought he could see two yellow-green eyes staring out at him. Maybe his imagination was running wild, but he was glad Dr. Kate had said Lotus could come along for company.

He looked down at the little dog sitting calmly at his heel and his racing heart slowed a little. Dogs can smell stuff people can't — hear, too. Maybe even ghosts. To be on the safe side, maybe he should come back tomorrow before the sun went down. Tomorrow he wouldn't hang around showing off the new card trick David had taught him to the other kids whose parents were "stuck in traffic." He started to back away, but Lotus was looking forward to the visit. She stood on her hind legs and scratched the door eagerly. A moment later, it opened. McCreery's nose stuck through the crack.

"Come in," Bess said, holding the door open.

He hesitated.

"It's all right. The little dog can come in, too. She and McCreery are great friends, but I don't know her name."

This was a good start. He knew something she didn't. Maybe things would go his way after all. He flashed the smile he had been practicing in the mirror and answered, "Lotus, Lotus Kumar."

Lotus wiggled her hind end and panted excitedly. McCreery seemed as pleased as she was about the visit. He tossed his head in the direction of the stairs, and the two dogs raced each other upstairs, a route they apparently knew well.

She turned to him. "So, what dirty work has David sent you to do this time?"

He had never seen anybody flick her eyelashes so fast before. "I'm sorry you're too old for dog shows and everything, but I'm not and I've decided I want to be in this one called Housatonic. You might have heard of it."

She peered over her reading glasses like he was as welcome as a toothache. "Housatonic? You and that puppy dog? Tell David he's got to do better than that."

He jiggled his leg, and his cheeks turned red. "No, really, it's my idea. I reee-ally want to go."

"Well, good luck then, and in case you're interested, I'm the one who started Housatonic way back when." She started to open the door.

"No, wait! I need your help," he said, bouncing up and down on his heels. He reached in his pocket and pulled out a roll of bills. "I've got money. David's paying me to train Breaker. He made me promise not to steal from my dad any more."

She held up her hands. "Put your money away." Her eyebrows scrunched into a frown. "Perhaps you've forgotten what I said when you took Breaker. If you want to show him, I won't stop you. Just don't expect me to help."

He looked down and saw the sole of her shoe had come

loose. He pushed the money toward her. "I wouldn't be so quick to turn the cash down. You could fix your shoe, for example."

She eyed the offending object indifferently and signaled him to follow her. The flap, flap of the loose sole punctuated their way down the dark hall. To the right, a door opened onto a cheerful living room with overstuffed chairs. Fresh garden flowers in a cobalt blue vase sat on a round coffee table in front of the fireplace. Even a boy whose own room would never appear on the cover of *House Beautiful* knew this room didn't look like her. She continued on, eyes straight ahead, past the dining room with twin mahogany buffets holding matching sets of antique dishes. At the end of the hall, she stopped and took out a key. "My private office. Mona's not permitted."

Benny nodded. That explained the cheerful living room.

She held out an arm and swept Benny inside. A sliver of light snuck through a gap in the floor-length, dark draperies. Old dog show catalogues and dried newspaper clippings were strewn everywhere, even under the keyhole desk. On the walls, the flocked wallpaper was barely visible, hidden by what seemed like a hundred old black and white photos. A series of younger Besses holding silver trophies and handsome Standard Poodles with various colored coats stared out from them. It felt kind of creepy like an old black and white horror movie where an old woman who had nothing to live for except faded memories was plotting something ghastly for her handsome young nephew. He was about to tell her he had to get home and take out the garbage when she snapped on a lamp on a round table next to a wing-backed chair. She brushed some crumbs that might have come from dog biscuits and sat, motioning him to the chair opposite.

"Is that smell old poodle fur?" he asked, wriggling his

nose like a prairie dog popping out of its hole.

She gave him a withering glance, and he shrank into his seat.

"Poodles do not smell," she corrected in a growl scarcely above a whisper. It was a lot more effective than the shouting he had gotten used to before his parent's divorce. "Poodles don't have fur like other dogs. It's real hair and grows, like yours. Consequently, it doesn't smell, unless the owner never shampoos it." She peered at him with big eyes. "You do shampoo occasionally yourself, I imagine?"

He rubbed his hand over his bangs. They ruffled back down over his forehead like falling dominoes. He would have given anything if his bangs would slick back like his mother's favorite movie star, or tumble in dark curls over his forehead like David's, but no matter how much goop he squeezed on, they came out like he had shampooed with Vaseline. "Sorry, no offense."

She softened at once. "None taken. You didn't know." She crossed her legs and turned full face to him. "You were saying you wanted my help. I can think of three reasons against it. First, it takes a lot of work to be in a dog show. Second, you don't like poodles which are the only kind of dog around here — except for Lotus, of course, and third, Breaker isn't settled down enough for you to handle him in the ring."

He grimaced. His plan wasn't working. He thought about bolting, but then he imagined his mother's smile when she saw him holding the blue ribbon and slogged on. "I can work hard when I want to, and I like some poodles. For example, I like McCreery and I like Breaker. If you helped me, I'm sure I could manage."

She shook her head. "It'd never work."

He squirmed in his chair. His favorite TV show was coming on in twenty minutes, and she was wasting his time. He stood, preparing to leave. "All right. If you won't help me with Breaker, I'll take Lotus."

Her next words were softer than he expected. "Lotus is a sweet dog with a cute personality and a pretty little face, but she's not registered with AKC — the American Kennel Club. You can't enter her in an official dog show."

"No problem," he insisted, waving her objections away with his hand. "A dog doesn't need to be pure-breed for Junior Showmanship. David says…"

He clamped his hand to his mouth, sure he'd just lost his last chance, but all she said was, "David's quite the man for all seasons."

"Oh, yes, ma'am. He's a real clever guy. Dr. Kate's crazy about him." He cringed and covered his mouth again.

Her thick eyebrows shot up. "Your shrink knows about this idea of yours?"

"It was practically her idea. I mean mine." He blushed. "What I mean is she thinks it'd be fantastic if I had a hobby going to dog shows. And by the way, here's a hint in case David ever brings her over here: she hates being called 'the principal.' She says we're a team all working together."

"Really?" she answered absently, as if she weren't really listening. She rose. "I'm hungry. You hungry? Mona made a coconut layer cake."

He flashed a relieved smile. "I'm always hungry. My stepmother doesn't like my baby fat. She has me on a diet." He thrust out his stomach and patted it tenderly.

She rolled her eyes and headed toward the kitchen. She signaled him to follow. She grabbed two plates and two forks and placed them and a three layer cake on the table. "Sit," she invited. She cut two large slices and placed one in front of Benny. "David's favorite," she explained, licking a finger. She sat and took a large bite. A sprinkling of coconut fell onto her shirt, but she didn't notice. She looked across the table, deep into his eyes, as if she wanted to know a part of him that couldn't be seen.

He squirmed uncomfortably. What was she up to? He was the one trying to con her, not the other way around, but that's how it was beginning to feel. "So, anyway, I was hoping you could give me a few pointers," he said, redirecting her back to the purpose of his visit. "The Housatonic Dog Show is practically here, so it won't be that much work."

She brushed his words onto the floor along with a few stray crumbs. "Here's what I'll do. I'll teach you about dog shows and handling, but only until Housatonic. After that, you're on your own."

He narrowed his eyes suspiciously. Something didn't feel right. The old woman had something up her sleeve, but what? Still, he was getting what he wanted, wasn't he?

A creaking noise at the door made them both turn to look. A nose appeared through the crack and then a head. McCreery padded softly into the quiet room, his nails clicking on the linoleum. He looked first at one and then the other, as if deciding, and then made a tight circle on the floor between them, measuring the space so as to divide it equally. He sank down gracefully with one paw draped over the other and waited patiently as if expecting news.

Benny turned to Bess with a guilty look on his face. In his worries about Breaker, he had forgotten all about McCreery. Breaker was his dog now, but McCreery had a special place in his heart and he always would. "I think McCreery should come along on Breaker's workouts. He'll be jealous if the puppy gets all the attention. You're too old to run around any more, and he could use the exercise."

McCreery blew out a happy puff of air, so he decided he was on the right track.

Bess clasped her hands together and smiled approvingly. "Good idea. No reason for him to sit around getting fat and lazy. Besides, you're right about his jealousy. He's been top dog around here for a long time, and he's not planning to yield to his son any time soon."

Benny scrunched up his nose, considering. He would hate to hurt McCreery's feelings, but he needed Breaker to win at Housatonic. "Can't there be two top dogs?"

"Obviously not," she answered, fluttering her eyelashes.

Benny decided he'd worry about it later. He held up his hand for a high five. "Deal?"

She hesitated, unsure what it meant. Then she remembered something she had seen on TV and slapped back. "Deal!"

Chapter Twenty-Four

Without Benny, the kitchen seemed empty like a book without words. Bess sat quietly for a minute wondering if somehow the boy had outsmarted her. She shook her head. No, that wasn't possible — unless her son David had.

She heard a noise behind her. She turned, supposing it was McCreery. Instead, Mona stepped out of the pantry. "Eavesdropping again?"

Mona attempted a hurt expression and held out a jar of apple butter with "Umpawaug Valley" on the label. "I was hunting for this when you and Benny came in. You know how a person can live without apple butter for months and then all of a sudden gets the hungries for it? Before I could announce my presence, Benny was pouring his heart out and doing a good job of remembering all of David's hints while he was at it. The poor kid would've been flummoxed if I'd popped out from nowhere."

Bess rolled her eyes.

Mona held up a thick piece of rye bread with a questioning look. Bess studied the cake and then the apple butter. She stuck the cake in the fridge. Mona pulled another slice of rye bread out of a white bakery sack and popped both into the toaster.

Bess peeked inside, as if it were possible the bread had vanished somehow. "For your information, I'm not in the least deceived by David's transparent ruse to involve me in Breaker's show career. He should be ashamed using the boy like that, but he'll find out the joke is on him."

"You don't say?"

"Strange, I'm not sure the boy likes poodles any more than he used to, but he really wants to be in that dog show. I'm certain of it."

"Can he win? The boy I mean?"

Bess reached across the table for the apple butter. "Possibly. It's a little country show only worth a point or two — unless Hannah packs it with her dogs — and I'll be teaching him." She screwed up her mouth determinedly and gave the jar a strong twist. "The lid's stuck."

Mona pulled a gadget out of the junk drawer. "Here, I ordered it from a catalogue. Something to help old ladies like us with no men handy for opening jars."

Bess gave a disgusted grunt, but took it anyway. The lid opened on the first twist, and the smell of overripe apples filled the room. She wiped her fingers on the hem of her shirt. "When David sees I can turn my back on a winning dog, he'll have to believe I'm serious. Maybe then he'll stay out of my business."

Mona frowned prettily. "But what about the boy? Won't winning build up his hopes all the more?"

Bess slathered a swath of apple butter across her toast. "Maybe, but maybe he'll be satisfied. He doesn't seem like the type who can stick with anything very long."

Mona reached for the jar. "I have to agree with you there," she said, surprising her sister.

"The best outcome would be for Hannah to take Breaker like I wanted in the first place. A puppy that looks like him deserves a show career. David knows that much, and if he doesn't, Hannah will be sure to inform him."

"You mean, if you can resist a winning puppy?"

"Exactly."

Sonya placed a frosty martini glass at her husband's elbow. "I thought Benny promised to turn over a new leaf. I had to take out the trash myself three times this week."

Benny's dad kept his eyes on the Red Sox batter. "He's training a puppy for the old lady next door. At least he's stopped whining about getting a dog."

"That's all well and good, but who's going to train Benny? That's what I'd like to know."

"He got an 83 on a math test, and he actually finished his homework every night this week. I checked. If he keeps that up, he and I will be partners yet: Neusner and Neusner, Attorneys at Law."

Sonya cringed. Her insides felt like a size ten foot trying to squeeze into a size two shoe. Dr. Kate had reminded them both in their meeting last week that Benny's academic horizons were limited, but his father still couldn't face facts. "So you approve of this dog business?" she asked evenly, skirting the issue.

He nodded. "For now, as long as he keeps up his schoolwork. Holding the dogs out as lure may help him stay focused. It's the carrot-and-stick approach coaches use to keep their athletes' eligible academically."

"Mmm," Sonya murmured thoughtfully. "And his mother? What about her?"

"If he has another good week, he can see her on her birthday." He picked up the glass and stared into the clear liquid like a fortune teller. "I only hope she doesn't let the boy down."

CHAPTER TWENTY-FIVE

Housatonic was a small time country event compared to Westminster, but to Benny's eyes it was as confusing as a shopping mall with no signs on the stores. Pedigree dogs of all sizes and shapes were heading toward a large canvas tent, and as far as Breaker was concerned, every one of them looked and smelled delightful. Off to one side, a refreshment stand displayed a blinking, neon hot dog slathered with yellow mustard. Benny wished he had one right now to calm his stomach.

David swept his arm in an arc across the campus and announced, "Once upon a time all this was part of the famous Danbury State Fair. Back when Bess and Mona were girls, every school in Connecticut closed on a Friday and kids got in free."

"Cool," Benny exclaimed, remembering with a shudder the homework piled up and waiting for him at home. Summer School had started last week, and his dad expected him to be stuck in his room every night hitting the books.

They loaded the mountain of paraphernalia a poodle needs to look his best onto a cart and started for the grooming area. Benny gripped Breaker's lead tightly, but so far the puppy had managed the excitement without getting too rambunctious. Four Pekinese on intertwined leads passed nearby, and he didn't let out a peep.

They stopped at a table near the entrance so David could buy a show catalogue. It listed the name of every dog entered, the dog's parents, and the owner. Serious breeders studied it like the Bible.

Breaker reverted to his old self as they approached the grooming area. He strained at the lead while Benny stumbled along behind, the sides of his blue blazer flapping like fins. They careened their way down the length of the tent, past more than one handler who raised an eyebrow or snickered at the sorry display.

Benny gulped as he saw Bess waiting in the section where most of the poodles had set up their gear, her arms crossed in a silent expression of distaste. She grabbed the lead and gave a no-nonsense yank downward. "Sit," she ordered. Like an Olympic obedience champion, Breaker sat. She circled the puppy, studying every inch. When she finished, she handed the lead back to Benny. "Here, try and do likewise."

"Greetings, Mother," David said, bringing up the rear with the cart. He removed his blue blazer, the twin of Benny's, and pointed to the portable grooming table waiting to be set up. "Care to lend a hand?"

She sniffed and turned to Benny. "Good luck, son. Just keep telling yourself, 'I'm in charge,' and you'll do fine." With a cool look at David, she left, presumably to find a seat in the spectators' section.

"Bess still seems mad at you. I thought you two made up," Benny said. He hated when his mother looked at him like that, and it probably didn't feel any better when you were old.

David shrugged indifferently. "I'm not worried. If Breaker makes a good showing today, she'll be hooked."

Benny tried a weak smile. Maybe David was the one fooling himself because he wanted her to be happy so much. He signaled Breaker onto the grooming table. The puppy hopped on board immediately. Grooming is part of a poodle's life, and Breaker was learning. He could be shown in puppy trim today, so the job was easier than in another six months, but even now the judge would be looking for a top-knot that would grow into a full mane. Before Benny was through, Breaker's top-knot needed to look and feel like brown velvet fluff. Unfortunately, the puppy decided the shiny metal object was a delightful doggie toy and kept nibbling on the handle. Benny waved a liver treat under his nose. Distracted for the moment, Breaker allowed him to fluff out his tail and ears. The puppy looked so fine Benny spit in his hand and slicked back his own bangs. They were ready to win.

Benny scanned the crowd of handlers and dogs gathering for the various classes. At a bare six months of age, Breaker would be shown in the youngest class of puppy dogs. He was pretty certain Hannah wouldn't pass up the chance to show off Chicory, the black puppy that looked so much like Breaker.

Hannah must have been looking for them, too, because her hand shot up and waved them over to the ring where the American Eskimo dogs were finishing up. A stack of crates was piled up beside her. Two of Breaker's sisters were soft-mouth wrestling at the end of Hannah's lead, and a third was waiting in a crate off to one side. A man Benny assumed to be Hannah's handler was putting the final touches on a full-grown male, scissoring his coat, resetting the lines of the trim and smoothing out the finish. The way the dog stood patiently made the job look easy, but it took years of practice to do it right. Benny could hardly believe that under the fancy haircut the dog was the same as McCreery and Breaker, but the funny part was the dog didn't look that silly. He had the same winning smile and mischief in his eye as the two poodles Benny had grown to love.

Hannah pulled her glasses down to the end of her nose and stared at Benny like he was a cockroach on a fancy dinner she had paid a lot of money for. "I didn't know you were entering Breaker in Junior Showmanship," she told David in a thin voice.

The color rose in Benny's cheeks, and David laid a warning hand on his arm. He could imagine how Hannah would feel if she missed the chance to compete against Breaker after carting so many dogs to the show. "You remember Benny Neusner," he told Hannah. "He'll be handling Breaker today in the class for six-to-nine month puppy dogs. Bess has been training him herself."

Appeased, Benny leaned down and peered inside the crate at Hannah's feet. "Where's Chicory?"

Hannah shifted uncomfortably. "He got a sliver of glass stuck in his paw last night. Someone broke a soda bottle and failed to clean up properly. The vet said it was only a surface wound but enough to keep him home today."

Benny shuddered, imagining how he'd feel if something like that happened to Breaker.

Hannah nodded at a young puppy dog that was waiting patiently for his turn in the ring. "Looks like Breaker will only have one dog to beat in the first class — his brother Licorice."

Benny wrinkled his nose. Had Hannah named all the puppies after food? "Looks like you've got your hands full even without Chicory," he said, pointing at Hannah's three puppy girls.

David nodded. "There could be enough for a major."

Benny frowned. "What's that?"

"A major win means defeating a substantial number of the same breed at a single show. The number of dogs needed varies in different sections of the country and from breed to breed," David explained.

Hannah stepped in to clarify. "For a major, it usually

takes winning several classes at a single show. Otherwise, there wouldn't be enough dogs to beat. The class between Breaker and Licorice is only the start."

David nodded. "The really big shows are worth five points. To become a champion and be invited to a show like Westminster dogs need to earn fifteen points. They have to win two majors, each worth three, four or five points, and they must win under different judges. The remaining points can come from shows worth any number of points as long as the total adds up to fifteen."

Benny wrinkled his forehead. "Wouldn't one major be enough?"

David laughed. "Two are supposed to keep mediocre dogs from accruing enough points from cheap wins against slim competition."

Benny plopped down onto the edge of a crate as if exhausted at the mere thought. "Sounds like a lot of work."

Hannah's smile widened as she readied a surprise. "Chicory's three sisters will be in the same class, and you'll never guess who's offered to help."

Benny and David turned together to look down the aisle to where Hannah was pointing. Bess saw them and waved. Her smile could have lit up a parking lot. She was holding the lead of a graceful black female who, like the others, had grown considerably in the past few months. Breaker had grown, too, but the change didn't seem as dramatic in a puppy they saw every day.

They were interrupted by the sound of someone blowing into a microphone. "Testing, testing," a man's deep voice announced. "Standard Poodle males, six-to-under-nine months, in ring three."

"That's you. The steward will give you a paper with a number to put on your sleeve and show you to your place," Hannah said helpfully. "The judge will signal you to come up for inspection when it's your turn."

Bess had taught Benny that every kind of dog was judged against a standard written by the national organization for that breed. PCA — the Poodle Club of America — wrote the ones for all three varieties of poodles: Toys, Miniatures and Standards. The judge picked the dog that came closest to meeting the written standard, or at least she was supposed to. Bess hinted that occasionally someone picked a particular dog for reasons that had little to do with the standard, but most judges were hard working, superbly trained experts on many different breeds.

Benny hurried to where other dogs and handlers were already collected around the entry to the ring. No one wanted to take a chance on missing a class. He checked his watch against the time Bess had shown him in the judging program and saw his class was right on schedule.

He took his place behind Licorice, not that it was much of a line with only the two puppies. Still, this was his first competition — and Breaker's — and once David took his seat at ringside, he was hit with a touch of nerves. He looked around for a friendly face and recognized Licorice's handler as the man he had seen earlier grooming Hannah's dogs. He was middle-aged, tall and reedy, with black wire-rimmed glasses and kind eyes. He was attaching a paper number to his arm with a rubber band. Two other papers stuck out of his jacket pocket. Licorice waited quietly on a loose lead.

Benny wiped the light sweat blistering his forehead and dried his hand on the side of his pants. "I'm Benny, Benny Neusner," he said, his inexperience sticking out like extra elbows.

The man gave Breaker an admiring once-over and offered Benny his free hand. "Felix Barnet," he said with a buck-toothed grin. He was about to say more when the show steward signaled them both to circle the ring. "Good luck, Benny Neusner," he said kindly.

Benny double wrapped the lead around his hand. "I'm in charge, I'm in charge," he repeated under his breath. He completed the circle and then moved to the side, watching carefully as the judge put Licorice through his paces. The inspection went exactly the way Bess had described, and he felt his confidence growing.

The judge waved Licorice off to the side, and all eyes turned to Benny and Breaker. Benny leaned down and whispered into Breaker's ear, "This is it, boy. Here we go." They stepped up to the judge, and Benny felt the color rise in his cheeks as it occurred to him for the first time how embarrassing it would be if they messed up, especially with Bess there watching. Fortunately, Breaker got a helpful dose of stage fright himself. He stood calmly for the judge's hands-on inspection and walked sedately down and back without a hitch. The judge ordered both dogs to circle the ring once more. Then he handed Benny the blue ribbon.

David held up a high five as Benny and Breaker danced out of the ring. Benny slapped back, but his gaze was still on the ribbon. He rubbed his thumb over its silky softness and handed it to David, eyes lingering.

David studied the dark blue silk. "Breaker's first win. Yours, too. How'd you like to have it?"

Benny's eyes widened, but he'd been fooled before. "It's not a trick? For keeps?"

An old sadness bubbled up in David and escaped in a sigh. "No trick. For keeps."

If Hannah was upset by Breaker's win, she did a good job of hiding it. Benny only had time to slip the ribbon into his jacket pocket before she was standing in front of him with her hand outstretched. "Congratulations," she said, nodding at David and pumping Benny's hand up and down.

Benny wondered where Bess was. His stomach rumbled

and he remembered he'd been too nervous for a real breakfast, just a half dozen jelly donuts and a quart of orange juice. "Maybe Bess is getting herself a hot dog," he said. "A couple of foot-longs with double chili cheese and sauerkraut would taste good about now. And a slice of pepperoni pizza if they have any."

Hannah and David rolled their eyes and smiled. "I'll go," David offered and left.

Hannah studied Benny with new interest. "You'll have a bit of a wait before you and Breaker go up against the other winners. All the male poodles need to compete in their classes first."

He glanced at the ring where Felix was waiting to take in the black dog in full coat he had seen earlier. The big dog pranced in place like a thoroughbred race horse at the starting gate. "Him, too?" he gulped.

"If he wins his class."

"And that's it?"

She shook her head. "Not really. The whole routine is repeated for the females. Winner's Dog and Winner's Bitch compete for Best of Breed. Jim and Holly Wren have brought their champion DandyGirl. She'll be hard to beat."

"And that's it?" he squeaked. He was tired just thinking about it.

She laughed her deep rumbly laugh. "I'm afraid not. The winners of each breed in the group compete against each other. Poodles are in a group called Non-Sporting."

"You mean poodles have to compete against dogs like Dalmatians and bulldogs?"

"All the winning Non-Sporting dogs go up against each other. They are judged against their own standard. If a bulldog's wrinkles fall short or a Dalmatian's spots, some other breed will win. Sometimes it seems like Non-Sporting is where they put all the dogs that don't fit someplace else — except Toy Poodles compete in the

Toy group. It's a little confusing at first."

He bobbed his head vigorously. "I'll say. And that's it?"

"Just one more. The seven Group winners go up against each other, and that winner is Best in Show."

He sighed. "It sure is a lot of work."

She made her excuses and left Benny to himself. His mouth was watering for those hot dogs, and he wondered where David had disappeared.

The announcer called for Bred-by-Exhibitor male dogs. Jim Wren was at the head of the line holding the lead of a beautiful black boy. Benny hadn't seen Jim earlier and decided he and Holly must have arrived late. The dogs went through their paces, and Jim's won easily. Jim stuck the ribbon in his pocket and looked around.

"Over here," Benny called from the sidelines where he was still waiting for his snack. "Congratulations," he said, shaking Jim's hand.

Jim looked proudly at the beautiful dog sitting quietly but alert by his side. "Yes, DandyBoy is having a good day. We're hoping to finish his championship today. Then we'll enter him in Specials and build up his record. Plenty of stud fees for a dog with a big record."

Benny had been gossiping too long, and Breaker was tired of it. He preferred to become better acquainted with DandyBoy and tried nosing under his tail. "Oooh, that's gross," Benny said, yanking him back.

Benny was pretty sure he couldn't hold out much longer without sustenance when he spotted David heading toward them with a white cardboard box. Breaker saw him, too, and broke free of his lead. He landed on David's chest with his two front paws. David barely saved Benny's lunch.

Jim hid a smile and excused himself to go search for his wife.

"Do you think it was a good idea to let Breaker get the upper hand just now?" David asked, wiping a glob of chili cheese off his cheek with a paper napkin. "What happened to 'I'm in charge?'"

Benny looked around guiltily, hoping Bess hadn't noticed his slip up, but he didn't see her on any of the folding chairs at ringside.

David guessed who he was looking for. "I spotted my mother on my way to the refreshment stand. I was going to say something about Breaker's win but decided it wasn't the time."

Benny wrapped a string of mozzarella around his finger, scraped it off with his teeth, and swallowed hard. "Maybe she's in the ladies room crying over how much she wishes she'd taken Breaker in herself." He was kidding, but from what he'd smelled of the Porta Potties, she wouldn't be spending a lot of time in there.

Benny's guess wasn't far off. Even though it wasn't much of a contest, Bess couldn't hold back a surge of pride when the judge had pointed at Breaker. She was determined not to give in to it. She picked the show catalogue off the empty seat beside her and stuck it in her purse. She was half-way to her car before she turned back. She needed to prove to herself, as much as to anyone else, that she had no regrets. Puppies didn't win against mature dogs like DandyBoy or Black Bean, the seasoned black male Felix was handling for Hannah. She could leave gracefully once Winner's Dog was chosen. It would be time enough then.

At last all the male Standard Poodle classes were finished, and it was time to choose the best of them. Breaker, Black Bean and DandyBoy lined up with the other class winners. The judge walked down the line and looked them over with obvious pleasure. When it was Breaker's turn to be called out, he stood calmly as the judge determined that all his bones and muscles were as they should be, but when the judge examined his bite, the puppy did a soft-mouth nibble on the judge's hand. In the front row at ringside,

Bess couldn't help smiling. McCreery had done the same at his age.

The judge pulled a large linen handkerchief out of his pocket and wiped his fingers. "Take him down to the end and back."

"I'm in charge. I'm in charge," Benny repeated under his breath as Breaker took off at full gallop. He was supposed to match his pace perfectly to the dog's, but he failed to keep up with the rambunctious pup. Feet flying, he trailed along behind until he arrived at the end of the ring a full lead behind Breaker. Miraculously, Breaker stood quietly at attention like he was supposed to, waiting for the command to return.

Benny straightened his tie and took a deep breath. He gave the signal to move forward, but instead of trotting back down the ring to where the judge was tapping his foot impatiently, Breaker yanked the lead from his hand and leaped high into the air. The crowd gasped, as much at the height of his spring as at his impertinence. Benny reached into his pocket for a liver treat. Breaker leaped for it, nearly bowling him over. In the split second it took Breaker to swallow, Benny regained the lead. He looked around anxiously, uncertain what to do.

The judge motioned with one finger for him to come back to the start. This time Breaker obeyed. The tall judge leaned down and whispered in his ear, "I'm going to forget what I just saw. Now, try again."

Benny held the lead firmly and shook his finger sternly at the grinning puppy. "You heard the judge. No more fooling around." Breaker shook his coat back into place and pawed the ground eagerly. He gave the signal and off they went.

From her seat in the stands, Bess could tell something special was happening. She had experienced it only a few times in her life before at the end of the lead. Every muscle in Breaker's body extruded a palpable electricity that lit up the ring like flashing cameras pursuing a Hollywood starlet. It was as if generations of champion Umpawaug poodles had come to life in that one dog. Breaker was doing what he was born to do and loving every minute. The crowd felt it, too. A ripple of applause broke out at ringside as he and Benny made their final turn and came to a stop at the end of the line. The judge gave Breaker a final look and called out Black Bean. It was time to wait again.

The judge moved quickly through the remaining dogs. When he was finished, he walked slowly down the line, hands behind his back. He nodded to one, two, three dogs, telling them to step forward. Black Bean and DandyBoy were among them. Benny was pretty sure Breaker was in the line for the finalists. His whole body tingled with excitement, and he had to fight to keep himself still. He could tell Breaker was feeling the same. The judge made one more pass at the long line. Motioning with his hand, he told Benny to stand in front of Jim in the short line. The judge spun on his heel and faced the remaining dogs. "Thank you," he said and signaled they were excused.

In the stands, Bess held her breath, a half-eaten sandwich forgotten on the seat beside her. A fly buzzed around it, unnoticed. The judge walked slowly down the short line, studying each of the four dogs carefully. When he stopped in front of Breaker, her heart beat faster. What if the judge asked him to go around the ring again? It was customary, if not actually required, for the finalists to strut their stuff one more time so he and the people at ringside could get one last look. Benny had managed to get Breaker back in charge the second time, but who knew what he would do given another chance, now, when the end was so near?

The judge walked back to the head of the line. He opened his mouth, started to ask the dogs to circle once more, and then thought better of it.

Benny squeezed his eyes shut and wished with all his might. He opened them when he felt someone standing close in front of him.

The judge leaned over and whispered in his ear. "That was the worst display I've seen in all my years of judging. Try to do better next time." Then he handed him a small silver bowl. Breaker stuck his nose inside, curious whether there was something good for the winning dog to eat, and gave a disappointed sniff. He wasn't exactly showing his best Winner's Dog manners, but Benny was too preoccupied to care. Hot prickles behind his eyelids threatened to turn into tears as he rubbed his fingers gently across the engraving: "The Bess Rutledge Trophy — Winners Dog."

Amid the polite applause, David edged through the crowd to where Benny and Breaker were waiting for the show photographer. He swiveled his head in all directions, scanning the crowd for Bess. Their eyes met and held. She tucked her purse under her arm and left.

Chapter Twenty-Six

Benny was in a rush to get home and polish the Bess Rutledge Trophy. He had taken it to school every day for a week, so there were a bunch of fingerprints he needed to wipe off. His mother's birthday was tomorrow, and he wanted it to shine like new. He had almost reached the gate when he spotted Steffie sitting on the long bench.

"Whoa!" he said, his mouth hanging open. Steffie was smearing on some black lipstick that she must have kept hidden in her backpack all day. Ms. Kim would've had a fit if she'd caught her with it. The color matched the black smudges under her eyes. Two tufts of orange hair stuck out from each side of her head like horns. Her red high tops were the only part of her outfit that wasn't black. "You going Gothic on me?" he asked, disappointed his little flower girl was gone. "Not that you don't look totally cool."

"It's because we Aspies don't know how to interact appropriately in social situations."

"How'd you get your mom to let you dress like that with the chains?" He was hoping to pick up a few hints.

"Easy. The List says Aspie's can't stand tags, so I cut the labels out of all her clothes. Now her friends can't see the names of the expensive stores she buys her stuff at. She was so mad she said she's finally given up on me. I can wear whatever I want and make a fool of myself."

Benny's gaze went to her nose.

"It's not a real stud if that's what you're wondering. I used Elmer's on a brass thing I found in my dad's tool box. It'll come off, I think." He bobbed his head like she'd said something profound. Personally, he thought she was taking this List thing a little too far, but he couldn't help admiring the way she handled her mom.

"So how are things going with Dr. Kate and that friend of yours, David?"

He shrugged. "Not so hot, but I can fix that. My dad had a late meeting with a client last night, and Sonya and I watched one of her chick flicks. A boy convinced his mom a certain guy was in love with her, and, sure enough, they got married. Her first husband got killed in a horrible train wreck, so it worked out okay. I picked up some really cool tips."

She slipped the lipstick into her backpack. "I hope you're right. Love can be tough on a person."

His heart gave a little flutter. He had seen her and Adam yesterday with their heads bent over a thick calculus book. Adam had said something, and Steffie stared up at him with a goofy-looking smile like she understood what he was talking about.

Benny gathered up his courage. "I saw you and Adam yesterday," he said unable to smother a little pout.

"Yeah, Adam's cool, but he's just a friend. Nothing serious."

He swallowed hard. It hadn't occurred to him things could have gone as far as she said they hadn't. "Sometimes I think I must be an Aspie myself. I've decided I like dogs better than people, at least some of them."

"Good point. Dogs are cool."

"I think Bess might be an Aspie, too. Can old people get it?"

"Depends," she answered noncommittally. She reached into the bowels of her backpack and fished out some nail polish. She held it up to the light. "It's supposed to be black, but I think I goofed." She checked the label and shrugged. "Oh, well, my mother'll still flip out over Midnight Blue." She swiped the brush across her thumb nail and blew. "So, any news?"

"You mean about the pizza party Friday for everyone who does their homework all week?"

She made a face. "Hardly. Did you tell Dr. Kate about 'you know what?'"

He stuck out his chin defiantly. "Maybe."

She swiped a blue streak down the middle of her thumb nail like she was more interested in that than him, but he could tell she was upset. "I saw a program on TV where a kid our age got put in jail for having drugs in school," she said. She sliced an index finger across her throat like a knife and stuck out her tongue. With the black lipstick circling her mouth, she looked like Morticia.

He gulped.

"Don't worry. If that happens to you, I'll bake a cake with a file in it."

He leaped to his feet, his hands balled into fists. "Ha! Ha! Very funny. I suppose you'll blame it on being an Aspie, but it sucked." He shrugged into his backpack and headed toward Gallows Hill Road, pumping his legs harder than he ever had before in his life.

"Just kidding," she called after him, her voice cracking.

He didn't answer. His head was spinning. For the first time in his life he had found a school where he felt safe and a girl who was his best friend, or at least she used to be. What if they both were slipping through his fingers, and all because of a secret he couldn't tell even her?

CHAPTER TWENTY-SEVEN

"**S**he's here!" Benny shouted from the front porch loud enough for Kate to hear upstairs with her office door closed. His mother's birthday was the only thing that could cheer him up after the way Steffie had treated him. He and his mother had made special plans, and nothing could ruin them now that her car was sputtering up the driveway.

He checked in his pocket for his wallet and, reassured, tugged on the beak of his new red and black checkered cap. He flung open the gate and jumped up high, holding the money in his hand so she couldn't miss it. He had hauled a jillion magazines and mowed David's lawn twice to earn enough money for dinner for two at the Spinning Wheel, but it would be worth it to see his mother's big smile.

He squinted as the car grew closer. Who was that in the passenger seat next to his mother? His jumps grew lower and slower, so by the time she cut the engine, he was standing quietly, shoulders sagging. The passenger door opened, and a man he had never seen before stepped out. The man was shorter than his dad with a fuzzy mustache, and if Sonya ever met him she would have had a fit the way his stomach hung over his belt buckle. Why a woman as beautiful as his mom was wasting her time on a guy like him was more than he could figure. Maybe she was having one of those mid-life crises he'd read about in *Reader's Digest* when he was working on a fake book report. The article said it happened to women when they turned thirty, and here his mom was already four years older.

"Benny, honey, this is my friend James," his mother introduced. "I know you'll be great pals. He's a Spiderman fan, too."

James thumped Benny on the back a couple of times and turned to his mother. "You're too young to have a son this old, Sweet Pea."

If there was anything Benny couldn't stand it was people talking about him like he wasn't there, so now he was twice as glad he hadn't offered to shake hands. He was only going to do it to make his mother happy anyway. He pasted on a smile and handed his wallet over to her. "It's all there. Enough for the tip and tax, too." He stuck his hands in his pockets and rocked back on his heels.

She thumbed through the crisp bills like a Las Vegas dealer and stuck them in the cleavage of her gold and black ruffled blouse. It was a good thing she had that "girl's secret treasure chest," as she called it, because she couldn't fit another thing in her shiny black pants.

She gave Benny a pat on the cheek. "Good for you, sweetie. We'll save this for next time. James has promised to take me to the Spinning Wheel for my birthday dinner tonight." She handed back the empty wallet.

Benny deflated like a leaky balloon. "But Mom, you said it was our turn."

"Now, Benjamin, don't go getting into one of your moods. This is Mommy's day. Try not to spoil it." She ran her fingers down his arm like a piano keyboard. "We'll have plenty of time together before we drop you off at your dad's. We'll stop at Chicken Lickin' for a little snack. You can pay for that. We'll order fried everything, and Sonya will never know." She poked her son conspiratorially in the ribs.

"Didn't you say you had a special package for Mommy?"

He held out the box he had been hiding behind his back like a boy on his first date. Hearts of all sizes in red crayon were scattered across the white tissue paper. A red yarn bow was tied on top.

She tore open the paper and held the gold-capped amber bottle up to the light. "Sonya's favorite! Thanks, sweetie." She dabbed a little scent behind each ear and tilted her head so James could get a sniff.

"Delicious," James proclaimed with a wink. He rubbed her neck and made her giggle again.

"Me, too?" Benny asked, sniffing like a rabbit.

"Sure," she said, offering the other side. "Well, if that's all, we'd better get going." She turned and stood by the driver's door, waiting. Benny rushed to open it. She slid in and pointed him to the back seat.

As Benny slammed the door, Kate stepped out onto the porch. "Bye, Benny," she called, but the engine muffled her voice and he didn't hear. She looked down. The Bess Rutledge Trophy was lying on the bench. For days Benny had been telling anyone who would listen how proud his mother would be when she saw it. She grabbed it and rushed to the gate.

"Wait," she called after the speeding car. He couldn't have heard, but she saw him looking through the rear window at her, waving after him with the cup. He turned and faced forward, and the car sped onward.

CHAPTER TWENTY-EIGHT

Benny headed downstairs from Dr. Kate's office, shoulders sagging and eyes on his feet. The silver cup dangled carelessly from one finger. He watched it slide onto the floor, rocking back and forth like an empty carriage on a Ferris wheel. He didn't care about the stupid cup any more. He'd told Dr. Kate to keep it, but she made him take it back. He was glad he'd forgotten it last night. All his mother was interested in was her stupid dinner with that James person. He slumped onto the bench.

"Mind if we sit?"

Benny jumped. He was so caught up in misery he hadn't noticed David and Breaker joining him. Breaker's puffy tail waved back and forth like a hummingbird. Benny tried to ignore him, but the puppy nudged his arm with his nose like a sheepdog herding a lamb. Benny hid a grin and pulled the puppy closer, as if David might snatch him away.

"A dog can be a great pal," David said.

"Better than some people," Benny muttered under his breath.

David had a pretty good idea about Benny's problem. Dr. Kate had surprised him with a phone call this morning. She only wanted to talk about Benny, not his dinner invitation, but he was pleased anyway. Maybe she was beginning to trust him with the boy.

"Dr. Kate told me about your mother's birthday. She heard about it from your teacher, so it wasn't private. I'm sorry, but you can't go on licking your wounds forever. You've got to get back up on the horse and ride."

Benny stood, his jaw clenched. "You calling my mother a horse?"

"What I mean," David said, measuring his words like a thrifty housewife, "is nothing takes your mind off troubles like plunging back into work. A dog show my mother never misses is coming up. We could take Breaker."

Benny jutted his neck out like an angry turtle. "You're kidding, right? Breaker doesn't want to be in any stupid dog show, do you, boy?"

The puppy sniffed his face with a worried frown.

David took a deep breath. He didn't want to lose the boy now. He had seen his mother's expression when the judge handed Breaker the trophy at Housatonic. His heart used to twist into jealous knots when her face lit up over a dog. Now he'd give anything to see it again.

"Can you believe it?" he asked, putting all the enthusiasm he could muster into his voice. "Breaker winning a five-point major at six months? Even I never expected him to beat DandyBoy. If that doesn't bring Bess to her senses, nothing will."

Benny stepped off the porch and kicked the grass. Sonya would kill him for scuffing up his good tie shoes, but he didn't care. "Good for you, but it's not my problem. Bess is your mother, not mine, and mine doesn't give a damn what I do."

David stood, too. He wished Kate were here to help. He tried to remember what would have worked for him at Benny's age. He picked the silver cup up off the floor and traced the words with his finger. "I know how you feel. When I was a kid, I wasn't crazy about dogs, but I faked it.

Once, I insisted Bess let me enter Junior Showmanship even though I knew I'd hate every minute of it." He lowered his voice confidentially. "I wanted her to love me."

Benny stared like David had just shed an invisibility cloak. He squeezed his hands into tight fists. If Dr. Kate had been there, she would have said he was fighting his emotions, rushing to do the very thing that would cause him pain. "I'm giving Breaker back to Bess. She's only pretending he belongs to me anyway."

David caught him by the elbow before he could bolt. "She won't keep him. She'll hand him over to Hannah." He brought his face in close, locking Benny's eyes. "You can't make a person love someone, not even a dog. You should have figured that out by now."

The muscles around Benny's mouth twitched like over-tightened rubber bands. David froze in place as his words echoed back to him with a deeper meaning than he had intended. Man and boy stared at each other as in a mirror.

David broke first. "That didn't come out right. I didn't mean it the way it sounded."

Benny looked away. He picked up the silver cup. "Come on, Breaker," he said, signaling the puppy to follow. "Sorry, David," he called back over his shoulder. "Sorry, sorry."

The knock on the door caught Bess unawares. Mona was out, and she wasn't expecting anyone herself. Whoever it was, McCreery's ears twitched, but he stayed in his dog nest, his chin resting comfortably on his toy fish, untroubled by the unexpected visitor. Bess pulled back the kitchen curtain. It was the boy, holding the silver cup and looking around nervously in the gathering dusk. Breaker was sitting beside him, calm for once. She considered pretending she wasn't home. She hadn't completely recovered from Housatonic.

It had been years since a novice puppy had gone Winner's Dog. The last time was McCreery at Stamford and before him, Jester at Oakdale. The last thing she wanted tonight was a debate with one of David's emissaries. Still, she could handle a mere boy.

"Well?" she asked, opening the door. Benny seemed to have grown. Even though she was standing in the doorway and he was on the step below, he towered over her.

He thrust the silver cup at her. "Here. It's got your name on it."

She took the cup and turned it slowly in her hands, enjoying the cool, smooth feel of it. When she was done, she handed it back. She never even glanced at the puppy.

Benny stuck his toe in the door before she could close it. "Wait, the cup's yours for keeps. Breaker, too. He's your dog no matter what you pretend. My dad won't let him in the house. And by the way, I think you should know David wants me to keep on being his handler."

"What did you tell him?"

He stuck out his lower lip. "I told him it's between you and him. I've got my own problems."

She narrowed her eyes. The conversation was taking an unfamiliar twist. For once, she didn't think her son was behind it. "You and Breaker beat some pretty good dogs and their handlers at Housatonic. I'd have thought you'd be eager to get back into the ring."

He shifted uncomfortably, a fish in a net. "What for? I only did it for my mother, hoping she'd be proud of me. You know, like David did when he was little. Well, she couldn't care less, any more than you did."

Her mouth dropped open. "David? What are you talking about?"

He had been scared by that look before, but he was determined to finish what he'd come to say. "You know. Pretending he cared about your stupid dog shows so you'd pay attention to him. It was dumb, but he couldn't think of anything better. He was only a kid." He waited, leg jiggling. If Bess was anything like his mother, he was in big trouble.

She braced herself against the door jamb, swinging her head back and forth like a loose gate in the wind. "No, you're wrong."

Breaker pulled free and put his paws on her shoulders, sniffing her face with a worried frown like McCreery had done a hundred times before.

Benny tipped his head back and made a loud guffaw that echoed through the damp twilight. "You don't know much, do you? David's still doing it for crying out loud. Trust me, he doesn't care about Breaker's show career for his own self, and he definitely doesn't mean for you to leave the poor dog out in the puppy shed and pretend he's not there."

The sound of an approaching car intruded, and they both turned to look. Benny grabbed Breaker's collar, but the puppy was content to watch. Mona climbed out loaded down with two brown grocery bags. She stopped in her tracks when she saw the three of them in the doorway. She looked the scene over briefly, then continued up the walk without a word. First Benny, then Bess stepped aside so she could pass. Mona turned and looked up at the sky. The evening star was visible through the trees. She held the door open. "It's late and it's cold. You'd better come inside."

Bess studied the puppy for a long moment without a word. Then she proceeded into the house, Breaker dashing in first.

Benny turned and started to leave, but he felt someone watching and looked back over his shoulder. Mona was standing in the lighted doorway, and, unmistakably, she gave him a wink like they were partners in a conspiracy. Well, maybe they were. Everyone had gotten when they wanted, hadn't they? Breaker would live in a house and have one more person to love him — two counting Mona. David would be happy because his mother wouldn't be all depressed any more. For himself, he was out of dog shows for good, just like he wanted. Everything was terrific. So why wasn't he feeling so hot?

CHAPTER TWENTY-NINE

Benny headed for the school office, the attendance sheet stuck in his pants pocket, tossing M&Ms and catching them in his mouth. Now that he wasn't spending every afternoon trying to teach Breaker some manners he had plenty of time to develop other hobbies — like this one. He had the best luck with the red ones, not that any went to waste. A little dirt never hurt anyone. In fact, he was so busy with his new life, he'd hardly had a minute to miss Breaker.

Good thing David was away on a business trip with a client. He didn't even know Bess had agreed to keep Breaker. He would probably say Bess needed help with the dogs, but that was stupid. She didn't need help, especially from a kid like him. She was practically the world's leading expert on poodles — or at least she used to be before she got old. She could hire anybody she wanted. Besides, nobody knew whether she was going to show Breaker or turn him into a house pet.

Benny held the candy wrapper up to one eye, hoping a piece was stuck to the bottom. Disappointed, he crumbled the paper and stuffed it in his pocket. Ms. Jeanette had taught them all about keeping the planet green, and he did his part by not littering.

Thinking of Ms. Jeanette reminded him about the awful fight he'd had with Steffie. He intended to give her the cold shoulder the next time he saw her, but when he spotted her sashaying toward him, he forgot all about it. He had never seen anyone quite like her before, at least not in real life. She was wearing Capri pants that looked like painted on yellow skin. It was a mystery how she had gotten them over her knees. They rode low on her hips, and her skinny, red tank top was kind of short so he could see the jewel she'd stuck in her navel. He hoped it was like the nose stud and the glue would wear off.

He gulped. "Wow! Did Dr. Kate see you looking like that?" He tried to keep his eyes off the soft bulges sticking out of the tank top, but he couldn't help himself.

Steffie shrugged and hooked a finger under a spaghetti strap. "She's going to talk to Mother during their Parent Helper meeting today. Big woop. She won't show up."

Benny grimaced. Kids almost never got kicked out of New Hope School, but parents did it for them when they didn't come to their Parent Helper meetings. Dr. Kate believed parents needed to make time for their kids. In person. His own dad was pushing the envelope. Too many phone conferences because he was too busy to meet with her at the school.

Steffie cleared her throat. "I'm sorry I upset you the other day." She tugged the hem of her tank top. "I always get crabby at my time of the month."

His cheeks burned. At least she hadn't tried to blame it on The List. "It's okay. My mother's the same."

She nodded at the garden chairs at the edge of the flower garden. "Got a minute to sit? I finished my test early and am on kind of a break."

He looked down at the attendance sheet and nodded.

She sat about a foot away from him, checked him out of the corner of her eye and moved her chair so it was touching Benny's. He casually rested his hand on the arm. She did the same with hers, leaving a tiny space between them. There was an awkward pause, and then he asked, "So, where'd you get the new clothes?"

"My mom. One of her New York shopping sprees. She's on a kick to get me a boyfriend." She pointed at his new red high tops. "You look cool yourself."

He leaned down, wiping a little smudge off the toe, and saw that Steffie's own high tops were a thing of the past. The shoes she was wearing now, if you could call them that, were mostly a bunch of silver straps and looked like something Sonya would wear to a club. He'd hate to have to get any place in a hurry in heels like that.

"I bought the high tops myself," he said. "I'm going to keep my own money from now on after what happened on my mother's birthday."

She touched his arm. "Sorry, Adam told me. Maybe next year."

"Yeah, maybe." His arm felt all tingly where she had touched him. He rubbed the spot, not sure if he was trying to wipe it away or make it last.

She crossed her legs and dangled a shoe off the end of her painted toes. "My mom'll try anything to make me popular. She thinks a boy friend will cure my Asperger's. She even hinted it'd be all right if I had sex."

His eyes bugged out. "Really? You sure?"

She gave him a sly look. "Pretty sure, but it could be my Asperger's getting me mixed up again."

"I wish my mom thought sex would cure me. She'd be happy if I was a baby all my life. I don't think you should tell Dr. Kate about the sex part though."

"She wouldn't care. She's a Freudian. They all believe in sex and stuff like that."

He shook his head. "I wouldn't count on it. You can ask her yourself. She's always telling me thinking's okay, but doing's different." He considered a minute. "Exactly how's your mother going to find someone for you to have sex with? I'd be happy to help."

"Ballroom dancing. Miss Bolyne's dance class."

He didn't see what good that would be. "I think I've heard of it."

"Three nights a week. I have to miss *Cosby* and *America's Funniest Home Videos*."

He felt sorry for her. He wasn't prepared to give up his favorite TV shows for a lame dance class, not even for sex.

She grabbed onto a strand of hair that had come loose from her up-do and twirled it around her finger. It reminded him of a travel movie Ms. Jeanette had shown them about Greece where old men played with their worry beads. He wondered what Steffie had to worry about.

She started to speak, stopped, drew in a deep breath and started again. "Try not to get mad, but you really need to listen. Drugs are bad for you, and you can get you in a lot of trouble if you're caught."

He got to his feet, his fists curled into balls. "I'm warning you, Steffie."

"What if you're dad finds out? He'll yank you out of school, and I'll never see you again."

Benny gulped. He hadn't thought about that. Nobody had ever cared enough to think about him before. She deserved to know the truth, but before he could get it out, she interrupted.

"Getting kicked out would be the dumbest thing you ever did, so try not to be stupid."

Benny's eyes narrowed. In the old days, he would have punched her one for an insult like that. "Stupid, am I? Well, I'm not so dumb I can't see you're not my friend." He tapped the side of his face and faked surprise. "Oh, wait. The List says you can't make friends, so I guess stupid me is wrong again."

"Then you'll be happy to hear my news," she snapped back. "My parents are taking me to Europe for the whole summer, maybe longer, so you won't have to put up with me any more."

His mouth dropped open, but no words came out. He turned and ran as fast as he could, his backpack slapping against his spine like he was punishing himself.

She wiped the back of her hand across her nose and sniffed. The tears would make her mascara run, but it didn't matter. She had just lost the best friend she ever had, and all because she cared.

Chapter Thirty

Benny was rocking on David's porch glider feeling sorry for himself. He was only there because he needed a place to hide. A pesky fifth grader who had a crush on him had chased him all over campus and he'd barely escaped, as if he'd be interested in a girl who was only ten. Remembering how close she came to kissing him made him feel faint all over again, and he gasped in big mouthfuls of air until his heartbeat felt normal.

He fished in his pocket for a half-eaten granola bar, wiped the lint off with his shirt sleeve and polished it off in two bites. Now what? Redding was the most boring place in the world, and he had the whole summer ahead with no one to do anything fun with. His mother had her new friend James, so it was no use asking if he could spend a few extra weeks with her, Sonya had put him on another diet and Steffie was off in Europe. At least she couldn't tell anybody about the pills.

He was thinking the fifth grader had probably gone back to class by now and it would be safe to head back to Summer School when he heard the sound of a powerful engine. If David found him hanging around, he might think he missed him. Fat chance! He wasn't about to forgive him for the last time that easily. He started to run, but he was too late.

"Benny, wait!"

Benny stuck his finger in his ears and continued running.

David sprinted after him and grabbed him by the elbow.

Benny stopped struggling, but his eyes were heavy with tears. "I'm sorry but we can't be friends any more. You'll just have to get over it."

David dropped his arm and smiled like he was really glad to see him. "Actually, I was hoping to run into you. Bess has something she wants to tell you."

Benny screwed up his face. "You mean *ask*. She's got something to *ask* me. You can tell her for me that if she wants me to handle Breaker, she's out of luck. My own mother doesn't give a damn what I do, so why should I care about yours?"

"I know how you feel..." David started, but Benny interrupted.

"Don't start that 'I know how you feel' crap again. You're not me."

David removed his cap and ran his fingers through his hair, like he was trying to regroup. "I've missed you. Breaker and McCreery have, too."

For a moment, Benny felt a guilty pang about the dogs, but he shoved it back down.

"I thought we were real friends," David said. "Real friends know people make mistakes and forgive each other."

"Yeah, as long as I do all the forgiving," Benny shot back, but the fire had burned out. A noise behind him made him turn and look. Breaker and McCreery, ears flying, came racing around the corner. McCreery won by a nose.

"That old dog isn't about to let his son beat him," David said with a chuckle, "but he'll have his hands full one of these days. I can't ever remember a bigger rivalry between generations."

McCreery nudged Breaker aside with a "gotcha" gleam in his eyes, put his paws on Benny's shoulders and stretched his neck to lick a few crumbs off his chin. Not to be outdone Breaker squeezed in and got in a few licks, too.

"They're happy to see you."

"I'm happy to see them, too," he admitted with a sheepish grin. He reached into his pocket and slipped out two biscuits he'd had been keeping handy, just in case. He handed them to the dogs, and they ran off to enjoy them in their separate spots.

David replaced his cap. "So, what should I tell Bess?"

Benny picked some mud off the bottom of his shoes and pretended to think. "I might have a little time to drop by, if it doesn't take too long. I've got my laundry to do tonight. Nothing like nice clean clothes to put on in the morning." He spit on a finger and rubbed a blotch of chocolate off his shirt front to show he meant it.

David hid a smile. He took a tennis ball out of his pocket and tossed it from hand to hand. The dogs danced around his feet, hoping to snatch it in midair. If they hadn't both grabbed at the same time and bumped shoulders, they would have succeeded.

Hands on hips, Benny swiveled right, then left, easing the crick in his back. "If you feel like tossing a couple of balls to the dogs, I could probably put off the laundry. I changed my underwear a couple of days ago, so it's not that bad."

David laughed and stuck out his hand. "Friends?"

Benny took it and shook. "Friends."

Benny found Bess under a tree leaning over a metal wash tub. Inside, Breaker stood half covered in suds, head hanging, tangled ears dripping. A ripe odor rose from his wet coat. Benny slapped a copy of the *NSH Gazette* over his nose. He had brought a copy of the school paper so she could read his article about Breaker's big win. He hated to write essays for English class, but a newspaper story was different.

He staggered back, rotating his arms like a windmill. "P.U. What's that stink?"

"Skunk," she answered matter-of-factly. She'd had too much drama from the dogs today to appreciate his. "Breaker's been trying to catch it for days. Got a little too close this time." She dipped a sponge and slopped more suds across Breaker's back.

Benny peeked under the grooming table where McCreery was resting with a smug look on his face. "For once McCreery seems happy that Breaker's getting all the attention," he said with a grin. The old dog got to his feet, let Benny give him a pat, and slunk off before Bess could stick him in the tub, too.

"I see you," she called but didn't order him back. She'd had enough of his holier-than-thou attitude for one afternoon.

Benny turned his attention back to Breaker. A rivulet of shampoo rolled down between the puppy's eyes and slid off the end of his nose. "He sure looks skinny with his coat matted down like that."

Bess nodded at an open can of tomato juice. "Pass me that," she ordered sharply.

Benny handed it over. "I never knew skunks stank this bad. I'll be smelling it in my dreams, or should I say nightmares?"

She poured the tomato juice over Breaker's head and down his back. He shivered from head to toe, mostly from humiliation, and his bobbed tail resembled a flag in surrender.

Benny poured the red liquid and watched it roll

off Breaker's nose into the murky water. He sniffed and wrinkled his nose. "Does that stuff really work?" He turned over the can and studied the label to see if "cure for skunk stink" was listed as a recommended use.

"It better. If it doesn't, I'll have to cut him down."

"Cut him down?" he squeaked, shielding his crotch.

"Oh, for heaven's sake," she snapped. "Shave his coat."

He unclasped his hands. "I knew that." He studied her face. Her short gray curls formed a topknot that looked pretty much like Breaker's before the skunk encounter. "Seriously, Bess, who ever dreamed up those crazy poodle hair-dos?"

She launched into the speech she had given hundreds of times. "The clip is a tribute to their days as hunters. Poodles are bird dogs bred originally to retrieve ducks in the icy waters of Northern Europe — probably Germany or Russia. No one's sure. The puffy chest kept their vital organs warm, and the bracelets on the joints were for the same reason. The hind end was shaved so they wouldn't sink down and drown."

He studied the puppy with new eyes. With his wet coat matted down against his skin, he looked pretty much like any other hunting dog. He handed her the last tomato juice can. "So chasing skunks is in Breaker's genes?"

"Birds, not skunks." She sniffed cautiously. "Better, but not good enough. We'll have to do the whole thing all over again tomorrow."

"We?" Benny squeaked. "I think I'm supposed to mow my dad's lawn. We like the place to look nice."

She peered at Benny over her glasses, thick eyebrows drawn together. "You should be doing this yourself. He's still half yours."

He shook his head. "If that's what you wanted to tell me, thanks anyway. I've given up trying to impress my mother." He gave Breaker a pat. "I'd better be going. I've got a lot of important stuff on my agenda today." It was one of his mother's favorite expressions.

She wiped stray suds off her cheek with the back of her hand. "Hold on! I thought you wanted me to get back into dogs."

"Not me. David. Like I said, he wants you to be happy."

She dropped the sponge into the tub and rested against the table. "I know. I finally get it. But what about you and your mother?"

He reddened and scuffed the dirt with the toe of his shoe. "It's hopeless."

She brightened. "I'd like to help. It might make up a little for not appreciating my son all those years."

He kept his eyes lowered. "Sorry, it won't work."

"Don't be so sure. From now on, no more half-hearted gestures. You have my full support." She gave him her most brilliant smile. "How does six a.m. tomorrow sound?"

He bugged out his eyes and bobbed his neck like a flamingo. Was the woman serious? Hadn't she heard a word he'd said? Maybe she was getting deaf. Old people did sometimes. She was right from the beginning. He was too young and she was too old to be messing around with dogs. So what if Breaker had been a super star at Housatonic? What good did that do him? He was about to tell her so when he noticed her face, all smiley and hopeful. If he let her down now, she'd get depressed again and who would David blame? Him! It wasn't fair. It really wasn't. Maybe he could trick her into picking someone else to help her — maybe even David.

He changed his frown to a grin and said, "Dog shows are too much work for a boy like me. I've already got lots to do. For example, I should be home picking up my room. Cleanliness is next to godliness, I always say. And I've been thinking about asking Ms. Jeanette for more homework."

She smiled innocently. "Very sensible. You and Breaker

made a great team at Housatonic, but that was just a one-shot deal, a thing of the past. I understand."

He exhaled a huge sigh of relief. That went better than expected. He decided to hang around a bit longer just to be polite. His dad was taking Sonya to the Spinning Wheel again, and she had left a frozen dinner on the counter for him. Mona always had something delicious cooking, and he might get invited to dinner if he played his cards right.

She refilled the tub with fresh water and squirted in shampoo from a bottle that had her own handwritten label. She dipped a brush and resumed scrubbing. "Even if the smell goes away, I may have to cancel Breaker's appearance at Quinnipiac next month. No handler."

"Quinnipiac? Sounds foreign."

"It's an Indian tribe that used to live not too far from here. Now it's the name of the biggest dog club in New England outside of Boston. Actually, I used to be President."

"Well, I hope you find someone to help you, but I feel sorry for Breaker — having to wear that sissy hair-do and all."

"Feel sorry all you want. The dogs love it: standing alone in the winner's circle, the crowd roaring, cameras flashing."

His eyes grew round. "Cameras? Do they have TV so everyone can see you, even people who can't come because they're too busy?"

"Sure," she answered nonchalantly. "CNN, Animal Planet — at least at the really top shows." She waited a minute to let the lure of TV fame really settle in. A show big enough for national television could be years away for Breaker — if ever — but this was no time to burst the boy's bubble.

He thought it over, imagining how impressed his mother would be. "Say, when is this Quinnipiac, anyway?"

She shrugged and answered nonchalantly, "A couple of

weeks. Fourth of July weekend, actually. Plenty of time if we work hard." She doused Breaker with fresh water and asked, "Toss me that towel, will you?" It was the distraction Breaker had been waiting for. As she raised her hand to catch it, he leapt free of the tub, spraying water where he landed.

"Come back here," she scolded, wiping the spray off her face. She might have been ordering the wind. He stuck his hind end up in the air, tail wagging, and dashed back and forth in front of her. Her finger tips barely skimmed his coat as he passed. He came closer, teasing. She lunged, and her feet flew out from under her. The puppy froze in place.

Benny rushed over and knelt beside her. He had never seen an old person so helpless before, and it scared him. "Are you all right, Bess?"

She raised up on one elbow and then to a sitting position, wriggling fingers and toes in turn. "No broken bones," she pronounced.

At the sound of her voice, Breaker moved closer and sniffed the back of her hand gently. She shuddered, like she was remembering a different fall.

She held both arms out to Benny. "Give me a boost." He grasped her hands and eased her up. She stood, testing her weight. She took a careful step forward, then another. "See, I'm fine."

She called Breaker over to her and gave him a pat. Then she signaled Benny to empty the heavy tub. He dumped the water onto the bare spot where the grass had worn down from the long hours she had groomed dogs there over the years. They both watched the water slide in rivulets over the hard dirt and disappear.

She turned and locked eyes with Benny. "Listen, Benny, I've given a lot of thought to what you said the other night about how I've treated my son. I've loved my dogs, and that's not bad, but I've put them above the people who loved me, especially David. How he learned to be kind, I don't know. Probably my sister Mona."

He started to speak, but she held up a hand for silence and continued. "I'm not going to lie to you. I'm seventy years old. I've been selfish all my life, but I like to think I can change."

Again, he tried to interrupt, but she was too quick.

"I'm not going to pretend I can change completely. I won't always do the right thing, but I do promise to try. I want one last chance at Westminster, and I need your help, but I'm not just thinking about me. You'll get what you want, too. If a Westminster win doesn't get your mother's attention, nothing will. So, what do you say? Can we be partners: Rutledge and Neusner?"

He waited, testing whether this time she was finished. He decided she was. He drummed the side of his cheek with his fingers like he was trying to decide. Really, there wasn't that much to think about it. Like Dr. Kate said, some people never change, but maybe Bess could. What she said made sense. They would both get what they wanted. He burst into a grin. "You mean Neusner and Rutledge."

She stuck out a hand. They shook and looked away awkwardly, uncertain what came next in their new partnership.

"By the way," he said, his face brightening with inspiration, "my parents are going out tonight. Sonya left me a frozen dinner on the counter — Vegetable Tofu Surprise — but I ate a big lunch. I can bring it over, and we can share if you're hungry."

She laughed her croupy laugh. "Thanks, anyway. Mona's making fried chicken with mashed potatoes and gravy. You're invited if you want."

He coughed to cover the sound of his tummy rumbling. "I think I can make it."

She still had something to say and looked Benny in the

eye. "I can teach you everything you need to know about being a handler, but dogs can tell how a person feels about them. Breaker is handsome enough to do some winning no matter who takes him into the ring, but unless he has a special bond with his handler he won't win at the really big shows. Some dogs want to win for their own sakes, but for Umpawaug poodles, their connection with the person on the other end of the lead is what counts. It's made for some seemingly impossible wins."

His face turned red like a schoolboy with his first crush. "No problem. Breaker's my friend now." The puppy danced over to Benny and placed two muddy, front paws on his white shirt. They grinned at each other until Benny took a dog biscuit out of his pocket and tossed it for Breaker to chase.

A horn honked nearby. Benny jerked up his head, face alight. He still hadn't forgiven his mother for her birthday, but something inside him couldn't help hoping.

"My mom! Wait 'til she hears I'm gonna be on TV." He grabbed his backpack, not bothering to slip it on, and dashed for the split rail fence. "Tell Mona I'll come another night," he shouted over his shoulder. He swung one leg over the top. The other leg was still stranded on the other side when he halted abruptly, shoulders slumping. "My mistake," he said, pasting on a fake smile. "Maybe tomorrow. I'll tell her the news tomorrow."

Bess felt a lump growing at the base of her throat as she watched the boy lumber slowly down the hill. Was this how it had been for David all those years ago, waiting for her to come home? She thought of the promise she had just made to Benny and remembered all the promises she had made — and broken, to her son David. She hadn't mentioned Westminster, but she knew Benny was thinking about it, and so was she. How many times had she tried and disappointed herself again at the last minute? Would it happen again this time, another broken promise to another boy? She pulled her arms tighter across her chest, as if locking the promise inside. Maybe this time would be different. She would try.

CHAPTER THIRTY-ONE

For the first time in months, Mona was greeted by the aroma of fresh coffee she hadn't made herself. The dinner table was set for three, and pink and white impatiens were arranged in a Newcomb pottery vase she recognized from childhood. Most surprising of all, Bess was dressed for the occasion in black pants fresh from the dry cleaners and a red pullover that matched her lipstick. The latest edition of the NHS Gazette was open in front of her. Benny had dropped it on the grooming table before he left.

Mona noticed the extra plate. "Someone special coming for dinner?"

"I invited Benny. His parents left him home alone again tonight, and I thought some of your special fried chicken might cheer him up." She took a sip of coffee and said, "He did a good job on this article. He even spelled 'Housatonic' right. There's a drawing of Breaker and Benny, too, by Mary Theresa A., age five. At least I think it's them. The one with four legs has a crown, and the two-legged one is holding something blue."

"Impressive," Mona murmured, pouring her own coffee. She stood back, hands on hips. "Are you going to tell me what you're up to, or do I have to guess?"

Bess kept her eyes on the newspaper, flipping to page

two. She adjusted her glasses to study a drawing by Joy K. of a mother holding a baby. "Benny and I have reached an understanding about Breaker, a kind of partnership. No big deal."

"Humph," Mona scoffed. "Glad to hear it. Now maybe life can get back to normal around here."

Bess jerked her head up. "You're not planning to leave? Didn't you say the cabinets in your condo aren't finished?" She coughed, hoping to disguise her worry.

Mona sat. "I'm taking a little trip to Boca Raton to see for myself how things are progressing. Care to come? We'll be back by the first of August."

Bess hesitated. Once Quinnipiac was behind them, the shows she planned to enter Breaker in were over for a while. She could take McCreery with them, and David and Benny could manage Breaker. "I thought you'd be glad to get away from me."

"And here I thought you hoped to get rid of me."

Bess crossed her arms. "Oh, for heaven's sake. I'll never understand you if I live to be a hundred."

"I plan to, so you might as well, too. It'll give us both time to figure things out."

Bess tilted her head for a better view of her twin. "Do you ever think about Papa's tree?"

"Papa's tree?" Mona echoed, her face relaxing into a smile. "People used to come from all over to see it. A live oak in Connecticut — right on our front lawn."

Bess nodded, the glow on her face matching her twin's. "If I could figure out how he kept warm water flowing around it all winter, I'd grow one myself."

"That's ridiculous. What on earth would you do with a live oak?"

"I've been thinking I might take a drive over to Madison one day soon. The pasture we played in as kids probably has been bulldozed by a developer, but back in the day it seemed like heaven to me — the little trail, the black-eyed Susans growing on either side."

"Our special place," the sisters caroled in unison. They peeked at each other out of the corners of their eyes and looked away quickly.

Bess held up a gardening catalog for Mona's inspection. "I'm going to order myself some pink japonica for out front, and I think I'll get some of those old-fashioned roses to go along the back where the kennels used to be. Growing a garden is kind of like raising poodles, don't you think?"

Mona drew in her chin, straightening her back. "I think you're nuts. That's what I think."

Bess tucked the catalogue under her arm and swung her legs around. "I might have expected you to say something like that. For your information, that new clerk at Myers' Pharmacy asked me the other day if we were related. He said I reminded him of you."

Mona sniffed. "Really? For your information, that happens to me all the time. Personally, I don't see the resemblance. Do you?"

Bess shook her head. "Definitely not, but it wouldn't hurt to look."

The twin sisters hoisted themselves up and walked to the antique bull's eye mirror hung at the end of Bess' front hall. The glass was small and the gilt frame was hung high, so they had to stand close together and stretch their necks upward to include both faces in the round opening.

And that's how McCreery found them when he came downstairs from his afternoon nap. He didn't interrupt, but he couldn't help wondering how long those two old fools were going to stand there, trying to decipher the obvious, before someone remembered to feed the dog.

Chapter Thirty-Two

McCreery's jealous eyes burned into the back of Bess' neck as she pulled the wood-paneled station wagon out of the driveway, but he would have to get over it. She had her hands full with Benny and Breaker. Quinnipiac wasn't Westminster, but it was the most important show in New England this holiday weekend. Half the cars racing past them were heading for a day's outing at Lake Candlewood; the other half sported bumper stickers saying "Show Dogs on Board" or lettering on the sides to announce a kennel's name. Sometimes small dogs' crates were stacked so high they showed though the back window. No doubt about it. Five point majors would be up for grabs today.

She leaned back in her seat, painfully aware she was one of those little old ladies in big cars who can barely see over the steering wheel. Her mind should have been focused on what was ahead for today, but she couldn't stop thinking she should have given McCreery a chance at Westminster. Then nobody would be able to match Umpawaug's record, not even Hannah. Well, too late now.

"Too late for what?" Benny asked, jerking his head around in time to see a sad look flicker across her face.

She hadn't realized she had spoken out loud. "Nothing," she fibbed. "No, not nothing. Dreams left unfinished.

That's what growing old is all about, son. Then one day, almost without warning, the ordinary things a person used to do without a single thought, like spreading toothpaste on a toothbrush or opening a jar — things that were cause for celebration as a young child — become hard again, and doing them a little longer is the only thing left because all the dreams are gone."

He began tapping his heels together. "Hey, I thought dogs shows were supposed to be fun. I don't mean to be rude, but old people's brains must kind of dry up or something because all they do is talk about the good old days. Well, I'm here to tell you, being young isn't all it's cracked up to be."

She stared at him over the top of her glasses, and he thought for sure she was going to land them in a gully. Even when she was paying attention he was afraid her big old clunker wouldn't make it around the steep, windy curves. His mother said Redding's roads were nothing but paved-over trails that cows had cut through the woods in the olden days when they trotted back to their farms for milking, and Benny thought it must be true. His classmates Chad and Eric were crazy about roller coasters and loved the way Redding's roads twisted and turned, plunging down sudden hills, but personally his stomach could use a rest right now. He had to gobble his breakfast so he wouldn't be late, and the cold sausage and pepper pizza wasn't sitting too well on his stomach.

"I don't recall mentioning anything about the good old days, or did my dried up old brain forget? In case you're interested, age has nothing to do with it. Plenty of people scarcely older than you are old already."

He had no answer, and they drove in silence until they passed Stormfield, the home where Mark Twain had died. He had heard that Mark Twain was born under Haley's Comet and died the next time it appeared seventy years later. He hoped it wasn't due again for a while. "What about dying? Do old people think about that a lot?"

"Not my favorite subject."

He slid back in his seat. "Mine, either."

She glanced out of the corner of her eye. "Don't worry. Your mother makes bad choices, but I don't think she's going to die any time soon."

He wiped his finger under his nose, hoping she wouldn't notice. Something tickled the back of his neck. He reached behind and felt Breaker's cool, wet nose.

"What's he doing?"

"Saying he likes you. I should've put him in his crate, but I got tired of chasing him around."

Benny looked out the window. Only the hum of the car's engine interrupted the silence. A herd of black and white milk cows huddled together under an old apple tree. On the side of a red barn hay was stacked in a mound. "Not to change the subject, but do you think we'll be on TV tonight if Breaker wins?"

"TV? Good grief, no. Quinnipiac's not that big. Maybe a story in *The New Haven Register*.

"I'm pretty sure he'll win. Everyone says Umpawaug Poodles are the best in the world. Even Mona."

The car swerved again. "She does?"

"Sure, as long as you're not around." He turned and stared out the window. A weather-beaten vegetable stand, the work of some farmer, stood unattended. "Sweet corn, three dollars a dozen," was painted on a hand-lettered sign. He had one more question. "Bess, do you think I'm one of those young people who's old already?"

She raised a curious eyebrow. "Why do you ask?"

"Because I wish for things I can never have. Like for my dad and my mom to be married again. We'd all live together in one big house — Sonya, too — and I'd never have to miss anyone ever again." He hung his head. "I guess that's dumb?"

She didn't answer.

He tapped his foot. "Sorry, sorry, Bess. I didn't mean it about old people's brains."

She waved a forgiving hand. "I'm not mad. I don't know the answer." A slow smile crept across her lips. "Like I would. Me, who's spent my whole life wishing for something just out of reach."

They snuck a peek at each other and laughed. Breaker wriggled excitedly, too, wanting to be in on the act.

He grinned. "I guess we are kind of alike."

She flexed her fingers and steered with her palms, a bittersweet smile on her face. "A couple of wishful thinkers."

He settled back in his seat. The same sad look Bess had worn earlier came and wrapped itself around Benny, but he was looking out the window, and nobody saw.

Bess eased the Country Squire into the parking spot marked "Reserved for Officers" and led the way to the section of the field house where Standard Poodles traditionally set up their grooming tables. She took the last empty space up front. Hannah and her dogs were comfortably settled at the far end. Today Breaker and Chicory would go head to head against each other for the first time. Today's win could belong to either dog, but over their lifetime careers, the one with the greater heart would come out on top.

Bess spotted Nancy Valentine, an old friend, who waved and hurried over. As usual, Nancy was elegantly turned out, this time in a yellow halter dress with a designer label. Bess had avoided spilling half her coffee down the front of her polo shirt, but her glen plaid pants could have used a good press after sitting in the car.

Bess peeked in Nancy's handbag where her champion Toy Poodle had been known to travel. "Pipe Dream not here today?"

Nancy shook her head. "I'm judging Toys, remember?" Her Julie Andrews hair-do swirled back into place perfectly.

Bess urged Benny forward and said, "This is Benny Neusner. He's doing the honors today."

Nancy gave the pubescent boy the once-over. A new pimple decorated the middle of his forehead. She raised her eyebrows at Bess, inviting an explanation that didn't come. She reached down and gave Breaker a pat on the head. "Hoping for a second major today?" she asked, straightening up. "This handsome puppy could do it. He's the image of McCreery at that age."

Breaker was so pleased at the compliment he hopped up on Nancy's spotless dress before Benny could pull him off. Benny gasped and waited to see what she would do.

She squeezed Breaker's muzzle like he was good enough to eat and brushed off invisible paw prints. "Don't worry. With two Toys and a Standard at home I'm used to it a few smudges now and then."

Benny felt a tug on the lead and saw Felix Barnet and Chicory approaching. Except for Chicory's black coat, Benny wouldn't have known him from Breaker.

Felix bussed the ladies' cheeks and shook hands with Benny.

"I suppose Hannah's bringing half the kennel again today?" Bess said, giving Breaker's handsome littermate the once-over.

Felix grinned slyly. He and Bess were friends, but they were rivals, too. "Besides Chicory? Just another puppy from Susie's litter, a girl named Crumpet. Hannah's in a hurry to finish her and begin breeding those beautiful Umpawaug faces. Not that she won't wait a couple of years for Crumpet to mature."

Benny rocked back on his heels. "Chicory must be worried about going up against Breaker. He won a major at Housatonic, remember?"

Felix smiled so broadly he forgot to disguise his overbite. "It wouldn't surprise me if both these dogs finished their championships in puppy trim like their father."

Benny wrinkled his nose. "I still don't know why everyone gets so excited about a dog being a champion? I think Breaker looks nice no matter what."

Bess and Felix exchanged an amused look. "Let's put it this way," Felix said. "Only finished champions get invited to Westminster."

Benny's eyes grew round with understanding. "Oh."

Bess gave a quick glance at the littermates who were busy inspecting each other's credentials in a series of undignified sniffs. "Aren't you getting a bit ahead of yourself? We've both seen dogs that were gorgeous as puppies turn into pet material when they hit adolescence."

Nancy nodded at the two puppies. "Well, they both look like winners today. All I can say is I'm glad I'm not judging."

Benny looked around. "Speaking of winning, where are the reporters?"

"Never mind the reporters. Keep your eye on Breaker," Bess snapped, embarrassed the boy's inexperience was hanging out like stained underwear on a clothesline.

Felix cleared his throat as if for an announcement. He waited until everyone's eyes were on him. Then he said, "Hannah has important news to share. She'll fill in the details as soon as she gets here, but I can't wait. They caught the guy that stole McCreery. He's confessed everything."

Bess gasped and steadied herself on Benny's arm. Breaker looked from one to the other, a worried frown between his eyes.

Felix pulled Chicory in closer. "After what happened to McCreery, Hannah installed a silent alarm and motion detector floodlights. I happened to be there when he arrived, and we had the creep on the ground before he had time to finish his story. It was a wood paneled station wagon, by the way."

Benny banged his fist into his palm. "I wish I'd been there. I'd have taught him a lesson he'd never forget."

"The guy runs a puppy mill," Felix continued. "Apparently, he was trying to add a little quality to his stock. The police have closed him down, thank goodess."

"Thank goodness," Holly echoed.

Bess signaled Benny it was time to move on. He kept a tight grip on the lead as Breaker pranced and bobbed his way through the section where merchants had set up booths to sell all kinds of dog toys and paraphernalia. He was pretty sure Bess already owned most of it. He was thinking about buying a deck of cards with pictures of dogs to show the kids at school when a loud cheer caught his ear. He turned to see a German Shepherd leap into his owner's arms at the end of an Agility run. Breaker caught the excitement and began pulling in that direction.

An athletic-looking Australian Sheep Dog, its body quivering in anticipation, was poised at the start of the obstacle course. His handler, a boy a year or two older than Benny wearing blue overalls, gave the signal. The dog charged up a ramp, dove off the top into a tunnel, dashed out the other end and zigzagged through a line-up of poles. Each step of the way, the boy moved smoothly along at the dog's side, giving hand signals and whispering words of encouragement. When they reached the finish line, the dog jumped into the boy's arms, her tail wagging joyfully. The boy hugged back with a gap-toothed grin.

"Awesome!" Benny exclaimed ofver the applause of the crowd.

A cut-down cream Standard Poodle was waiting to go next. Benny turned to Bess. "Did you ever enter an Umpawaug Poodle in Obedience?"

She nodded at Breaker dancing on his hind legs in the direction of an attractive King Charles Spaniel instead of heeling. "What do you think? Poodles are great athletes and natural born show-offs so they do well in Obedience, but I stuck with conformation." She hesitated. "Years ago I considered entering one of my bitches in field trials. She would dive into bone-chilling water after anything that flew quicker than any dog I ever knew, but I got busy with other priorities and never followed through."

He reeled Breaker back in, straining at the effort. "People like my dad think conformation classes are just overblown beauty pageants."

She scowled. "There's a little more to them. Conformation started decades ago as a way for experts to identify the dogs with the best traits, so their genes could be passed on to the next generation."

The show steward called for Breaker's class, and they lined up quickly. The judge was Winston Samish, one of the grand old men in the poodle game. He and Bess had co-owned a dog a few years ago, but he wouldn't let friendship enter into his decision today.

Winston told Breaker and the six other dogs to circle the ring once and then line up along the side. Because Hannah had gotten her entry in early, Chicory and Felix were first to be called. Felix was a veteran handler with a puppy to match, making Chicory the hands-down favorite. Breaker's brother went through his paces flawlessly, showing off his perfect manners. Winston gave him one last look and called the next dog forward.

Benny's heart pounded while he waited for the other four puppies to be examined, but at last it was Breaker's turn. He stood like a statue while Winston examined him from nose to tail. He even let Winston raise his lips to check his mouth without moving a muscle. Winston jotted down a couple of notes and then ordered Benny to take Breaker up to the far end of the ring, turn, and bring him back down again.

From his first step, Breaker seemed to do everything right. Tail straight, head high, he sashayed his funny little butt from one end of the ring to the other. He seemed to be telling the other hopefuls, "Better luck next time." Only the future would tell whether Breaker would carry McCreery's prize-winning features into adulthood, but looks aren't the whole story in the show ring. The thrill of center-stage, a passion for pleasing the crowd, the lure of the spotlight occasionally can thrust even a mediocre dog into the winner's circle, and Breaker was far from mediocre.

Winston ordered Benny to take Breaker down to the end of the ring and back for a second look. "I'm in charge, I'm in charge," Benny whispered, trying to remember everything Bess had taught him. All those practice sessions were really paying off! Breaker was taking to his show career like he was born to it. The puppy pranced along cheerfully at Benny's side, watching closely for any signal. When they made the final turn and came around to face Winston again, Benny was sure they were in the running.

But the contest wasn't finished. Winston walked down the line one more time. He studied Chicory, then Breaker, back and forth between the brown and black littermates. He signaled Chicory to step out of line and trot around the ring once more. Felix held the lead loosely and Chicory moved forward. The puppy's joy at being in the ring shown through in the jaunty lift of his head and the delicate way his feet barely touched the ground. He seemed to be reminding the world that he was an Umpawaug poodle, too.

They made the final turn and were heading down the last stretch when out of nowhere, Felix seized up with a monstrous sneeze. Chicory broke his gait and looked up at Felix anxiously.

A disappointed groan traveled through the spectators. At the biggest shows, a tiny fraction separated the winners and losers. Still, Quinnipiac wasn't quite in that league. Felix pulled himself together and finished his tour around the ring, taking his place at the head of the line. It was all over except for Winston's decision.

Winston squared his shoulders and walked to the Judges' Table. He reached for the American Kennel Club's official record book where the winner's name would be preserved for all time. He pulled a silver pen from his suit coat pocket, inspected it as if he was about to sign the Magna Carta and wrote the name with a flourish. Then he took the small stack of ribbons from the show steward and held the blue one out ostentatiously in front. He walked to the center of the ring.

"First!" he shouted in a loud voice and pointed straight at Chicory.

Bess' couldn't hear Winston shout "Second" over the applause, but she saw him point at Breaker and hand Benny a red ribbon. She pushed through the crowd, past the show photographer posing the winner. A beaming Hannah stood in the middle with Felix and Chicory on one side of her and Winston on the other.

Benny was in the grooming area, blinking back tears, his arms wrapped around Breaker's neck. "Sorry, Bess, sorry. I've let you and Breaker down."

The dog did look miserable. A good show dog wants to win with every fiber of his being, and it seemed Breaker was as disappointed as Benny.

"Nonsense," she insisted brusquely, ruffling Breaker's topknot. "No telling what makes a judge pick one dog over another. One favors heads, another the set of the tail. Some won't put a brown up over a black." She reached and pulled the red ribbon out of Benny's blazer pocket where he had stuck it. She ran it through her fingers tenderly, as if she didn't have a closet full of others, not to mention solid silver trophies. She studied it, debating, and thrust it at Benny. "Here, you keep it."

He wiped his nose on his sleeve. He studied her face and was reassured by the encouragement he saw there. "I guess it's not so bad."

"Chicory was lucky today. Another day will be Breaker's turn. There's plenty of time for him to earn all the points he needs."

He gave her a weak smile.

"That's better. What do you say we give him another chance at Bar Harbor over Labor Day? A second major will be up for grabs, and Chicory will be there."

Breaker placed his paws on Benny's chess and grinned into his face.

He ruffled his topknot. "You'd like that, wouldn't you, boy?" He turned to Bess with a grin. "You're right. Plenty of time. We'll show Chicory how it's done in Bar Harbor. Just see if we don't."

CHAPTER THIRTY-THREE

Kate heard a knock on her office door and checked her watch. It must be David. He had phoned this morning with an idea he wanted to discuss. She had tried putting him off. She had too much on her mind to spar with him, but when he said it was about the school, she yielded.

She waved him to a chair and sat in her usual spot. "You had an idea?" she prompted, getting right down to business. His amused smile told her he expected no less.

He followed her lead and came straight to the point. "Benny's told me all about the teachers' theme for Summer School. 'A Day at the Circus' sounds like fun, and I was thinking a striped tent and a cotton candy machine would take it up a notch. Maybe add a pony ride."

She cocked her head. "No doubt, but those things aren't exactly in our budget."

He waved away her objection. "I'd like to donate them. You probably have a whole list of things the school needs, but I want to do this for the kids. It could be kind of a 'thank you' to the teachers, too, adding a little zip to their hard work."

"Well, yes…"

A "but" was coming and he interrupted. "Please, I'll write another check for an equal amount, and you can spend it any way you want."

She leaned back and laughed. "I usually don't have people begging to give the school money."

"My pleasure. If it makes you smile like this, I might have to do it more often."

They fell into an awkward silence, both of them wondering whether he was really doing it for the school, or for Benny, or maybe even for her?

"Benny's asked if he can bring the dogs and do a circus act with them. Bess is fine with it, but I told him he needed to check with you." He grinned sheepishly. "See, I'm learning. He needs to speak for himself."

She smiled, but the worry when he mentioned Benny must have shown on her face.

He leaned forward. "Problem with Benny?"

She dropped her chin. She knew the boy was hiding something, but he wouldn't say what. She only hoped he hadn't gotten into something over his head. "You know I can't discuss him," she said, but there was no sting in it.

"Benny's a good kid. Whatever it is, I think we can trust him."

Her eyes moved over his face, as if trying to read the man he truly was.

He reached for her hand, and she didn't pull away. He fingered her filigree bracelet tenderly, perhaps remembering she had worn it the day they met. "I'll keep an eye on him. I know you can't tell me anything, but I'll let you know if I learn something."

His hand around hers felt warm and gentle and strong enough to keep her safe. She longed to lace her fingers through his and hold on forever. "Thank you," she said, freeing her hand.

He exhaled deeply, a shift in the wind. "So, now that that's settled, I make a mean beef stroganoff or we can go out."

She rose and crossed her arms protectively across her heart. All her instincts warned her against becoming involved with him. Yes, he was attractive. Yes, he was intelligent. Yes, he seemed kind. But there was always the possibility of heartbreak ahead. He was inviting her to step into a loosely moored boat wearing the wrong shoes. Would he grab her hand and pull her to safety, or would she fall into the foamy waters and sink?

"I'm not very good at dinners," she said.

He turned on his heel, the tips of his ears reddening. "I'll call your secretary for an appointment."

She shivered, like a ghost was walking over her grave. In a way he was a ghost, a phantom reminder of feelings long dormant inside her. She had vowed never to leave herself open to that kind of hurt again, and now, after years of building a protective wall around her well ordered life, he was threatening to tear it down. How could she be sure the ending would be different with him? She couldn't. No one could tell the future. Isn't that what she told her clients? David had been patient, but now he was walking away, maybe for good. Perhaps what Benny had told her was true. She needed more in her life. Benny trusted the man. Why shouldn't she?

"Wait," she called at David's back. "A man who crunches numbers and cooks? How can I turn that down?"

He spun around. His face relaxed into a smile. In his mind's eye, he pictured her sitting across from him at a candlelit table overlooking the waterfall at Cob's Mill Inn. "Spinning Wheel? Seven o'clock?"

She returned a real smile. "Seven."

CHAPTER THIRTY-FOUR

Bess sat alone at the breakfast table with a month of unopened mail stacked up beside her. She never should have let Mona talk her into the trip to Boca Raton in the heat of summer. It was good to be back in Connecticut where a person could sit under a shade tree with a cool drink and eat a lobster with real claws. Ignoring the heap of envelopes — mostly bills — she began flipping through the latest issue of her favorite dog magazine. The lead story about Fandango, Picture Perfect Pete's star offspring, threatened her mood. If Fandango had the snappy temperament of his famous father, it wouldn't help the poodle gene pool for him to be receiving all this attention. Maybe Breaker could do something about that. He would be going up against Fandango at Bar Harbor. Then people would discover which dog deserved to have his photo on the cover of *Dog World*.

"Knock, knock," David called, opening the kitchen door. Breaker almost slipped inside behind him, but David stuck his foot out in time. "Muddy paws," he explained. "I was helping the school kids water the garden, and Breaker was chasing the hose. You know how poodles love water."

"Do I ever! I'll say hello to him later."

He stood back and gave his mother the once-over. "The

trip's done you good. Your color's back." He gently brushed the sleeve of her shirt. "You and Mona must have done some shopping. Pretty, I always liked aqua on you."

McCreery crawled out from under the kitchen table where he had been catching up on his beauty sleep after the long drive from Florida. He rubbed his muzzle against David's leg and looked up with a grin. David ruffled his topknot and smiled back.

"It wouldn't hurt that dog to spend a little time outside with Breaker. All he did the whole time in Florida was lie around in the air conditioning." She grabbed his collar and urged him out the door.

David poured two cups of coffee and handed her one. He held the steaming cup up to his nose and sniffed. "Mmm, fresh beans from PJ's. Remember when you were in that funk and only had that awful freeze-dried stuff?" He lifted the lid of a white cardboard container on the counter. "And croissants!" He held the flaky pastry up to admire like a great work of art.

Bess waved an indifferent hand. "Have one."

He took a large bite and then another. "Thanks, I'm starving," he said with his mouth full. "Breaker got me up hours ago. He takes as much energy as the kids at the school. Even Kate says so."

If she noticed the warmth in his voice when he mentioned Kate, she didn't comment. She lowered her coffee and asked a little too casually, "How's Benny doing by the way?"

David carried the box of croissants to the table and sat. He reached for a small pitcher shaped like a one-eyed pirate's head and poured cream into a mug from the rim of a tri-cornered hat. "Benny's fine. He's been practicing with Breaker every afternoon. I think he only missed once when his mother actually showed up."

Bess glanced at the door. "I'm surprised those dogs

haven't been barking to come in. Usually, McCreery can smell a croissant a mile off."

She walked stiffly to the kitchen window and pulled back the curtain.

David wasn't expecting her to say more, so he wasn't surprised when she fell silent. Still, something felt terribly wrong. She was leaning heavily against the sink, her head bowed. He rushed to her side, placing his hands on her shoulders to steady her. "Bess? Mother?"

For a long moment she didn't answer. When she did, her voice was so soft he almost missed it. "Poor Benny. He had his heart set on Westminster."

David gently nudged her aside and looked out the window. The dogs were racing back and forth across the grass. Breaker loved to be chased, and McCreery was up for the job. David wondered why he hadn't seen the change before. In the month Bess had been gone, Breaker had morphed into an all-together different dog. His legs were too long, his neck was too short, and his back sloped down like a whippet's. His feet, while still quick, no longer landed in steps so light a prima ballerina would perform as a dancing eggplant to have them. Only his face still kept the distinctive Umpawaug features of his ancestors.

Blood pounded in David's ears. "He'll grow out of it, right? It's just that awkward adolescent stage?"

She picked up the *Dog World* and tossed it into the trash. "Don't let your imagination run away with you."

"We can't give up. I'll keep him at home with me for a while."

She turned her back, dismissing him with a wave of her hand. "Do whatever you want. You will anyway. Sell him as a pet. That would be the kindest."

It wasn't the time to argue. David opened the kitchen door a crack. Breaker rushed past his father and raced inside. He placed his paws on Bess' shoulders and sniffed her face anxiously.

David reached for the lead hanging on the back of the door. "Come on, Breaker. You're staying with me."

The puppy whimpered, holding fast to Bess with his front paws. David snapped on the lead and stepped toward the door. Bess stood without moving, her face a mask to hide the pain.

David tugged again on the lead. "Come," he insisted. He opened the door. Breaker followed but kept his head turned back on Bess. She stepped forward and slammed the door behind them.

David hunkered down and took the puppy's head between his hands. "It'll be all right, you'll see," he said, hoping he sounded more confident than he felt.

Breaker rubbed his muzzle across his arm, and David had the fleeting thought the puppy was wiping away tears. David put on a smile he didn't feel. "It'll be fun. A couple of bachelors bunking together." Then he remembered Benny and dropped the cheerful act like an overfilled sack. He wasn't sure how a champion poodle looked, but from what he had seen on his mother's face, Breaker would never stand in the winner's circle again. Benny's hopes would fade like disappearing ink, just like Kate had predicted.

Breaker tossed back his head like an unbroken colt trying to free himself. He grabbed David's sleeve between his teeth and tugged in an invitation to play. In spite of himself, David couldn't hold back a smile. Breaker might look different on the outside, but inside he was the same as the rest of his Umpawaug ancestors. A human was unhappy, and it was his duty to use his entire armament to turn that mood around.

The Umpawaug magic took hold, and David started to shake off his gloom. Bess hadn't said for sure the puppy's looks were gone forever. Maybe there was still a chance. Breaker gave another tug on his sleeve, urging him further into the game. David ruffled the puppy's topknot, and then, in a quick shift of mood, urged the puppy back on all fours. What was he thinking? Breaker was a run-of-the-mill, garden variety dog with an abundance of charm and personality. Like Bess said, he would make a wonderful pet for someone who would love him for the dog he was. She had faced the end of her dream. He must do the same.

Chapter Thirty-Five

Dr. Kate had founded the New Hope School as kind of a one-room school with many rooms. Benny's class was for students who needed the most support regardless of age and was held in an old carriage house. She opened the door and flooded the room with sunlight. All the students looked up from their work except Benny who was concentrating on a video about sea creatures he had seen a dozen times. She signaled two strangers, a heavy set woman and her five year-old daughter, to enter ahead of her. The girl hung back and hid behind her mother.

"Go on, Keisha," the girl's mother urged gently. "Life is full of first days. You just have to get used to them."

"Mom can stay as long as you want," Kate promised. She had deliberately scheduled Keisha's first day to begin after her mother got off work, so she could be available if needed. Keisha was starting kindergarten and just learning to read, but she would fit into Benny's class where students were taught on their own individual levels and older students helped with younger ones. That is why a boy as old as Benny and a five year-old girl like Keisha could be in the same class. In spite of the differences in their ages, they were similar in their emotional needs.

Kate resisted the temptation to tell the class they should

welcome Keisha. Ms. Jeanette would have reminded them how they felt on their first day of school; over-doing it would only backfire. This time Ms. Jeanette's efforts didn't seem to be taking hold. The students kept their heads buried in their work so the new girl couldn't see their expressions, but Keisha must have heard Benny's "not another new student," under his breath which spoke for them all. Only Eric put on a smile and said, "Welcome, Keisha. Wanna be friends?"

Keisha turned and buried her face in her mother's ample stomach. "Keisha's a little shy," her mother answered for her. "She's new to our family and has a lot to get used to."

A short boy named Aaron raised his hand, eyes bright. "I'm adopted, too. From Russia."

"I thought this was a school for big kids," Benny groused, looking back and forth

between his teacher and his meeting doctor. "Keisha's a baby."

Ms. Jeanette came and stood beside Benny. "Keisha's part of the team now, like you, Benny. Do you think you can help us?"

"I will," Matthew piped up, saving Benny from answering. "Me, too," echoed Jack.

Keisha's mother leaned down and lifted her daughter's chin. "Would you like me to sit by you for a while?"

The girl looked around the room with big eyes and nodded, making the yellow ribbons on her short, thin braids bounce. Ms. Jeanette pointed to a chair at a round table where Matthew was seated and pulled up a larger one for her mother. She nodded at Kate. "We'll be fine."

Kate was half-way out the door when a piercing scream cut through the room. She spun around. Keisha, wide-eyed, was frozen in place, her arms hugging her body. "A fly! A fly!" Sammy leaped up on his chair, as if the fly would attack from underground, and began screaming, too.

"Keisha's terrified of flies," her mother called over the commotion, explaining the obvious. "Hush, baby. Life is full of flies. You just have to get used to them."

"I'll get it," Benny said, rolling up a handy workbook. He whacked the workbook against the back of a chair, barely missing Harrison. "It's dead," he announced, holding the fly up by one wing for inspection. He gave Kate a crescent-moon grin. "I told you I was a good hunter."

"Okay, boys and girls. Where do you need to be?" came Ms. Jeanette's sensible voice. "It's almost snack time. If everyone finishes their work, I can read the princess story to the class."

Kate threw Benny a warning glance, expecting to hear a complaint about a "baby story for sissies," but he looked pleased. As always, the boy was full of surprises.

Keisha was settling in nicely with her mother's help, so Kate signaled Benny it was time for their meeting. David had stopped by yesterday to let her know about Breaker. He had offered to tell Benny, and she had agreed. Today she would help Benny deal with the fallout. They had found it remarkably easy to come up with the plan. Maybe they were learning to work as a team.

Upstairs in her office, she expected Benny would be bursting with the news, but he was strangely quiet.

"Thinking about Breaker?" she suggested, hoping to ease the way.

He snapped open the lid of his lunch box and rummaged through the empty packets until he found a lone grape he had somehow overlooked. Catching it in his mouth, he said, "Not really." He rubbed a finger lightly over the photograph of his mother taped to the lid and slammed it shut. He stuck the lunchbox in his backpack and pulled out a stack of trading cards. One by one he studied the exotic cartoon figures. When he got to the bottom of the pile, he wrapped them with a rubber band and stuffed them in his pocket. "He'll be fine."

She wished it were true. When David told her about Breaker, her first thought was how hurt Benny would be, and then to her surprise, her second was about David's own disappointment. Remembering it now, she realized she hadn't retreated into the old blame game, saying "I told you so" because David had taken a risk that ended in heartache.

Benny rolled over onto his back and clasped his hands behind his head. "I am kind of sad about Breaker. Bess says there's no such thing as the perfect dog, but show dogs have to be almost perfect." He glanced down at his own over-sized feet and blushed.

Kate was back in the moment. She wiped fake sweat off her brow. "Thank goodness that's not me. I would hate needing to be perfect for somebody all the time."

Benny bounced to his feet and balled his hands into fists. "I warned you. No talking about my mom."

Kate's breath caught in her throat. Standing over her chair, his face twisted with rage, Benny looked more man than boy. She struggled to hide her fear. He needed her to believe in him in order to calm himself down. She sat still, heart pounding.

He took three deep breaths like she had taught him and sat.

"Good job getting back in charge, Benny."

He glanced at the clock and squirmed impatiently. She wanted him to enjoy the feeling of mastery and end on a positive note. Besides, she had derailed him with her comment about needing to be perfect. She would have to figure out what was going on with herself to make her lose her empathy like that. "I know you wanted to hear Miss Jeanette's story, and I've got some time this afternoon," she said. "Would you rather meet then?"

He nodded and hoisted his backpack onto his shoulders, his need for prolonged goodbyes a thing of the past. "I think I'll head over to Bess' after school. She isn't half bad for an old lady once you get to know her, and she's got to be bummed about Breaker."

Kate thought his sadness was about more than Breaker. Steffie hadn't returned to school so far this year. Maybe she never would. "That's a kind thought," she said. "Bess will be glad to see you."

"I'm glad I'm young and can roll with a little change in plans," he said.

She ducked the invitation to debate.

He spun on one leg and held up a finger. "Hold on! I just had the best idea of my life. I can't wait til Bess hears."

Kate was afraid Benny's idea would lead to more heartache. She waited to hear if he would tell her.

"I better not blurt it out all at once. Like I said, old people's brains need to get used to new ideas." He noticed the school newspaper lying on the coffee table. "I'll bring her a copy of the *NSH Gazette*. That'll ease her into it."

"Sure you don't want to talk it over here first?"

"Can't wait."

"Okay, see you later then."

"Not if I see you first."

She gave him a small smile. It was an old joke from a movie he liked.

She shut the door behind him and sank back into her chair. Benny had shown a lot of maturity today. For the first time since he had brought up the idea of going to Westminster, she thought he might be up to the challenge. David had said there was a chance Breaker would pull himself together again, but Benny wasn't known for his long attention span. For his sake — and David's, she hoped it would happen, but by then would the boy still be on board?

CHAPTER THIRTY-SIX

B enny found Bess in the puppy shed with McCreery on top of the grooming table. He held the newspaper up to her face and read the headline in a voice loud enough to be heard over the buzz of the clippers: "Champion Poodle is New Hope School's Neighbor."

She snapped off the clippers and rubbed a stray clump of poodle hair off her nose with her sleeve. She reached for the paper. "Hmmm, an interesting drawing of McCreery by Keisha, age six. Such pretty blue eyes. And a feature article on the famous Umpawaug Kennels by Carol Gale." She squinted at the class picture. "Which one is she?"

He ignored her question and pointed to the photo of him with his arm around McCreery. "Ms. Jeanette took it with her digital camera and put it on our school website where everyone in the world can see it. My mother will be as excited as me."

"Nice," she said, turning to the next page.

"It's good for you, too. The *Gazette* could be your last chance to be famous now that Breaker's ruined." He gasped and pressed his hand to his mouth. "Sorry, I guess I shouldn't have said that."

She dropped the newspaper onto the counter. "That's all right. It's the truth." She turned her back and reached for McCreery's brush. The swishing sound it made moving across the dog's coat was the only noise in the room.

Benny hopped up on the counter where Breaker had come back to life eight months ago. He raised his feet over his head, back against the wall. He pulled the red ribbon he and Breaker had won at Quinnipiac out of his pocket and rested it against his chest, tracing the floret with his finger. "Feels like my mother's favorite blouse," he said to himself. He stuck it back in his pocket and straightened up. "I'm bored."

She handed him the brush. "Here, McCreery would love you to finish grooming him. Believe me, I've got plenty to keep me busy." She sat on the rusty folding chair and picked up the newspaper again.
He tossed the brush back into the tattered shoe box with the other grooming aids. "Miz Rutledge," he sing-songed, "McCreery only likes me because I'm young. He can't help it if you're all worn out."

She flushed. Last week at Betty Johnson's Beauty Boutique a blue haired sixty year-old raced to open the door like she was a helpless old lady who couldn't kick it open with her shoe any more.

Benny rolled the ends of the red ribbon into tight circles and let them drop. "My body may be stronger than yours, but how'd you like to have so many feelings inside they make your head swim?"

She smiled sadly. "We have something in common. Neither of our bodies does everything we want."

"At least your brain's working."

She shuddered. Lately she had been afraid whenever she forgot something. Had she always been like that only now she noticed it more? Mona would know.

He came around to the front of the grooming table and grabbed hold of McCreery's chin. He turned the old champion's head this way and that, his brows drawn together in deep concentration. Satisfied, he let go of the dog and turned to Bess. "I have an idea," he announced, excitement plain in his voice. "How old's McCreery?"

Hearing his name, the dog turned his head in Benny's direction. He seemed to sense something important was in the works.

"McCreery? He must be about ten."

Benny's face fell. "Years? That's pretty old for a dog, isn't it?"

Bess stood and fished the brush out of the box. "Not that old — at least for an Umpawaug Poodle."

Benny spun around on one leg and came back all smiles like a puppet head with a different face painted on each side. "Breaker may be ruined, but McCreery's still a great looking dog. You said so yourself."

"So what?" she asked, sounding juvenile. She knew where he was heading.

McCreery seemed to know, too. He jumped off the grooming table, shook out his coat, and positioned himself the way he had done dozens of times in front of a judge.

"So we could take McCreery to Westminster."

Bess froze in place. Only her eyes moved, stopping on the red second place ribbon. "Westminster? You think I'm still thinking about Westminster?"

Benny flicked out his hands, his neck thrust out like a turtle's. "Du-uh! "Remember what you told me on the way to Quinnipiac? Westminster's been your dream your whole life. So why didn't you ever try? She jerked her head back like she had been hit. "Plenty of reasons, that's why." .

"Maybe you should figure it out." His face lit with inspiration. "Maybe Mona knows. You could ask her."

Bess pulled her thick eyebrows together. She pulled McCreery by the scruff of the neck into an empty crate and banged the door shut. "Dream time's over."

Benny stared at his feet and swallowed hard. A bitter taste in his mouth made him want to punch somebody. Instead he slipped his fingers through the grate of McCreery's crate and gave him a little scratch. "Sorry, boy, I tried. Hope you like the newspaper," he told her and left.

CHAPTER THIRTY-SEVEN

The autumn day was crisp and warm, and a blanket of colorful leaves covered New Hope School's playground faster than the Nature Club could rake and bag them. Heading toward Benny's classroom, Kate realized the year was slipping away fast. In a month, it would be Thanksgiving, then Christmas, and in the blink of an eye, the school year would be over. Next year Benny would be too old for New Hope School, but he still had a lot to master before he would be ready to move on to Joel Barlow High. What she heard as she entered the classroom didn't reassure her any.

"Margaret's eating boogers again," Benny announced in a voice meant to be heard by all. He beamed and looked around for his classmates' approval. He wasn't disappointed. Heads popped up all over the classroom waiting to see what would happen next.

"Gross," Joel crowed, wrapping his hands around his neck and sticking out his tongue.

"Gross," repeated George, depositing his own nose booty down the side of his jeans.

Kate sighed and glanced at Margaret scrunched down in her chair. The girl's thick brown hair fell over her face, a shield against a prying world. Why her mother let a blossoming twelve-year old wear tights and a tank top was more than Kate could fathom. Both arms were pocked by open sores where she had worried the skin away.

"What are you boys supposed to be doing?" Kate asked, encompassing Joel and George in one glance. "And Benny, you're supposed to be a leader, not tattling on people." She passed by Margaret's desk and dropped a clean tissue. "Here," she whispered, "and try not to pick at those scabs." She checked the clock. "Two more minutes until lunch."

On Ms. Jeanette's signal, the children rushed into the kitchen and jockeyed for their favorite seats. Out of the corner of her eye, Kate noticed Keisha passing half her cupcake to Margaret. Now that Keisha had been in school for nearly a month, she was feeling at home and trying to befriend the awkward older girl. Kate smiled. The children could be a handful, but there was a reason why they were called "special."

A loud thud jolted her out of her reverie. Benny was on his feet, his chair tipped over behind him. He was holding a styrofoam container over his head ready to dump. To his left, Keisha was frozen in fear. To his right, Sammy took shelter under the table.

"I told her, 'No Thai food!'"

Kate moved in front of him, protecting the other children. "What's going on?" she asked, keeping one eye on the container. "Sonya! She and my Dad had a date at the Thai restaurant in Westport last night, and she gave me their leftovers for lunch."

"You can have half my sandwich," Jacob piped up bravely. "It's good — peanut butter and jelly."

"Nice words, Jacob," Kate said, holding Benny's eyes. "Do you want to put your lunch back in your locker, Benny, or toss it away?" Things went better when Benny had a choice. Still, she wasn't sure it would work this time.

He started to lower the box. She held her breath. None of the other children moved.

Slam! The box crashed down, peppering the kitchen with slippery pad thai noodles. At least he had aimed away from the table where the others were seated. His face was still red, but she could tell he was struggling to get back in charge.

Kate stood quietly in place. "What do you say we invite your Dad and Sonya to one of our meetings?"

He studied his shoes. His lower lip quivered, and she thought the crisis had passed. "Not her. Just my dad."

The door burst open and Clarence from Mr. Michael's room dashed in, his long stringy hair swinging back and forth. He crouched down, trying to hide the wet splotch on the front of his pants. "Forgot my book," he explained lamely and crab-crawled to the bathroom.

Kate held out the phone, but the mood was broken. Before she could stop him, Benny dashed out the door. He had only gone a few yards when he skidded to a stop. A poodle was lying on the grass in front of him with his legs splayed in the air like a Thanksgiving turkey.

"McCreery!" he shouted and held out his arms. The poodle leaped to his feet and careened toward him, ears flapping, mouth open in a wide grin. Before he could duck, the dog made a direct hit against his chest. Benny windmilled his arms and managed to keep his balance.

The rest of the class had been drawn by the noise and gathered at the door. Only Sammy stood back and clung to Ms. Jeanette. His feet danced up and down in place and his hands slapped his sides.

"Sammy's a sissy, Sammy's a sissy," George teased.

Keisha rushed to Sammy's side and took his hand. "I'll sit beside you. Life is full of big dogs. You just have to get used to them."

While the other students guffawed and pointed, the poodle ran in figure eights from Benny to his classmates and back again. Each time the dog circled back, Benny grabbed for his collar, but the dog was too quick.

"Hey, Dr. Kate," Benny called. "McCreery's acting weird."

Taking advantage of the distraction, the poodle charged and collided against Benny's chest with a thud. He tumbled onto his back on the ground. He leaned in to lick Benny's face, and the boy got his chance. "Gotcha," he said, snagging the dog's collar. He looked around for applause. The dog made a sidewise leap and twisted free. Benny looked at his empty hand, disbelieving. "I had him," he whimpered.

"I'll catch him," Margaret called from the classroom door. She had been hanging out in the bathroom when the commotion started. She zipped up her culottes and headed for the excited dog. She crouched and held out her hand. "Good doggie, it's all right," she crooned.

The poodle flopped over on his back like he had hit a glass wall. Four walnut-shaped feet stuck up in the air like a giant dead insect's. Margaret slipped beside him and rubbed his belly. If a dog could purr, he would have.

Benny heard a noise behind him and turned. A second brown poodle was heading toward the classroom. Bess was right behind him. She was holding a rectangular pan covered with aluminum foil. "Mona made devil's food cake for Funhouse Friday," she called, unaware of the commotion.

Benny looked back and forth between the two dogs, a puzzled expression on his face. "If that's McCreery," he said, pointing with his chin at the dog beside her, "who's this?" He tipped his hand at the dog now sitting politely at his side.

Bess stepped closer and signaled the dog to stand. Her eyes grew wide. She walked around the dog slowly, studying him as if she had never seen him before. She handed Benny the cake pan and threw her arms around the dog's neck.

Benny's mouth dropped open. For a minute he couldn't

speak. Then he turned to his classmates like a master of ceremonies. "Hey, guys, Breaker's got his looks back! We're going to Westminster!"

Kate stepped forward and gave a warning cough.

He turned to Bess. "Right, Bess? I'm going to be on TV?"

She straightened up, avoiding his eyes. "We'll see."

He jammed his fist in the air. "Yes!" he shouted like he hadn't heard the caution in her words.

Benny and his fellow students headed back to class. Bess left with both dogs following close behind. Kate stared after her and couldn't help wondering. Had she really heard a little catch in Bess' voice when Benny mentioned Westminster?

She gave herself a mental head slap. She was overanalyzing again. Of course, Bess would be guarded. No one had thought Breaker would ever appear in the show ring again, let alone head off to Westminster. Naturally, she would keep her hopes modest, but some intuition told Kate that Bess' hesitation had more to do with Benny than Breaker. Westminster would bring out the finest handlers in the world. Could a boy like Benny compete against that elite group? Kate would try to keep his expectations realistic, but the genie was out of the bottle. She only hoped he had gained the maturity to handle whatever disappointments still might lie ahead.

CHAPTER THIRTY-EIGHT

David knocked on his mother's back door with his knee and prepared to wait. It was early and she might still be asleep, but she opened the door promptly fully dressed in corduroy slacks and a blouse with a sweater vest. He brushed past her, his hands holding something hidden under a green checkered dish towel.

She lifted the towel and peeked. The aroma of warm blueberry muffins wafted up to her. She cast a suspicious look at him. "Beware the Greeks and all that."

"Careful, they're still hot. I remember how much you like them."

She arched an eyebrow. "Overnight guest?"

"I wish. No, I made them myself. Even picked the blueberries and saved them in the freezer for a special occasion." He stuck his head in the fridge and called out, "Any real butter in here? I'm not thinking about cholesterol while I can smell those muffins."

"Probably hidden behind the heavy cream," she said, prying two muffins out.

He thought she was kidding, but there it was. He pulled out a chair and sat. "I heard about Breaker. Fantastic!" He crossed his legs and looked at her. "What's next?"

She studied him over the top of her glasses. "I'm surprised

you're so interested. I thought you'd drop the act once you got me to keep Breaker."

He sat forward. "It's not an act."

She set two plates on the table, poured the coffee and sat, too. She was stalling for time. She met his eyes, struggling shyly to hold his gaze. "You mean it, don't you?"

He reached across the table and covered her hand with his own. "I love you. When are you going to get it?"

She let it rest there a moment and then withdrew gently. "Sometimes I wonder if it would have been better if I'd taken you with me all those times on the road."

"Benny's got you thinking, too, hasn't he? Watching him makes me remember the times you were gone. Not that Mona wasn't wonderful, but still. . ."

". . . I'm your mother," she finished for him.

He stood and retrieved the coffee pot. He topped off their cups, as if he, too, needed time to think. "Yes," he said, "but now I see your point of view. Like you said, I was never interested in dogs except for what they meant to you. I hated Junior Showmanship. And spending night after night in hotel rooms, always missing school, never having friends? That's no life for a kid."

"That's what I thought," she whispered, her gravelly voice shaky, "but now when I see how lonely Benny is, hanging around every afternoon like — well, like a dog — hoping his mother. . ."

He sat again and faced her, his shoulders squared confidently. "The difference is I knew where you were. You'd be home when you said." He hesitated. "Not that I wasn't afraid you loved your dogs more than me."

She winced. She had been afraid of that for years.

He drew in a bracing breath and leaned forward. "I might as well go ahead and say it. Lately, I've had the idea that you never went to Westminster because you felt guilty about the way you treated me."

She waved her hand dismissively. "You've been spending too much time with Benny's shrink."

He crossed his arms protectively, but now that he had said it, he wouldn't take it back. 'No, really. I've watched your face when you look at Benny. Every time his mother lets him down it almost breaks your heart. I think it's about me."

She wanted to stop him, but her mouth was dry and no words came. He was wrong. All those times she had tried and failed to achieve Westminster were just coincidences. She tried to tell him, but he held up his hand to stop her.

"Forgive yourself. I have," he said. He turned and walked to the window, swallowing the feelings that would have crushed them both.

She shook her head, trying to make sense of the thoughts spinning around in her brain. Could David's idea be true? Had she been holding back all those years because of a bizarre notion she was paying him back for all the hours she had selfishly neglected him for her dogs? She had heard people could stab themselves in the back like that, but she never imagined it could happen to her.

She reached behind her for the loving cup that had rested on the kitchen counter ever since Benny returned it. She tilted it back and forth like she was trying to read a faint message etched inside. She rubbed a finger around the rim a final time and placed it in front of the chair where the boy always sat. He would find it there the next time he came.

David pulled back the kitchen curtain. "I'm surprised the dogs aren't in here sniffing around for a muffin. As I recall, McCreery's crazy about blueberries."

She brushed at her cheeks with both hands and straightened up in her chair.

"Mona's taken them both to the living history exhibit at Putnam Park. I think they're supposed to be colonial dogs or something."

They shared a smile. It was so like Mona to fuss at Bess about raising dogs and then co-opt them for her pet projects.

He started to leave, nodding at the muffins on the counter. "I'll pick up the muffin tin next time I come."

"Sure you won't take a couple? Maybe share them with someone?"

"If you mean Kate, I wouldn't mind." He studied his toes, looking boyish. "I like the whole package: the woman, the school, the kids. I think I might have found my own special passion. I admit Mona's not the only one who's envied you that."

She rose and gave him a quick hug, something she hadn't done for years. "Go on, get out of here. I can't sit around here all day chatting about muffins. I've got dogs to take care of."

⚜ ⚜ ⚜

The knock came again and then Mona's voice. "Bess? I forgot my key. Open the door."

Bess shook herself awake and checked the clock on the mantle. Four-fifteen. She must have fallen asleep on the sofa after lunch. Last year's PCA catalogue lay open on her chest. She had been reading her ad. For thirty years she had altered the lyrics of an old show tune to announce Umpawaug's news. What would this year bring? "Happy Days are Here Again" or "Fools Rush In?" Breaker wasn't the first Umpawaug puppy that had transformed a mismatch of adolescent bones into a stunning maturity, but no one knew yet whether his old sparkle and determination to win had returned along with his looks. The Liberty Bell in Philadelphia would tell the tale. If he did well, he might just finish his championship in time.

She shuffled to the kitchen in her stocking feet and opened the door. McCreery and Breaker slipped through and hurried to sniff their dinner bowls. It was too early for their supper, but it never hurt to try. The surprise was Mona. She was wearing a long brown skirt covered by a coarse blue apron. A red petticoat stuck out underneath. A homespun blouse, brown shawl, and white colonial cap with a black ribbon tied in front topped off her outfit.

Bess staggered back and pressed a hand against her chest. "What in the world?"

Mona smiled cheerily and stepped inside. "It's the annual Patriot's Weekend at Putnam Park. We're doing a living museum all about life in General Putnam's camp and how he helped George Washington defeat the British. Lots of cannons and stuff. Very historical." She shifted a black iron kettle from one wrist to the other and waited for her sister's response.

Bess looked her twin up and down. She recognized the scent of the perfume Mona had given her for their birthday. "And you're supposed to be a camp follower?"

Mona flounced her red petticoat. "So very amusing!"

Bess heard the click of dog nails on the wooden floor and watched them circle down in their own corners where they could eavesdrop undisturbed. McCreery choose under the kitchen table; Breaker curled up on the mat in front of the back door. They had earned a bit of a rest after their day reliving history with Mona.

"Thanks for letting me take the dogs," Mona said. "A few of the boys preferred climbing on the canons, but the others wished they could take Breaker and McCreery home. One little girl even followed us to the car. She reminded me of you as a kid."

"Those dogs like nothing better than showing off for a crowd," Bess grumbled.

Mona knew her twin was secretly pleased. "I suppose

that's what makes them great competitors in the ring," she said agreeably.

Breaker raised up from the mat and rubbed his muzzle against Mona's skirt. Then he turned and did the same to Bess. McCreery lifted his head, scooted out from under the table and nosed Breaker out of the way. Breaker resisted, but only for a second before stepping back, tail between his legs. His upset lasted only a moment before he slipped around to the other side.

"McCreery still insists on being top dog," Mona observed.

Bess flicked her eyebrows, surprised her sister noticed. "Normally, I wouldn't let two intact males live in the same house, but McCreery's managed to contain his jealousy and keep the peace, at least so far."

Mona reached down and scratched the top of McCreery's head. "I have to admit it's hard to tell father and son apart now that Breaker's got his looks back."

Bess shrugged, feigning indifference. "McCreery has always gotten himself up for every big show."

Mona dropped into a chair. "Big show? For McCreery? You can't be serious."

"Just the Parade of Champions at the Liberty Bell in Philadelphia where the old fellows strut their paces," she answered nonchalantly. "A kind of Veteran's Day Parade for dogs. People want to see the top-producing stud dog of all time. Sixty-five champions — so far."

Mona bent down and took off a shoe. A pebble that had caught inside fell out and rolled under Bess' chair. "I bumped into David at the Living History. He said you two had a good talk."

Bess stabbed the pebble with her toe. It spun across the room. McCreery considered chasing it and dropped his chin onto his front paws again. "We had a few words about Westminster. Things like that," she answered evasively.

Mona studied her twin closely. "Do you think you'll actually make it this time? You won't just be letting yourself down. It'll be Benny, too.

Bess nodded. "I know." She stared into space, cocooning into herself. "David says I never went to Westminster because I feel guilty about the way I treated him as a kid. I think he's been hanging around with Dr. Kate too much." She thrust out her chin, challenging a fight to conceal how much she wanted her twin's opinion — and how much she feared her son could be right.

A slow grin grew at the corners of Mona's mouth. "It could be something in our childhood. Personally, I've never had the slightest urge to take a poodle to Westminster."

Bess stood and threw up her hands. "Oh, for heaven's sake. You didn't think I was serious, did you? Freud!"

Mona walked to the counter and busied herself stacking dishes in the dishwasher to hide a smile. For whatever reason, Bess had changed. Mona didn't know why except Benny was part of it and David, too. This time there wouldn't be any false starts. She was sure. Her sister would make it to Westminster and handle the outcome whatever happened. She closed the dishwasher with a bang and headed for the door.

"I'm late. A few of us are in a tableau at Emma Goldhorn's Rest Home. Something to cheer up the old folks." She turned when she heard the staccato of dog kibbles hitting metal bowls. She watched Bess mix in three tablespoons of her secret champion-building formula while McCreery and Breaker stared up at her like she was a goddess. A slow smile appeared at the corners of Bess' mouth as her dogs bent over their dishes. She didn't even know she was doing it.

"My real estate agent called about my condo this morning," Mona said. "Something about the plumbing this time, I think."

A white cloth fell out of Mona's pocket, and Bess bent

down stiffly to retrieve it. She spread the handkerchief across her palm, studying the "M" their mother had painstakingly embroidered in pink. "Pretty," she said, handing it back. "Mine was blue. I lost it years back."

"It was a long time ago."

Their eyes met, remembering. The tenderness of the moment was too awkward for them both and passed quickly.

Bess opened the door and signaled her sister to go through first. McCreery roused himself and scooted past, nosing Breaker out of the way. The night air had an autumn chill, and the sky was black, no moon, only specks of blinking stars. She stood a long time in the driveway watching the tail lights on Mona's red sports car grow smaller and smaller, finally disappearing from view. She pulled her sweater tight across her chest and signaled the waiting dogs to follow her inside.

Chapter Thirty-Nine

Benny and Bess rested under a sugar maple in lawn chairs she had stowed in the back of the station wagon and looked out over the field where the Liberty Bell All-Breed Show was about to begin. Breaker stretched out on the metal grooming table, cooling his belly, and McCreery sat sedately on top of his crate. The shade of the ancient tree barely made a dent in the heat of Indian Summer. It was the hottest October day on record, and when it was hot in Philadelphia, it wasn't just hot; it was sticky hot.

Benny stuffed the last of his Philly cheese steak hoagie into his mouth and tossed the grease soaked wrapper into a nearby can. Breaker twitched his nose as the greased wrapper sailed by, but decided it was too hot to bother and lay his head down again. McCreery didn't even sniff.

"It's a good thing my mother decided not to come. She's not used to all this heat," Benny said. He patted his stomach. "I sure could use a nice, cool Frosty Freeze to top off my sandwich."

Bess took a can of diet lemonade out of the ice chest and handed him one. "Nobody can control the weather, but it'll be murder on the dogs."

"Probably global warming," he suggested importantly. "Ms. Jeanette will probably make me write an article about it for the *NHS Gazette*."

"I suppose you'll have a lot of work to make up for missing school yesterday."

He shook his head. "Naw. They had a field trip to the Mark Twain Library. I've been a million times. The yellowish papers with Mark Twain's real handwriting are sort of cool, but the rest of it is just a bunch of books."

She rose. "I'm going to have a look around. Keep Breaker in the shade and work on his coat. His tail needs fluffing out." She had something special to do, and she didn't need Benny nosing in on it.

He shook his hands and blew. "I think I'm getting blisters. I better take a break and come with you."

She was pretty sure he wanted to sneak down to the parking lot and see if a TV truck had shown up. She reached into the ice chest and dropped a few ice cubes into the dogs' water dish. "You stay here with Breaker. This is what they call a Benched Show. Dogs are supposed to be on their "benches" when they're not in the ring, so the public can educate themselves about the different breeds."

"What about McCreery? The public can educate themselves on him."

She flashed a fake smile. "Good idea. The Parade of Champions isn't until the very end. I'll take him with me." She snapped her fingers and McCreery jumped off his crate. He rubbed his muzzle along Bess' side while she clipped on his lead.

"McCreery will be the best looking dog in the parade," he said, stalling her departure. "How many old champions do you think there'll be?"

She considered. "Depends how many stay until the end in this heat. Even dogs needing points are dropping out." She considered going home herself, but she had to be certain before PCA whether the old Umpawaug sizzle had returned along with Breaker's looks.

Plenty of well-wishers stopped Bess along the way. A few recognized McCreery from the old days. He feigned the cool detachment of royalty until he spotted Felix bringing Chicory back from a potty break. McCreery ignored his handsome black son and pounced on Felix's chest with delighted abandon.

"McCreery!" Felix greeted, rubbing the dog's rump vigorously. McCreery wriggled happily. Felix turned to Bess. "If this old boy weren't in pet clip, I would have taken him for Breaker. He looks good enough for the show ring himself." Felix slid his glasses to the end of his nose. "You didn't, did you?"

She shook her head. "Parade of Champions."

"Well, I wouldn't put it past you. No telling what you'll do now the gleam is back in your eye." He lifted his own lead over McCreery's head and handed Chicory off to her.

She circled the lovely black dog. No question about it. Breaker's littermate would be stiff competition. His black coat had grown in thick and dark, and the Umpawaug face held true. Breaker and Chicory hadn't squared off in the ring since Quinnipiac when Chicory had come out on top. She handed the lead back to Felix. "Nice. I'd be ashamed if McCreery didn't produce good-looking get."

McCreery snuck a peek out of the corner of his eye and assumed an air of indifference equal to Bess' own.

"Hannah's got her heart set on a win today," Felix teased.

She didn't mind. Their long friendship didn't cancel the honest rivalry between them. It was different with Hannah. Impossible to believe someone could be that nice.

"The fire marshal sprayed the tent roof, but it's turning to steam," a new voice interjected. Jim Wren had slipped up behind them. DandyGirl sat sedately at his feet. Jim unscrewed the lid of a thermos, extracted an ice chip and held it out. DandyGirl took it delicately between her lips and slid it down her throat. "It feels like a hundred degrees under the tent. If too many people drop out, the five-point major will be broken."

"Hannah's heart will break," Felix said. "She's got her letter about Chicory's record stamped and ready to mail to Westminster."

McCreery tugged on the lead, and Bess turned to see Benny and Breaker skid to a halt, both panting heavily. She narrowed her eyes disapprovingly. Between the heat and Felix's goading she was in no mood for their shenanigans. There wasn't much time before Breaker's class would be called to the ring. "I thought I told you to keep that dog cool and calm. Now he'll need to be brushed out all over again."

Breaker dropped to his belly and covered his face with his paws.

"Sorry," Benny apologized, not looking sorry at all. "I thought you'd want to know there's a car with *Philadelphia Inquirer* on the door, but no TV van."

Jim said his goodbyes and hurried off. Felix was next. "See you for Winners," he said, leading Chicory away from the ring.

"Where's Felix going?" Benny asked.

"Chicory's entered in American Bred. Hannah must think he has a better chance in that class. If Breaker and Chicory both win their classes, they'll get their rematch for Winner's Dog."

Benny puffed out his chest. "Breaker's got Chicory on the run."

She nodded at a handsome white poodle at the head of the line. "Maybe, or maybe Hannah's worried about that dog over there. Fandango is Picture Perfect Pete's son. You may have heard of him."

Benny remembered the white Standard Poodle on the cover of *Dog World* and swallowed hard.

She signaled Breaker over to her. She held her hand out for Benny's brush and began attacking Breaker's coat with heavy strokes as though he had suffered more damage during his jaunt around the premises than he really had. Felix had hit a nerve. Breaker and Chicory each had one major and needed a second. Breaker had lost a lot of time during his homely adolescent phase and even if he won a major today he would still need five more points to finish his championship. In Chicory's case, a major win today would bring his point count up to the required fifteen, including the two majors. Even so, a championship in itself was no guarantee of a spot at Westminster. A dog couldn't just turn up at Madison Square Garden; he had to be invited.

Invitations to Westminster go to the top five dogs of every breed. They are given a deadline by which to respond. The remaining spots go to other Champions of Record on a first come, first served basis. Entries become open at an announced time, and there is always a bit of a scramble to get applications in quickly because places fill up fast. No one can be assured of a spot until their acceptance letter is in hand, and neither Chicory or Breaker had even finished his championship.

The first call for Breaker's class blared over the P.A. Bess stayed with Benny until he found his place in line and then hurried toward the Judges' Table. She made a habit of checking the judge's identity in advance, but this was the first time she had entered on purpose because of one. Reginald Hannaford had worked for her father when they were both kids. He had moved to Birmingham, England decades ago but stayed in the dog game. Now, after all those years, he was standing a few feet away. He was talking to a teenage girl holding a black Standard Poodle puppy in her arms. He said something, and the girl nodded back excitedly. It was like watching herself fifty-odd years ago. Today he would be judging her dog and wouldn't even know it.

She stood some distance away, hoping she wouldn't be noticed. There would be time to catch up later. She wasn't trying to influence Reginald's decision, not really. It was enough to know that a judge who shared her tastes would be making the decision. After all, Reginald was the one who encouraged her to concentrate on breeding beautiful faces — as long as they went along with loving temperaments. Wasn't she counting on that today?

The show steward hastened over to Reginald and tapped his watch. Bubba Silverstein was famous for keeping his shows running like a Swiss train. With the weather preying on the dogs, he was the right man for the job.

She made her way to the grandstand and climbed over a sea of legs to find Jim's wife Holly. "I hope Breaker can pull it off, but Fandango's tough competition," Holly said.

Bess had read that Fandango had finished his British championship a few months back. Reginald might even have been the judge who put him up. "It's hard for a judge to dump a dog with Fandango's record."

"Don't I know it." Holly was still smarting from her disappointment last year when the judge picked a well-known champion over DandyGirl even though she was clearly showing better that day. Judges aren't supposed to know who a dog is, but sometimes they can't help recognizing a seasoned competitor.

Bess waved her shirt tail up and down, hoping to let in a little air. "Frankly, I don't understand why Fandango hasn't been able to finish in the U.S. yet."

Holly pruned her lips. "According to Jim, he snapped at the judge in Baltimore."

An expectant silence filled the tent as Reginald stepped

into the ring. His shirt was soaked to the skin as if he had been standing in a rainstorm.

"You'd think he would dispense with a tie in all this heat," Holly said, fanning herself with her catalogue.

"Not Reginald. A judge doesn't appear without his tie."

Holly looked at her curiously. "I didn't know you two were acquainted."

Bess made an elaborate display of sniffing the air. "This stadium smells like mildewed sailcloth without a nice ocean breeze to carry it off."

"The firemen sprinkled the roof earlier, but it's not helping. The temperature might have dropped a few degrees, but now the humidity's worse."

Breaker was first in line, followed by an unknown black dog and then Fandango. Reginald's eyes widened when Benny appeared, apparently surprised by his age, but he turned his attention to Breaker without comment. Breaker stood politely to be examined and went through his paces as instructed. He never put a foot down wrong; Benny just ran to keep up. In what seemed like only a minute, their turn was over.

Bess glanced over at Hannah who was making an elaborate display of studying her show catalogue.

Holly leaned into Bess' ear. "Benny's come a long way. You've taught him well, Bess."

Next came the black dog with an unfamiliar handler. Holly flipped through her catalogue for the pedigree. It was Breaker's other brother. Hannah must have sold him. Holly leaned over and whispered, "McCreery can't put out champions every time."

"He looks like a decent pet puppy to me."

The judge waved the dog off and called out Fandango.

Holly sighed. "Look at that gorgeous white coat."

What happened next was so quick Bess wasn't sure how it started. A dog was loose in the ring. Benny had the presence of mind to grasp Breaker's lead and hold on. Fandango's handler wasn't as fast. Fandango bolted free and grabbed the loose dog by the neck. Reginald and Fandango's handler dashed across the ring to break up the fight before either dog became seriously injured, but Fandango wouldn't let up even when his handler recovered the lead. He twisted and jerked, fighting to free himself. The handler yanked down hard on the lead. Fandango bared his teeth and lunged. The handler barely got his hand out of the way in time.

A horrified gasp rippled through the crowd. Bubba Silberstein stepped forward and excused Fandango from the ring.

"One more incident like that, and Fandango will be banned for good," Holly whispered.

Reginald decided he had seen enough. He pointed at Breaker and called, "First," in a loud voice. Breaker realized his work was done. Before Benny could stop him, the puppy planted a wet smacker on Reginald's lips.

Bess couldn't hold back a laugh. Reginald glanced her way. An almost imperceptible flick of the eye let her know he had recognized her. Her smile hadn't changed in fifty-odd years.

Reginald moved the other classes along in good time and before long all the winners, including Breaker and Chicory, lined up for Winners Dog. Benny flapped his arms, like priming a pump, to dry the wet circles he had sweated onto his shirt.

Reginald called Chicory out first. His pleasure was almost palpable as he ran his hands over Chicory's head and body. He instructed Felix to move to the end of the ring and back so he could study his dog's movements. They were flawless. Regardless of Bess' desire for Breaker to win, she couldn't help feeling pride in this other puppy she had bred and seen born into the world.

Four other dogs went through their paces, and then it was Breaker's turn.

Bess held her breath and made a wish as Benny and Breaker stepped forward. As they approached the spot where Reginald was pointing, she was flooded with doubts. Reginald wouldn't show her any favoritism, but now she began to imagine the other possibility — that he would be overly harsh.

Reginald took Breaker through his inspection and then ordered him around the ring. Only when he was in full motion could Reginald and the crowd at ringside appreciate the full extent of his fluid grace. Benny took Breaker through his paces flawlessly. No one could have done better. Reginald finished up with the remaining dogs and then called the whole class out again. They all went around one more time, and then he dismissed everyone except Breaker and Chicory and two others he told to wait on the side.

"The judge is making quick work of it," Bess heard someone behind her whisper.

"We'll see," replied her companion.

Beth held her breath. In a way, Breaker's whole future rested on the outcome. If he won this class, he had a chance of finishing in time. Otherwise, Westminster would be put off for another year — if ever.

Back and forth Reginald went between McCreery's two puppies. Chicory had a body that wouldn't quit, but Breaker's face was pure Umpawaug. Bess' breath stuck in her throat when Reginald moved Chicory ahead of Breaker, but the contest wasn't over. Back Reginald came to give Breaker one last look. Bess could see he was tempted. He reached down and brushed his fingertips lightly over Breaker's downy topknot. It was something judges never do; he couldn't help himself.

Breaker closed his eyes and let out a sigh of poodle

ecstasy that would bring a stone to life.

Reginald straightened up and pointed straight at Breaker. "First!"

"Look here," Sonya said, holding out a plastic bottle of pills. "I found them hidden in Benny's room."

Benny's father turned the bottle slowly in his hands as if a magician's trick could make the contents inside disappear. The glue from the missing prescription label stuck to the tips of his fingers. He dropped the bottle and backed away from it, rubbing against his pant leg as though the glue and not the pills could kill. "That's it! No more New Hope School. Dr. Kumar's had her last chance."

Sonya patted his arm. "Where else would he get poison like this? Not from anyone in this family, that's for sure."

He closed his eyes and eased out a deep sigh. "And just when I thought we had a chance for Neusner & Neusner."

CHAPTER FORTY

"**P**ssst!"

David thought he heard a noise, but he must have imagined it. He had arrived at the school early to set up an obstacle course and hang the banner for the First Annual Field Day. Even Kate wasn't in her office yet.

"Pssst," came again.

He pushed aside a rhododendron branch and found Benny crouched frog-legged underneath. The ear flaps on his red and black cap must have itched on a pleasant fall morning, but the boy didn't seem to mind.

"Aren't you supposed to be in class?"

Benny looked around with narrowed eyes, making sure no one had spotted him. "Haven't you heard? My dad pulled me out of New Hope School. No more meetings with Dr. Kate, either."

"What happened?" David asked, afraid he already knew.

"Sonya found some pills in a cigar box under my bed, and my dad freaked. He thinks it's Dr. Kate's fault."

David held his breath. "Are the pills yours?"

Benny jerked back. "No way, but thanks for asking. Sonya and my dad didn't bother."

David exhaled. "So whose are they?"

Benny zipped his lips shut with a clenched thumb and forefinger. "Can't tell."

David sighed. Benny must be protecting someone important to him — maybe that strange girl he has a crush on, but as far as he knew she was off in Europe someplace. "Does Kate know?"

Benny thrust his lower lip out belligerently. "She can't tell. She could get arrested if she did."

David didn't know much about the rules of confidentiality, but he was pretty sure that if Kate knew an underage child was on drugs, she would be obliged to tell his parents. "Maybe you should tell your dad the truth — if you don't want to go back to Putnam Elementary, that is."

Benny shook his head. "Naw, he's hired a tutor to come in every day. I snuck out before he got there. My dad says maybe now I'll finally get somewhere."

David frowned. "Do you think sneaking out was wise?"

Benny screwed on a serious face. "I didn't have a choice. I had to see you."

David looked at his watch. The students would be arriving soon. Worse yet, Benny's tutor could be looking for him. "Can it wait?"

Benny shook his head. "It'll just take a minute. Now that Breaker's good-looking again, I think Bess and I should enter him in Westminster. We're partners, you know."

David sighed impatiently. "Even if Breaker qualified, do you think your dad would let you?" He hesitated. "Of course, if you told him the truth…" His voice trailed off.

Benny rolled his bottom lip, unconcerned. "Westminster's months away. My dad'll get over it. He always does."

"Only finished champions get to go to Westminster, remember?"

Benny flipped his arms out at the elbows. "Breaker won at Liberty Bell. He only needs five more points. I've heard Bess bragging about this big show called Poodle Club of

America. I'm pretty sure he could win it."

"A win at PCA would get anyone's attention."

"That's what I was thinking."

"I don't think you'll have a hard time convincing Bess. She probably registered him months ago."

"She hasn't mentioned it."

David started to walk away. "Go ahead and ask. She wouldn't miss PCA for the world."

"But David," Benny called after him. "What if she says no? She'd like it a lot more if you asked her."

David lifted his cap and smoothed his hair before replacing it. "I thought you two were partners."

Benny held up his hands in prayer. "Pleeease, David. Can't you ask her?"

The hunger in Benny's voice wrapped itself around David's heart, and he was tempted to give in. Then he remembered Kate's advice to let Benny speak for himself. He held both hands up like stopping a train. "If you want to go badly enough, you'll find a way."

Benny sank onto the grass and watched David head for the old apple tree. He crossed his legs and cupped his face in his hands. The itch on the back of his neck went on almost a minute before he noticed. He reached up, expecting to shoo away a bug, and found McCreery sniffing him gently.

"What is it, big fella? Breaker's going to Westminster, not you."

Benny thought he heard a low growl.

"You're right. It's a long shot for a puppy, but how else am I going to get on TV?"

The growl grew louder. Benny wasn't getting the message. McCreery circled around in front and posed like he was standing for inspection.

Benny pushed himself up on one knee and leaned forward for a closer look. Yes, it was like he told Bess back when they thought Breaker's show days were over: McCreery was still one terrific looking poodle, from the tip of his nose to the perfect set of his tail.

McCreery pawed Benny's arm impatiently and barked twice.

Not for the first time, Benny wished dogs could talk. Suddenly, his face lit up with an enormous smile. "I get it. You want me to take you to Westminster!"

McCreery raised up on his hind legs and pressed his front paws against Benny's chest. He grinned into Benny's face and barked twice more.

"I'll do it!" Benny promised, almost without thinking. Sure, Bess had refused before, but this time he would convince her. He didn't know yet how he would get her to change her mind, but he'd do it for McCreery. A promise is a promise.

CHAPTER FORTY-ONE

Bess threw a blue and white checkered cloth over the kitchen table while Mona laid out the eating utensils. David had dropped off a take-out lunch from the Spinning Wheel. November in Connecticut was a bit chilly for al fresco dining, but an indoor picnic would make a pleasant change.

Mona placed her own creation of fresh fruit, fall flowers and gourds in the middle of the table as a centerpiece. "David certainly has been dining out a lot in the past month," Mona observed with an arch look, "not that it isn't kind of him to remember his poor old mother and auntie."

Bess sniffed. "How would you know where he's been dining? I wasn't aware you were David's special confidante."

Mona unwrapped the sandwiches, placed them on two plates, and sat. "I keep my eyes and ears open. You must have noticed he lit his pipe with matches from Cob's Mill Inn."

Bess sat on her side of the table and eyed her sandwich suspiciously. "I guess a person would notice something like that if she didn't have anything better to occupy her time."

"Humpf," Mona scoffed. "I suppose you didn't smell the perfume when he opened the door of that fancy car of his. I'd say he'd just dropped his friend Kate off at her school."

Mona bent her head and sniffed her sandwich.

Bess pulled her glasses to the end of her nose in studied concentration. "I always seem to end up with the curried tuna. I suppose you prefer the fresh salmon salad?"

Mona closed her eyes, considering the question like a philosopher contemplating life's eternal truths. "Mmm, hard to say. The grapes make the curried tuna, but the salmon tastes divine with that layer of thin cucumber slices."

Without another word, each twin lifted half a sandwich off her plate and swapped it with her sister's. With a satisfied nod, they each took a large bite from the center of a triangle.

Breaker heard the promising sounds and roused himself from under the table. Benny had taken McCreery to school for a show-and-tell demonstration, or he would have been nosing in, too. Breaker rested his chin on the table top and stared at Bess' plate with moocher's eyes.

Mona lifted her chin, and Bess braced herself for a lecture on dog germs. Instead, Mona leaned closer and really studied the interloper. "He certainly is a good looking dog. Such a shame you can't show him at PCA."

Bess screwed up her mouth like she had ordered filet mignon and gotten liverwurst. "Not show him? What are you talking about?"

Breaker snatched a crust of bread that Bess had dropped and gulped. Hoping for seconds, he put his front paws on her lap and grinned into her face. Tuna on dog breath was a potent combination. She grimaced and guided him back down on the floor. "As a matter of fact, I'm taking Breaker to PCA next week," she said blinking innocently. "Luckily, I registered him ages ago, before his unfortunate adolescent phase."

Hoping the ladies were too occupied to notice, Breaker slipped around to the other side of Bess' chair. A poodle sized bite remained untouched on her plate. If he had been a St. Bernard, he would have drooled. Faster than a frog's tongue, he snatched. A moment later, he was safely back under the table, posing his most charming "Who me?" expression.

Mona's eyes grew wide. "You mean you intend to risk the Umpawaug name on a dog whose manners haven't advanced beyond basic toilet training? At PCA? Even I know everyone in poodles will be there."

Bess helped herself to bit of salmon that Mona had overlooked and slid it under the table. "I must have explained a hundred times," she said like a burnt-out schoolteacher. "Behavior doesn't count in conformation beyond rudimentary obedience."

Mona blinked back. "Exactly."

Bess grabbed up her plate and headed to the sink. Mona followed and laid her plate on top of her twin's.

"Oh, for heaven's sake," Bess said. "Benny and I are taking Breaker to PCA, and that's final. Benny's heart would break if we didn't."

"Oh, yes, Benny," Mona said, but her smile faded as she considered a new angle. "Do you think the boy's up to it?"

"Of course, I've been training him myself."

Mona nodded agreeably. "He has been working hard. I see him from my bedroom window every day, parading Breaker up and down, and there's poor, old McCreery trailing along behind them."

"McCreery? Why?"

Mona jutted out her chin. "You're asking me?"

They both stared at the old dog, resting under the kitchen table, a picture of contentment. He caught them watching and yawned lazily before closing his eyes again.

Bess turned on the faucet. The stream of water splashed on the dishes piled in the sink and soaked Bess' shirt. She studied the blotch indifferently and faced her sister. "This whole discussion's ridiculous. I don't know what you're talking about."

A smile played at the corners of Mona's mouth like she had just drawn to an inside straight. "Actually, I have a little surprise of my own." She signaled Bess into the living room and opened the lid of their mother's Victorian hope chest. "We always used to hide David's Christmas presents in here when he was a boy, remember?" Gently, she reached under the yellowing lace tablecloth they both remembered from childhood holidays and pulled out a thin, narrow box decorated with foxes and hounds on foil paper. Eyes bright, she held it out to her twin. "If you're going to PCA, you might as well have this."

"It can't be a necktie," Bess joked, flushed at the attention.

Mona blushed, too, failing to hide her excitement. "A little something I've been saving for the right occasion."

Bess fumbled with the paper, all thumbs, trying to save it.

"Here," Mona said, grabbing. She tore off the paper and handed back the slender box with *Sosnoff's Fine Leathers* embossed in gold. She held her breath as her sister lifted the lid.

Bess held the red leather lead up to the light. "Breaker" ran down the length in embossed gold letters. "It's wonderful," she murmured.

"There's one just like it for McCreery only in green," Mona said, hot tears prickling behind her eyes. It wasn't often she scored a home run with her sister.

Bess turned the lead over in her fingers, enjoying the feel of the fine grain. She looked up, almost shy. "Sometimes you amaze me, sister."

"I know. Sometimes I amaze myself."

CHAPTER FORTY-TWO

Bess stretched out on the comfortable chaise lounge, the sun warming her through the French doors, but her mind was too full for sleep. She wasn't surprised Mona thought taking Breaker to PCA was a bad idea. She had doubts herself, but a win at PCA was Breaker's best chance for an invitation to Westminster. True, he had two majors behind him and could pick up the remaining points at several smaller shows, but a championship earned in dribs and drabs would not impress WKC's invitation committee. Only a dazzling finish at PCA would catch their eye, and even then an invitation wasn't a dead certainty. She could wait another year, but she had learned her lesson. She wasn't about to put off her dream again, not at her age. PCA was a chance she had to take now, a million to one shot or not.

Still, she had a huge problem. She hadn't told her sister the whole truth, and the part she had left out was nagging her like the proverbial pea under the princess' mattress. The truth was she wasn't all that sure she would be going to PCA next week. How could she? She didn't have a handler. She and Benny were partners, but PCA was out of his league. All the other top handlers would be busy. Jim Wren had hands full with DandyGirl and DandyBoy, and Hannah would keep Felix hopping. She could hire a stranger, but the risk was even greater than with Benny. Like she had told him, an Umpawaug poodle's feelings toward the handler were paramount.

The front doorbell chimed and startled Bess from her reverie. She catapulted the recliner into its upright position and zigzagged past Breaker who danced around her feet. Mona couldn't have forgotten her key again. She was tucked away upstairs, napping with McCreery. The two of them had become buddies during their trip to Boca Raton. She had even caught him sprawled across Mona's bed once or twice. With her in it!

Through the peep hole, she discovered Benny, his fist tight around a bunch of fall flowers she recognized from Mona's garden. She opened the door, and he thrust the bouquet at her. "For you."

She sniffed. "Very nice. Perhaps you'd better come in."

His eyes flicked to the empty dessert plate beside the recliner.

"Mona made lemon ice box cake. Interested?"

"Sure. I'll put Breaker out so he doesn't go nuts begging." He held a treat over the dog's head and danced him out the door.

She sliced two big pieces and put the plates on opposite sides of the kitchen table. She left the cookie jar open at Benny's elbow. They both sat. She decided to let him speak first.

He scraped up the last crumbs with his fork and licked. He wasn't in any hurry to state the purpose of his visit while there was food left. He reached into the cookie jar and inspected his catch.

Her impatience won out, and she grabbed the jar. "Oh, for heaven's sake. Are you here to discuss PCA or not?" She hadn't meant to ask. It just slipped out.

Benny rubbed a finger in his ear to get the ringing out. What was she up to? This was a new Bess he hadn't seen before. She used to look like she had a lot of gas, and now her face was all open and hopeful. He had read in one of the magazines in Dr. Kate's waiting room how constipation was the curse of old people because they didn't get out and exercise enough. He knew from his own experience it could make a person crabby. He wondered if she had tried that new medicine the announcer on TV said everyone should ask their doctor about. Then he decided she was just excited about Breaker's new looks. He leaned forward, arms crossed on the table. "Tell me."

"Breaker has two majors but he still needs five more points for his championship. There are other ways to get them, but a win at PCA would finish him in one fell swoop."

Benny uncrossed his arms and leaned on his elbows. "I must be psychic. I was thinking the same thing!"

She pulled in her chin. "Breaker's a good-looking poodle, if I say so myself, but what are his chances? Nine hundred of the most beautiful poodles in the world will be there, and only one can win."

Benny narrowed his eyes. He smelled a rat. "You didn't mention Westminster."

"Westminster? Did you hear a word I said? He'd have to win PCA first."

He sat taller. "Yes, Westminster."

She crossed her arms. "Forget it. We're too late. The preparations for this year's show began days after the final toast was drunk to last year's winner."

He leaned back in his chair, unimpressed. "So? We shouldn't even try?"

She noticed a faint moustache was sprouting on his upper lip. For the first time she felt like she was dealing with a young man who knew what he wanted and how to get it. She drew a deep breath and blew out the answer. "All right, yes. If Breaker is invited, he can go."

Benny leapt to his feet, pumping his fist in the air, and

shouted, "Yes, yes, yes!" He was so busy celebrating he missed a guilty look slither across her face.

She hadn't told him the whole truth. She had no choice but to use him at PCA, but if a miracle happened and Breaker got invited to Westminster, he couldn't be Breaker's handler. He could come along for the ride if he wanted, but that was all. She had waited her whole life for this chance, and she couldn't trust a boy against that kind of competition. Jim Wren wasn't entering a dog this year. Breaker liked Jim, and Jim would handle him if she asked. He had hinted as much. Benny would earn glory enough if Breaker got the win he needed at PCA. Goodness knows it was a long shot, but he had surprised her before. The dogs seemed to sense something special about him. She realized with a pang, they weren't the only ones.

"Anything else?" he asked, voice calm and steady again.

She studied him closely, trying to read his mind. Perhaps he guessed she wasn't telling him everything, but how? For a moment, she had the fleeting thought that he, too, had a card hidden up his sleeve. "Not unless you have something to add."

He leaned forward, his expression determined. "I'll take in Breaker at PCA, but only if we can take McCreery to Westminster, too." She started to object, but he held up a hand and locked eyes with her. "With his record, McCreery can get invited easy. He wants to go, trust me. Every time I practice with Breaker he follows along." He lowered his voice confidentially. "I think he's jealous."

Bess' mouth opened and shut like a fish out of water. What was the boy's fascination with McCreery? She was certain he had grown to love Breaker, but apparently his affection never wavered from his first love, McCreery. If his devotion hadn't been so constant, he might never have found McCreery and saved the dog's life. The memory of it made her blanche, and she regretted having to disappoint him now.

"Jealous? What's McCreery got to be jealous about?"

Benny's eyebrows flew up, a mirror imitation of hers. "You're kidding, right? You think he doesn't notice how you ignore him? All you think about is Breaker. What about McCreery?" He squirmed uncomfortably in his seat. "I could be jealous that McCreery picked you, but I'm not. I know he cares about me, and he knows I care about him."

She didn't answer for a long moment. He was talking about more than the dog. "I suppose you think a novice like you is ready for Westminster?" she asked finally.

"Sure," he answered, but his voice wavered a little. "I won Liberty Bell and I'll win PCA, too. You'll see."

She was back on firmer ground. "To compete at Westminster you've got to be exceptional. Not just the dog, the handler, too."

Benny puffed out his cheeks, ready to object, but she waved him into silence. She needed to think. The whole idea was crazy. Breaker and McCreery? Up against each other at Westminster? At McCreery's age, he didn't stand a chance. His time in the ring had passed, like hers. On the other hand what harm would it do? No one would blame her if an unseasoned boy finished last with a dog whose sell-by date had passed. Besides, Benny had her over a barrel. If he didn't help her at PCA, Breaker would miss his chance. Still, she didn't want the boy to make a fool of himself. "I'll make you a deal. If you and Breaker win Junior Showmanship at PCA, you can take in McCreery at Westminster."

Benny wrinkled his nose like he had stepped in something nasty. "Junior Showmanship? That's for babies."

She peered over her glasses. "Think again. Any kid can't just walk in with a dog at Westminster. It takes ten wins in Open Classes at official AKC shows to qualify. *You* wouldn't be eligible."

Benny thought it over. Tough as it would be for Breaker

to win conformation at PCA, Junior Handlers would be tougher. The dog's looks didn't count, only his behavior. McCreery's whole future would depend on Breaker's manners. "How about I take McCreery instead? He could use the practice, don't you think?"

"Good try."

"Will McCreery and I be in the real class at Westminster — the same as Breaker?"

"If you win Juniors at PCA."

Benny's shoulder's sagged. This was McCreery's only chance at Westminster, so what choice did he have? He was about to agree when he had an awful thought. She couldn't be that devious, could she?

He held up a hand. "Wait a minute. You said I couldn't enter Junior Showmanship at Westminster, but what about the regular show? Do they let kids do that?"

She gave him a dazzling smile. "They don't need a rule against it. They never imagined anybody would put their champion dog in the hands of a mere child against the world's most experience handlers." She held out her hand. "Deal?"

Benny took a deep breath and started to shake, but at the last second he jerked his hand back like it was on fire. "McCreery and Breaker would be in the ring at the same time. Even I can't do that. Maybe if you take that medicine on TV for your constipation, you could help out."

Truthfully, she had considered handling Breaker herself briefly, but her trick knee had been bothering her lately, and she couldn't chance it. She scrunched her face into a frown, pretending to craft a solution, then flashed a toothy smile. "Jim Wren isn't taking a dog to Westminster this year. I'll ask him."

Benny's lower lip quivered. "I've been Breaker's handler his whole life."

Bess lifted her chin. "You've got a better idea?"

He considered for a moment. "Will I still be on TV?"

The lie was tempting. "Not unless McCreery gets into Group, and he'll have to beat Breaker and the rest of the dogs to do that. But they'll have streaming video on the website for the other classes. Anyone in the world with a computer can watch."

"No kidding? That's big."

She let his imagination fill in the details. Breaker was the boy's ticket to Westminster and vice versa. Benny would try his best, and, so far, his best had been good enough.

Benny stood. "High five?"

"To Breaker," she called, slapping back.

McCreery, who had slipped downstairs and was eavesdropping, jerked up his head. He tapped Bess' foot impatiently with his paw. Perhaps he only wanted his dinner, perhaps something more. There was a glint in his eye she hadn't seen for years.

She ruffled his topknot and pulled her eyebrows into a warning frown that encompassed the dog and the boy. "Let's not get ahead of ourselves. We've got to win PCA first."

Benny waved off the caution like a pesky fly. "No worry." He reached into his pocket and took out the cookie with the chocolate chips carefully removed. "Chocolate's bad for dogs," he told Bess importantly, as if she weren't the one who had taught him. He held the cookie over McCreery's head and zoomed it around like an airplane. McCreery quivered in place, eyes following every move. Benny laughed and slipped it into the dog's mouth. He had kept his promise. They were going to Westminster, he was certain of it, and Bess had done all the asking.

Mission accomplished, he rushed home and closed the door to his bedroom. For once, he couldn't wait to be alone. He pushed his math workbook onto the floor and opened his middle desk drawer. Buried under the scattered trading cards and old candy wrappers he found the spiral notebook his mother had given him when he first moved in with his dad. She said he could use it to write her letters if he missed her too much. An envelope with a blotch of dried soda and a book of stamps lay underneath it. He had never written before. He never had anything this important to tell her. He ripped out a sheet, smoothing down the little tabs the round wires had made, and licked the point of his pencil:

Tuesday

Dear Mom,

Its me, Benny. How R U? I'm fine. Well, I am going to be in a really, really big dog show called P.C.A. Its short for Poodle Club of America. But don't get you're hopes up to high (like Dr. Kate says). Its really, really big. Bess says if we win I can go to West Minister (sp.!). The one on TV. Can you come? All the other moms will be there.

I love you.

XXXOOOXXX

Benny

(Your son)

P.S. Please try.

P.S.S. I can't wait.

CHAPTER FORTY-THREE

When Benny boasted to David that his Dad would let him go to PCA, he only half believed it himself, but now it was really happening. He had worked hard and done everything Sonya and the tutor asked. The article in the *Philadelphia Inquirer* helped, too. His dad launched into a big lecture on the benefits of sports and clean living, but Benny didn't mind that much because afterwards he said he could go.

Bess had warned Benny that Junior Handlers would be different, but he hadn't realized until he lined up how strange it would actually seem. All varieties and shades of poodles, including a few whose lineage was debatable, were mixed in together, and the handlers were as different as their dogs. The boy in front of him wearing a hand-me-down brown suit was handling a mid-sized white fluff ball with a perky bounce to her step. The boy's loose hold on the lead told Benny he knew what he was doing. Behind him, a skinny girl was trying to stack her white Toy. The Toy was trying to make friends with a dog that looked more Papillion than poodle handled by a tall boy with deep, Latin eyes. A girl in green tights and a small brown dog rushed in last.

The judge entered the ring and passed her eyes quickly over Benny and the other young hopefuls waiting their turn to be called. He wondered how she would manage to decide among so many kids and dogs, but she immediately divided them into two groups according to a system only she understood. He was in the first group in front of a short girl who practically had to drag her cream Miniature to the end of the line. He was afraid the judge had put him in with a bunch of losers until she signaled a petite Chinese-American girl with the air of a star to stand behind him with her perfectly turned out black Miniature. He didn't care how long the judge took to make up her mind. If it took forever, he was determined to win.

Breaker seemed to sense how important the class was and followed every instruction perfectly. Benny made the first cut, and the second, and then the judge told him to wait while she brought back the other half of the group. He overheard someone at ringside whisper that the tall girl wearing a gray pleated skirt and dark tights was last year's winner. In the old days news like that would have turned his legs to cold spaghetti but no more.

At last, only ten finalists were left in the ring including Benny and Breaker. The judge called them out one by one. Benny couldn't help worrying about a long-legged girl wearing gold hoop earrings whose cream Standard Poodle seemed to know what she was thinking ahead of time. Based on the girl's looks, she would be too old for Juniors next year.

Benny was last to be called. He snapped to attention as the judge told him, "Take your dog down to the end of the ring and back."

He straightened his tie, made sure his blue blazer was buttoned, and moved forward. "Okay, Breaker, let's give it our best shot," he said, and the two of them took off. Every handler and dog knew the contest was down to the wire, and the people in the stands sensed it, too. Not a sound could be heard in the tension-filled bleachers. Then out of the silence a booming voice shouted, "Go, Benny!"

A horrified gasp rippled through the spectators. Benny recognized the voice and sensed the other junior handlers had turned to stare. He wanted to look, too, but this was his moment and he wasn't about to let anyone mess it up, not even his own mother.

"I'm in charge," he whispered, not making a single misstep.

"Way to go!" his mother's voice came again. Benny's heart beat faster, and his palms began to sweat. The lead grew wet and slippery and his grip slipped a little. He had to push his growing panic back down inside.

"I'm in charge," Benny repeated. All the times Bess had made him take Breaker around an imaginary ring came back to him, and the familiarity of the task made his confidence return. Breaker added a little more spring to his step and held his head higher.

Just a few more steps and their turn would be over. Benny imagined how wonderful it would be when the judge handed him the trophy. He pictured his mother's big smile, and he smiled, too, and his attention drifted for half a moment before he thrust himself mentally back into the real world. With a rush of relief, he realized that Breaker had covered for him and done exactly as they had practiced a hundred times.

The judge called out the girl in the gray pleated skirt for one more turn up and back, and Benny was afraid of what it might mean. Then the judge ordered the ten finalists to circle the ring a final time and line up near the judge's table.

Benny stifled an anxious yawn as the judge took one final look. He didn't understand why she was taking so long. Surely, she should have made up her mind by now. She turned her back and picked something he couldn't see off the table. She turned again and held out a small silver trophy.

"First!" she called in a loud, clear voice and pointed at Benny and Breaker.

Breaker leaped high off the ground and planted a kiss on Benny's face. Benny wiped it off with his sleeve and hugged Breaker back. He held the silver trophy high overhead for everyone in the stands to see and hurried out of the ring. He didn't even have time to dash into the stands and show his prize up close to his mother. He had to get Breaker to the Breed ring in time to show him in conformation. He had only finished the first part of his deal with Bess. If they had any possibility of a slot at Westminster this year, Breaker had to finish his championship today. Unless he could pull it off, they would be out of chances.

CHAPTER FORTY-FOUR

B ess appreciated Felix's offer to drop Benny off at his father's. The boy's excitement over winning Best Standard Poodle and finishing Breaker's championship had practically done her in. But who could blame him? Breaker had bested all the Standard Poodle boys and then gone on to beat the winning bitch Black Bean. All Bess wanted now was a nice hot bath and a good book, but tonight was the annual banquet where the election would be held for next year's Best in Show judge. It was an honor the Club bestowed on its most knowledgeable and trusted members, a contest as full of intrigue and machinations as the most heated duel between Presidential candidates. She had been chosen once before, but this time was different. This time she was running against Hannah, and even a monsoon couldn't keep her away.

PCA's official hotel made allowances for show dogs, so Bess sailed past the registration desk with Breaker leading the way. He waited patiently by the closet where she had stashed his dog food and watched her pour a generous helping into his dish. Sniffing cautiously, he by-passed the usual dry kibbles in favor of the tired ham sandwich leftover from lunch she had dropped on top.

She was freshly showered and clipping on her best pearl earrings with the matching choker when she heard a knock on the door.

"Hello, hello," Jim Wren called, poking his head through the open door. A room service waiter pushing a cart with a bottle of chilled champagne and hot hors d'oeuvres followed Jim and Holly inside. Breaker reached the company before Bess, skidding to a stop an inch short of toppling Holly over. Jim scrunched down on his haunches and stretched his arms toward Breaker who panted and bounced and generally acted silly like any ordinary dog. They made a handsome pair, smiling into each other's faces: Jim in is his formal plaid bow tie, Breaker smelling like a wet wool sweater from nosing into the shower.

"Are you going to smooch with that dog all night or pour the champagne?" Bess pretended to grumble.

Jim popped the cork and passed glasses all around. "To Breaker."

"To Breaker," Bess repeated.

"Don't forget Benny," Holly added. "You've brought him along remarkably well, Bess."

"Hear, hear!" Jim said, raising the bottle and offering seconds

Bess shifted uncomfortably, wondering how to broach her question. With today's win behind him, Breaker had a decent chance of making it to Westminster, but she still needed a handler. Even if Benny was up to the task, he was planning to take in McCreery.

Jim caught Holly's eye and smiled behind his champagne flute. "I'm taking DandyGirl to Amherst. How would you feel if I brought Breaker along? It wouldn't hurt for him to get used to a new handler — just in case you need one."

Bess tried to hide her surprise. Was Jim hinting he might take the job without her even asking? "That might be useful," she answered with no more emotion than if he was offering salt for some hot buttered popcorn, but Jim's and Holly's smiles showed they weren't fooled. Jim would be taking in Breaker at Westminster.

Jim checked his watch, emptied his glass and hurried the ladies into their coats. As the door closed behind them, Breaker scooted out from under the coffee table. Thankfully, someone had remembered to leave the hors d'oeuvres out on the cart where he could help himself. He nibbled each one daintily, taking his time, and then padded over to the king size bed. Nudging the pillows into a comfortable dog nest with his nose, he turned round and round in tight circles until he landed in the perfect spot. With a weighty sigh, America's top Standard Poodle closed his eyes and settled down for a quiet evening at home.

Bess made a good show of enjoying the awards banquet, but when the speeches were over and dessert was announced, she slipped out. The voting for Best in Show judge was about to begin, and she would have to absent herself in any case. The cocktail lounge across from the banquet hall was empty and dark except for the little lamps meant to look like candles on the round, wooden tables. Stale cigarette smoke hung in the air. She pulled out a captain's chair and sat. Her knee was throbbing after the long day, so she stuck her leg up on the opposite chair and waited. Before long someone would bring her the results.

As her eyes adjusted to the light, she noticed a tall figure in shadow standing across from her. "Mind if I sit?"

Hannah was the last person she wanted to chit-chat with, but she could hardly refuse. She waved at an empty chair. "Help yourself."

Hannah braced herself on the arms and eased down stiffly. She had worn herself out at the show and then finished the day campaigning for tonight's election. Bess would be amazed to know for whom, and Hannah hoped she would never find out. Bess had too much pride. "Congratulations on Breaker's win today," Hannah said. "Benny picked the right puppy."

ALMOST PERFECT

Bess tipped her head to one side noncommittally.

Hannah twisted her large hands nervously, hoping Bess would ease her path. When she didn't, Hannah forged ahead. "We've been rivals a long time. For myself, I've enjoyed the competition. No one's done more for the breed than you, Bess. You've never compromised temperament for looks. The dogs I've loved most have had Umpawaug in back of them, and they will as long as I'm able. I wanted to say I hope you win tonight. You've earned it." When Bess didn't answer, she rose. "I'm sorry I intruded."

Bess' hand fluttered out, but the words stuck inside. If she didn't speak now, a door would close forever. "You'll get the face right eventually," she said with a half smile. "Don't stop trying."

If they had more to say to each other, it was too late because Jim was coming through the door, holding up the Judges' Book for them to see. It was the equivalent of white smoke for the Pope's selection. "We couldn't decide. Hannah, your turn's coming in two years. Bess, you're up next. Congratulations to you both."

Hannah stuck out her hand, and Bess grasped it. "They probably think I'm going to die first."

⚜ ⚜ ⚜

Benny's dad refolded the newspaper and cleared his throat for a painful announcement. "I've made a terrible mistake, Sonya. The pills we found in Benny's room belonged to his mother."

His wife's hand flew to her mouth. "No!"

"David Rutledge, the man Benny's always going on about, tipped me off. He said Benny's mother acted like she was on something at the big dog show and nearly ruined the boy's chances."

Sonya handed him a plate of sliced turkey and scalloped

265

potatoes. "You can't think of everything."

He went on as if she hadn't spoken. "Benny admitted pilfering her purse so she couldn't take the pills. They weren't even her prescription. She lied and told the doctor Benny needed them."

"Sounds just like her," Sonya said, not quite hiding her satisfaction. She gestured toward his plate. "Your dinner's getting cold."

"I've offered to pay for his mother's rehab. It's the least I can do for the boy."

Sonya gasped. "And New Hope School?"

"Of course, and Dr. Kate, too." He pushed his plate to one side. "It's time I got to know my son better. Brains aren't everything in this world. Character counts, too." He picked up the paper again and found the page he was looking for. He folded it back and tapped the spot with his finger. "See, right here: 'Boy Wins at Poodle Specialty Show.' Sports section, but still, the Sunday *New York Times!*"

"Oh, my," Sonya murmured, grabbing the paper.

"Who'd have thunk it? A son of mine." He reached in his pocket for a handkerchief and blew.

She dropped the newspaper and came around to put her hands on his shoulder.

"You know, Sonya, I feel ashamed. All this time I've been wanting Benny to be someone he isn't, someone like me if I tell the truth." He sighed and studied his reflection in the matching metal salt and pepper shakers placed side by side on the table, as though seeing a memory and not his own face. "I remember the first time I saw my little son, back in the hospital when the nurse handed him to me. There wasn't that much of him to see all swallowed up by that big towel or whatever they had him wrapped up in, wearing that funny little white cap." He splayed his fingers in front of him, turning his hand back and forth, assessing. "His little button nose was smaller than my pinkie nail."

He sighed and rested his hand on his heart. "I looked into the future and saw my boy following in my footsteps — me helping him every step of the way. He'd grow up to be the best part of me, the part that would last after I'm gone." He choked and dropped his chin, staring down at his open, empty hands. Sonya started to speak, but he silenced her. He pushed back his chair and stood, rubbing his hands against his sides. Sonya came around to stand beside him, waiting. He started to speak, then hesitated again, a man considering one last time if he could part with a favorite family heirloom.

"Fantasies are all well and good, but reality isn't so bad, either," he said finally. "It's time I faced up to the fact that not everyone's cut out to be a partner in a law firm or even a college man. There are other talents in this world just as important, and I think my son's found his."

She bobbed her head and smiled encouragingly. "And he's only in junior high!"

He fumbled in his pocket for a handkerchief and blew. "I couldn't be prouder." He turned and looked around the room anxiously, like a man who has just realized he's misplaced his wallet. "Where is Benny, anyway?"

She shrugged. "Probably next door visiting the dogs."

"What do you say we invite him to come with us to Cob's Mill Inn tomorrow night for a real family celebration?"

She moved quickly to the wall phone. "I'll make the reservation."

CHAPTER FORTY-FIVE

Benny couldn't believe his eyes. Steffie was sitting on the bench in front of the school waiting for him. She had been gone for months, ever since her parents had pulled her out of Summer School and flown her off to Europe with them. He was eager to tell her the truth about the pills, but his mind was elsewhere at the moment. Underneath her camel's hair coat, she was wearing trendy denim jeans, a yellow collar shirt and lipstick that wasn't black. He wondered if it would taste like cherry if she let him kiss her.

"What happened to you? Your clothes. . .?" he asked.

She turned up her face, blinking her eyes rapidly. "I bought them myself. How do I look?"

He had the fleeting thought she might be flirting with him and tucked in his stomach. "You look great. Just like a normal kid." His hand flew to his mouth. "Ooops, sorry. Maybe I'm catching Asperger's, too."

She smiled. "I don't think it's something you can catch." Her voice was soft, without a hint of anger. "I gave my mother strict instructions to stop shopping for me. I've got my own style now, and she's not going to change me."

"That's terrific," he said and felt heat rising in his cheeks.

She scooted over to make space beside her. "I'm sorry,

too, for the mean things I said about the school. I finally figured out how special New Hope School really is. Smart kids can be dumb sometimes."

They peeked at each other out of the corner of their eyes and grinned. "Maybe," he said, "but I'd lots rather be smart like you. Sometimes my head hurts from trying to figure stuff out, and I can't keep my body still. It drives Sonya crazy, but lately she seems to be mellowing out a bit."

"Really?" she asked distractedly.

"I think it's because of my dad. Now that he's not so worried about me, she isn't so worried about him. She really loves him." He dropped his eyes. "Not like my mom."

She narrowed her eyes. "Something still bothering you?"

He rolled down his bottom lip. "I promised McCreery I'd take him to Westminster. He wanted to go so badly I couldn't say no. I made a deal with Bess, but I'm afraid she'll change her mind. She thinks he's too old."

Steffie sighed. "A person can't make a promise to a dog."

"A promise to a dog might not matter to you, but it does to me."

She looked down, ashamed. "I know. I'm sorry."

"That's okay. You were only trying to help."

"I'm really proud of the way you've made a success of your career with dogs. No one can ever take that away from you."

He squirmed with adolescent embarrassment. "I guess you're right."

She cleared her throat. The corners of her mouth were pulled down like Dr. Kate's when she was worried about one of the students. "I've got some news of my own."

He held his breath. From her tone of voice, he was pretty sure he wouldn't like it.

She straightened up, bracing herself. "I might as well

just say it. I'm leaving New Hope School."

He exhaled, relieved it wasn't worse. "Yeah, sure. We're both going to high school next year."

She tried a smile, but it trembled on her lips. "No, I mean right away. I only came today so I could tell you myself."

He jumped to his feet. He had never imagined anything this terrible. "You can't. You just got back."

She shrugged. "I'm used to it by now. Besides, Kingwood Academy won't be so bad."

He wasn't buying. "You're my best friend. Who can I talk to when you're gone?"

"Providence isn't that far. I'll be back on school vacations. Besides, you've got plenty of people to talk to right here: Adam, Dr. Kate, David, your dad." She tried again for a smile.

His leg bounced up and down like a paddle ball on a rubber string. "Yeah, but none of them are you."

She stood in front of him and laid a hand on his arm. He felt tingly all over, and his leg jiggled faster.

"Sorry," he apologized. "Girls get to me sometimes, especially pretty ones. It gives me thoughts in bed at night, but Dr. Kate says not to worry. It's normal."

She dropped her eyes. "Yeah, Dr. Kate talked to me, too. I've decided I'm not going to have sex after all, not for a long, long time."

"That's good," Benny said. "I mean, I guess it is. Just don't forget about me, okay?"

"I'll never forget you, Benny." She said it like a promise.

"Me, neither," he said, examining his high tops.

"My mother's given up on her Asperger's kick, and I'm never going to let anyone tell me there's something wrong with me again."

"That's great, Steffie." He really meant it even though his heart was breaking.

She studied his face as if she was trying to engrave it on her memory forever. "I'm sure I'll make lots of new friends at Kingwood, but none of them will be as special as you, Benny."

His high tops were toe to toe with her penny loafers. A rosy blotch colored his neck and spread until his cheeks were bright red. "I've heard a person never forgets his first kiss."

She smiled shyly. "I've heard that, too."

"Not that this would be my first," he added, hastening to cover his mistake.

"Whatever. It sounds like a good idea."

He leaned, and she leaned, and as their lips touched, Dr. Kate happened to look out the window.

"Asperger's? That's a good one," she said disgustedly and hurried downstairs to tell Steffie good-bye.

⚜ ⚜ ⚜

"You heard me," Benny's dad told Sonya. "His mother's suing for custody. Now that Benny's in the newspaper, she thinks he's going to be rich.

Sonya popped an olive in the glass and handed the martini to her husband. "She can't be serious. A silver cup or two won't pay the bills."

Benny's Dad took a deep swallow before answering. "She got some shrink to say she's off the pills, and she's hired a shyster lawyer. The worst part is the judge is bound to ask Benny's opinion. He's old enough now."

"Do you really think he'd choose that woman after everything she's done?"

His eyebrows lifted in surprise. Were those tears glistening in her eyes? For once, she sounded more concerned for Benny than hateful toward his mother. She and Benny had been spending more time enjoying each other's company and less arguing over his diet. Just last night he had come home to find them giggling and high-fiving when the guy got the girl at the end of one of Sonya's silly movies, and she was the one who had asked whether they could all take trip together next summer to a place Benny would enjoy. Was Sonya finally growing fond of his son? Did Benny feel it, too? Not that he expected or even wanted Benny's feelings for his mother to change. He only hoped his son would have the maturity to choose what was best for him on his day in court.

He sighed and placed his empty glass carelessly on the table. It teetered back and forth before falling on its side with a jarring note of finality. He reached for Sonya's hand and answered huskily. "She's his mother. He'll never stop wanting her."

CHAPTER FORTY-SIX

Benny plopped down on Dr. Kate's couch. "You know how you're always telling me to keep my feet on the ground and not get my hopes up? Well, you're not as smart as you think you are. I always hoped my mom would fight for custody of me, and now she's doing it."

Kate's blood ran cold. Benny's dad had warned her that his mother might do this, and now she was. Kate wasn't sure Benny had the maturity to handle the choice the lawyers would put in front of him. She drew in a deep breath, hoping Benny would give the answer that would free him. "Both your parents want you. The question is, 'What do you want?"

He pushed back his bangs and grinned broadly. "I want," he said and stopped. "I want," he began again. Then he dropped the mask, and his eyes flooded with tears. "I want to live with them both. Sonya, too."

Dr. Kate frowned. "Benny, you know that's not possible."

He rolled onto his back, staring at the ceiling as if the solution were written there. "My mom said she'd let me have a dog, any kind I want. A real dog, not a poodle."

"Is that your opinion or hers?"

He pushed himself up and sat. "I told her a poodle is a real dog, but she said I'd look better on TV with a different kind. Maybe a Pomeranian."

"So she's thinking about TV, not you or the dog?"

He stuck his chin out defiantly but didn't answer.

Kate drew in a deep breath and tried to calm her racing heart. "What about McCreery? And Breaker? Aren't they counting on you?"

He dropped his chin onto his chest. "My mom got all excited when I won PCA. I told her I'd done it for her, but that wasn't the whole story."

"What was?"

He stood and paced. He swung his arms back and forth in an arc. "I did it for me," he said finally. "For once in my life I found something I could do better than the other kids. It felt great."

She held his eyes. "Are you willing to give that up? For anyone?"

He grinned and spun in place on one leg. He had made his choice. "Thanks, Dr. Kate. Sorry, but I'd better get going. Sonya's making steak and baked potatoes for dinner, my favorite, and I don't want to miss it."

⚜ ⚜ ⚜

Sonya's mouth tilted in a skeptical smile. "Benny says the old lady next door is bringing two poodles to Westminster, and he's going to take one into the show ring himself."

Benny's dad cut a generous slice of Boston cream pie and slid it onto a clean plate. A proud smile played on his lips. "It's true. Dogs can't just turn up for a big show like that. They have to qualify."

"No wonder he's been so jumpy. More than usual, I mean. I thought once the custody hearing was over, he'd settle down again."

He scooped some custard off the edge of the knife with his finger and popped it in his mouth. "I can hardly

274

believe it's over myself. Thank goodness the judge didn't try to make him pick her or us, but she had to be swayed by how much he loves his school and the fact that we sent him there. Of course, he still gets to visit his mother whenever he wants." He picked up the plate and headed upstairs to where his son was finishing his homework.

"Should I buy tickets?" Sonya called after him.

He waved a big hand over his head. "Do bears sleep in the woods? Get a few extra. I'll pass them out to my partners."

CHAPTER FORTY-SEVEN

Bess smelled the aroma of fresh-baked oatmeal raisin cookies Mona had left unguarded on the counter. Good thing Breaker was at Jim's so they could practice together. If he had been home, not a single bite would be left. Not that McCreery was an angel. Now that she thought about it, where had he disappeared? Then she remembered Benny had dropped by earlier and said he would give his pal some exercise.

She picked a cookie with plenty of raisins and glanced out the window. Benny was heading into the puppy shed with McCreery. The boy was smiling, and McCreery was wagging his tail excitedly and studying the boy's every move. Westminster was only two days away, and they had no idea she was about to shatter their happiness. She tossed the uneaten cookie into the sink, turned on the disposal, and shrugged into her pea jacket.

The February chill crept down her collar, but her heart was too heavy to notice. She opened the puppy shed door and discovered McCreery standing patiently on the grooming table. Benny was aiming the clippers straight for his hindquarters.

"Benny, stop!" she gasped. "One mistake and it'll take months to grow out."

He didn't look up. "It can't be that hard. I've seen you

do it plenty of times."

She spoke quickly. "Well, it is. You shouldn't be fooling around like that."

He wheeled around, lips tight. "Westminster's in two days and somebody's got to do it. You're not."

She held out her hand, hoping it would hold steady, and motioned for the clippers. "Please."

He looked back at McCreery, hesitated, and then pulled the cord from the wall. His wrist showed where he had outgrown his shirt sleeve. The clippers clattered to the floor.

She gestured toward the milking stool. It hadn't been used since Breaker and the others were tiny puppies. "Sit, please. You need to listen."

He considered a minute and then perched himself next to McCreery on the grooming table. He circled the dog's neck with his arm. He could tell she had bad news. "You registered him, didn't you? He can go?"

She sat on the stool, leaning forward, hands clasped. "Yes, I registered him, but he can't go."

He bolted to his feet, hands balled into fists. "You're nothing but a rotten, dirty liar. You've been stringing me along all this time for your precious Breaker."

A tight band squeezed her skull. When she had promised the boy, the odds against him were overwhelming. The idea that he and Breaker could win Junior Showmanship at a show like PCA seemed ludicrous. Not to mention beating all those champion dogs for top Standard Poodle in America.

She sucked in a deep breath. "McCreery is ten years old, Benny. In his day he was the greatest of them all, but he's had his turn. It's time for the next generation."

"You're old. I don't see you giving up." He flung the words, past caring whether he hurt her or not. "You might try thinking about someone besides yourself once in a while. What about McCreery's feelings?"

She held his gaze, willing herself not to let the hurt show. "You don't understand," she answered calmly. "I *am* thinking about McCreery. A few years ago, a seven year old German shepherd went Best Show, but mostly the winners are youngsters. Do you want people calling him an old has-been?"

He jumped down. "It's not fair. McCreery's loved you all his life, and you've never given him a chance. He's waited and waited, hoping his time would come, and all you do is ignore him."

She looked from boy to dog to boy again. He was talking about more than the dog. "It means that much to you?"

He nodded, tears threatening.

She stood and began pacing. "Even if I change my mind, McCreery's not in show coat. That's not allowed."

Benny reached behind him and held up a book with a faded green cover. *Poodles in America* was written on the spine. The gold embossed letters were flaking with age and use. "I found this in a cabinet. The dogs have lots of funny-looking clips from the olden days. Maybe he could wear one of them."

Bess reached for the book. It fell open at a familiar page. Her finger traced the photo of a handsome dog in full coat. "Jester, McCreery's great-great-great grandfather," she said softly, voice choking. On the opposite page a youthful Hannah Washington was holding a silver cup beside a white poodle.

Benny paced impatiently. He was interested in today, not something that happened a thousand years ago. "So? What do you think? Could McCreery get into Westminster with one of those crazy clips?"

She flipped through the pages, considering. "I guess he could appear in a hunting clip," she said finally. "The technical name is the Historically Correct Continental — HCC."

Benny pumped his arm. "Yes!"

She looked at the boy's eager face, mirroring the naïve hopes she had felt with Hosannah decades before Benny was born. She tossed the book back onto the counter. "I'm sorry. I've let you get your hopes up for nothing. Even with the right clip, McCreery wouldn't stand a chance."

Benny clenched his fists, trying to slow his breath. "Who cares if he wins? It's the dream that matters. Remember?"

She shut her eyes. Her head swung back and forth in small, rapid movements like a wind-up toy. She felt off balance like he was the adult and she was the child. Had she really forgotten? Was Westminster only a dream for the imagination of youth, a fairy tale whose ending had become stale in the re-telling, or was she meant to grab this one final chance with both hands whatever the outcome?

She heard him open the door. She opened her eyes. "Wait! We'll do it. We'll take them both."

Benny turned and grinned, showing every one of the metal spikes on his braces.

She hesitated, then held up her hand. "High five?"

He laughed out loud and smacked back. "Don't worry. You won't be sorry."

Strange, she almost believed it herself.

Chapter Forty-Eight

Mona found Bess in the puppy shed up to her elbows in soap-suds. A wet poodle in a round metal tub looked up at her blinky-eyed. "I stopped by to wish you luck tomorrow. Westminster at last!" She sighed, like she was the one who had been waiting all these years. She shrugged off her coat, as if she planned to stay a while, and stepped closer to the sopping wet dog. "He looks splendid," she said.

Bess brushed her bangs out of her eyes with her arm. "He doesn't look his age, that's for sure."

Mona's eyes widened. She hadn't realized the dog in the tub was McCreery. "I don't know how you can be so relaxed. With Westminster tomorrow, a normal person would be getting Breaker ready."

Bess rubbed the tips of McCreery's ears gently between her fingers and shrugged. "Breaker's at Jim's. I'm sure he's been ready for hours. I promised Benny I'd groom McCreery myself."

Mona's mouth dropped open. "Don't tell me you're taking McCreery to Westminster."

Bess replaced the cap on the bottle of her special crème shampoo with just a hint of lavender for luck. "All right, I won't if it makes you feel better."

Mona tossed her head and sniffed. "I hope you know what you're doing. That dog has feelings, you know." She straightened the waistband on the emerald green sweater she had swapped with Bess two Christmases ago. It was her favorite.

Bess wiped some stray bubbles off her cheek with the back of her hand. "You won't believe me, but he wants to go so badly he can taste it."

Mona did believe her, and it was an odd sensation. "Does that mean Breaker and McCreery will be competing against each other?"

"First time ever for a father and son combination at Westminster," Bess answered, unable to hide her pride.

Mona studied her manicure, digesting the news. She had tried one of those new metallic blue colors, Midnight Passion. "So what happens if one of them wins Best Poodle?" she asked, satisfied her nails were perfect.

Bess turned the water on full force, spraying droplets over Mona's red suede shoes. "It'll never happen."

Mona stuck out her lip. "But if it does?"

"Then he'll have to beat all the other winners of all the other breeds in Non-Sporting."

"And if he wins Non-Sporting?"

"Then he'll have to beat the winners of the other six Groups — Sporting, Hounds, Working Dogs, Terriers, Toys, and Herding, the winners of twenty-five hundred champion dogs. Think of the odds."

Mona was impressed. "And that's it? He'll win Westminster?"

"Stop! Breaker's good-looking, but he's still a puppy. Only dogs with records a mile long ever win Best in Show."

"Like McCreery," Mona said, folding her arms triumphantly.

"McCreery? In the world of show dogs, he's ancient. A living relic — like us."

Mona looked again. She could have sworn McCreery winked, but it must have been a drop of shampoo in his eye.

"That's not what he thinks."

Bess stepped around in front and saw it, too. McCreery's old sparkle shone through, soaking wet coat and all. Bess reached for a towel and invited him to hop out of the tub. Both sisters stood back while he shook off the worst of the water.

"I have to agree with you, Mona," Bess conceded, adding to a conversation full of surprises. "McCreery hasn't looked this good in years. That treadmill has really gotten him in shape."

Mona gasped. "Treadmill? You don't mean you've been making that poor dog work out on a treadmill?"

"Don't be ridiculous," Bess snorted. "Do you think I'd make a dog of mine do something he didn't want? The doctor said it'd be good for my knee, and McCreery hopped aboard one afternoon when I turned it on. It's done wonders for us both."

Mona shrugged into her Chesterfield. "All I can say is that poodle has a strange look in his eye. There's no telling what he might have in store for you tomorrow."

Funny, Bess was thinking the same thing herself.

CHAPTER FORTY-NINE

Hands on his hips, head thrust back, Benny gulped in deep breaths like he had just finished an Olympic weight-lifting event. An empty dog crate with a bag of liver treats taped on top hung precariously off the back of the Country Squire. Off to the side, McCreery waited, his mouth open in a wide grin, his whole body shaking with anticipation. Benny pushed the crate the rest of the way in with his shoulder, and McCreery leaped inside without waiting for an invitation. He lay down with an air of calm expectancy, as if a few more hours wouldn't matter after a lifetime of waiting.

Benny flopped over at the waist and massaged his back. He cast a baleful eye over the rest of the paraphernalia show poodles require: folding table, towels, oversized metal tackle box filled with rubber bands and combs, not to mention hair spray and assorted beauty products. He turned to Bess. "Where's David? He promised he'd help me load the car."

Bess looked up from the map David had drawn of their route to Madison Square Garden and studied Benny carefully as if he was on exhibit himself. In the ambient light from the car headlights, she saw a sharp crease in his gray pants, and his dress shoes wore a fresh shine. A blue and red striped tie and a starched white collar were visible through the gap in his trench coat. His blue blazer would be underneath. The familiar checkered cap topped the outfit. If she didn't keep an eye on him, he would wear it in the show ring. As for herself, she always dressed to the nines for a big show. A silk man-tailored shirt, perfectly ironed, was covered by her signature red jacket so her friends would have no trouble spotting her. Not a spot was on it. A heavy gold chain and matching earrings were *de rigueur* for such an occasion; her fingers were unadorned. She had almost switched her usual black pants for a skirt, but changed back at the last minute. Too much like Mona.

She opened the collar of her camel hair coat and unclipped her mother's old-fashioned watch pin. She held it up to her ear and shook. The ticking was plainly audible. The hands read a few minutes to six a.m. She stood on tiptoes and peered through the trees. A soft glow was visible behind the drawn curtains of David's cottage. "Stay here. I'll see what's keeping David."

She expected her son would meet her half-way, but she made it to the front stoop first. Even then, she had to knock a couple of times before he opened the door. He was wearing a striped bathrobe. A pair of blue pajama legs showed at the bottom.

"Why aren't you ready? Are you sick?" She tried peering behind him, but he kept his shoulder in place.

He took a deep breath. "I'm sorry as I can be, but I can't go with you today. Lotus hasn't been herself all night. Kate didn't want to bother you before your big show, so she brought her over here." He leaned into her confidentially. "She thinks I inherited some knowledge of dogs from you."

She gave a skeptical cough and waited for him to go on.

He straightened up. "I don't think it's serious. The poor little thing probably ate something that didn't agree with her, maybe the anchovies in the Caesar salad, but I don't want to leave Kate alone with her."

Bess bit back the words on the tip of her tongue. This was the biggest show of her life. Mona was planning to watch on TV — if one of the dogs made it that far, but she thought her son would be with her.

"You feed that dog too much junk. She's getting pudgy." She would never admit how disappointed she felt.

He pulled his sash tighter against the cold morning air. "Kate has some medicine left over from Lotus' appointment with the vet last month. Her symptoms are pretty much the same. She'll be all right."

She stretched her neck, still trying to peek inside. "Sure I can't help?"

"Thanks, anyway. We've got it under control. If not, Dr. Hammer's close by."

She had one more card to play. "What about Benny? He's counting on you."

He gave an amused smile, seeing through her ruse. "Benny's his own man now. He doesn't need my help."

She returned a guilty smile, caught. "You're right. He can thank you for that."

"Thank us both, you mean. And Kate, of course."

Bess narrowed her eyes suspiciously. He had a secretive look about him she recognized from his childhood. There was more to his change of plans than he was admitting. What was hidden behind the door he was blocking with his shoulder? She peeked under his arm and saw a pair of women's shoes lying on the floor. They were the open-back style Kate preferred even in winter. Maybe Kate had embraced her advice after all and decided to take a chance. She swallowed the smile that threatened to spill out. If more had developed between her son and Kate than they wanted to announce, she needed to keep her hopes to herself. But with her whole heart, she wanted it to be true.

He took his mother's elbow and guided her down the

front steps. "You'll be fine. Benny, too. Holly and Jim will be there, and everyone here will be rooting for you every step of the way."

"You're right," she said, pulling up her coat collar. She no longer minded that he wouldn't be with her today. Westminster was her dream; it never had been his. Lotus was Kate's dog, and he belonged with her now.

He watched until he heard the car engine turn over. Then he closed the door gently. Waiting a minute for his eyes to adjust to the soft light from the pot-bellied stove, he tiptoed over to the big easy chair in the corner. He leaned down and kissed the top of Kate's head. She smiled in her sleep and snuggled deeper into the blanket he had thrown over her in the early hours of the morning.

Stepping softly, he moved behind her chair. His attention was on an old wicker laundry basket Bess had used in the past for newborn puppies. He knelt down and listened carefully. Lotus' soft snores drifted up. Pulling back the old towel he had draped over the handle to keep out the draft, he peeked. Yes, there they were: one, two, three, four. All alive, breathing softly. He leaned back on his haunches and indulged in a contented chuckle. McCreery's latest offspring!

Some people might disagree, but he thought his mother would be rather pleased — once she got over the initial shock. After all, there was a whole school next door full of children who would want a puppy to take home. It was just bad luck the puppies had chosen today to get born. He would have liked his mother to see them right away, but it wouldn't be fair to distract her with a basketful of newborns on the biggest day of her show career.

He cocked his head. What was that? He thought he heard a high-pitched squeak, so soft and quick he might not have heard it at all. There it was again. He pulled the towel back a smidgen to let in a little light. Yes, it was him all right: the brown boy with the big round belly, the one with his father's unmistakable Umpawaug nose. Even in his first sleep, he was using his sturdy hind legs to push his siblings out of the way.

"You've done well, little Mama," he said, stroking Lotus' crown with one finger. "Half Umpawaug, half New Hope School — an almost perfect combination."

CHAPTER FIFTY

B enny and Bess rode mostly in silence, too nervous for chit-chat. Benny read out loud from the map, and two hours later they made their turn safely onto 34th Street. Madison Square Garden, straight ahead! Colorful purple and gold spotlights swooped back and forth in the winter morning sky, announcing that America's First Dog would be chosen tonight. A New York City traffic cop with a whistle in his mouth waved white gloved hands in choreographed movements. He pointed at their car and blew. A string of greyhounds and a chunky bulldog ambled across the busy street in front of them. The whistle blew again, and they pulled up at the unloading dock.

Bess led the way to the grooming area downstairs, holding McCreery's lead. Benny never knew there could be so many kinds of dogs in one place. Twenty-five hundred dogs of every imaginable size, shape and color were squeezed in together. Spilling out into the narrow aisles, anxious handlers brushed and teased like Fifth Avenue hairdressers prepping runway models.

"The place doesn't even smell like dog," he said. He nodded over the top of his load toward the roped-off area meant for the dogs' restroom, but she was too busy pretending it was all old hat to reply. Besides, she had her hands full making McCreery heel with all the delicious dog aromas he could smell even if Benny couldn't.

Benny looked from side to side hoping to spot Breaker first, but the dog's sharp eyes beat him to it. He wriggled excitedly on the grooming table where Jim was completing a last-minute comb out. Benny knew better than to touch Breaker's coat, but he patted his muzzle where it wouldn't do any damage.

"Breaker looks good, Jim. You've done a great job," Bess said, her pride hanging out like a Fourth of July flag.

Jim hid a pleased smiled. "I'd say Breaker's got a decent chance today, but he's got some stiff competition."

Benny squinted and thought he spotted Hannah's tall figure off to the right. Breaker had beaten Chicory at Liberty Bell, but Chicory had won the first time the two brothers went up against each other at Quinnipiac. Felix would be taking Chicory into the ring tonight, and Felix was one of the best.

"Fandango's here, too, of course," Jim continued. "He's probably been sedated up to the eyeballs after the way he snapped at his handler at Liberty Bell."

Benny looked down the crowded aisle to where Jim was pointing. Fandango's striking white coat was easy to spot. He swallowed nervously knowing that the handsome dog had almost equaled his sire's record already. A win tonight would put him over the top.

Benny screwed his face into a frown. "You mean drugs?"

"Desperate handlers have been driven to it," Jim admitted.

"Not me, not even for Westminster," Benny said. "Too many people can get hurt."

A trio of black Standard Poodles moved quickly past them. Bess turned to Jim, a puzzled look on her face. "For a moment, I thought one of those dogs was DandyLady, but that's impossible. You retired her three years ago after she went Best of Opposite Sex here. She's probably sleeping on your bed at home."

"The best dog you ever sold us. We've loved having her, penchant for bathing in mud puddles and all."

Jim checked Breaker a final time and invited him down off the table. Breaker shook out, his tail whirring back and forth excitedly. He was still in a puppy cut, but his rich, chestnut coat was coming in nicely. Jim had scissored his growing mane the best he could. Usually poodles Breaker's age would be at home growing more coat to create the poodle's dramatic appearance, but what Breaker lacked in the showiness of a full coat, he made up for in the sparkle coming from inside. A poodle his age had never looked better, and he knew it. The glint in his eye fairly shouted "Step aside, boys. I'm here."

Benny looked back and forth between Breaker and McCreery, father and son. McCreery was in top form himself. The Historical Continental Clip suited him. His coat had enough gray mixed in to create a soft, warm undertone and conveyed an innate dignity and strength of character that came with age. Benny rested his hands on his stomach and pronounced confidently, "I think McCreery has a good chance, too."

McCreery's patience stretched only so thin, and he nudged Bess' arm. She tapped the grooming table with a metal comb and signaled him on board. "Feel like a snack while I'm finishing him off?" she asked Benny. "There's a row of concession stands along the far wall. You've got plenty of time."

He patted his stomach. The baby fat was almost gone. "Are you kidding? I couldn't swallow if my life depended on it."

After what seemed like an interminable wait, the P.A. blared out the first call for Standard Poodle dogs. Jim stuck out his hand and said, "Good luck, son." Then he hurried upstairs with Breaker.

Benny picked up the armband with McCreery's number and slid it up his arm. McCreery turned to look at him. They stared at each other deeply for a moment, as though reading each others' thoughts. Just like Benny's dog book said, some dogs and their people have special powers of communication. He and McCreery had proven it over and over, going back to when he had found McCreery sick and lying at the end of his dad's driveway.

He filled his lungs and eased the air out slowly like a leaky balloon. "This is it, big fella," he said and signaled McCreery forward. Bess fell in step alongside.

The noise rising from the crowd was so loud Benny thought half the people in New York must have come to watch. As they reached the portal to the stadium, his knees buckled slightly. McCreery looked back at him and tugged on the lead. No opening night jitters for this old champion; he was raring to go. It gave Benny the reassurance he needed. He straightened his tie, tucked in his stomach, and stepped inside.

Westminster Kennel Club! A tingling sensation traveled up McCreery's lead to the tips of Benny's fingers. He flexed them back and forth, reassured they were still working. The mundane smells of hotdogs and popcorn, human sweat and dog breath mingled with the residues of hope and loss. For a minute, he thought he might sneeze. Instead, his eyes were drawn upward. Row upon row of seats rose up to the ceiling, the highest so far away he could barely make them out, all filled with people wondering who would be chosen the finest dog in America. Somewhere in that crowd his father and Sonya were watching. He scanned the bleachers, knowing it would be a miracle if he could spot them.

A sudden flash of light caught his eye. A spotlight bounced off something shiny in the section for people who wanted the best view. He stopped, and McCreery stopped, too, wondering what could be holding them up. The dog didn't see what Benny saw: the distinguished man in a coat with a lambskin collar, the tall lady whose auburn hair fell in soft curls down her back. The flash came from a pin shaped like a lightning bolt that his Dad had given Sonya in a blue box last Chanukah. And then, unbelievably, he noticed a second woman sitting on his Dad's other side. Straight, sandy hair, so like his own, hung down around her face like a mantilla.

His arm shot into the air in a victory salute. They came, the three of them together, just like he had always dreamed. He knew the happiness wouldn't last, that it was just for tonight, but for tonight, life was almost perfect.

Bess tapped Benny's arm. He had forgotten she was there. She nodded to her right. A little group of reporters were gathered around Nancy Valentine dressed in a chartreuse silk suit. "The press love Nancy because she can give an interview in four languages," Bess whispered.

Benny recognized the CNN reporter with lots of hair holding the mike. The man posed a serious expression and signaled the camera man closer. "Ms. Valentine, what are your thoughts about the Standard Schnauzer? We hear he's the favorite."

Nancy smiled and flipped her elegant hands out to the side. "Gentlemen — and lady, how could I judge something like that, if you'll pardon my little pun." Every dog here's a champion — literally, and they seem to get more beautiful every year." She knew what she was talking about. Last year, she had been Westminster's Best in Show Judge.

Nancy waved Bess and Benny over. He tugged on the cuffs of his blazer and brushed the bangs off his forehead. "You remember Bess Rutledge — Umpawaug Kennels?" Nancy asked the reporter.

He gave Bess a toothy grin. "Yeah, sure."

Nancy put her hand on Benny's shoulder. "Here's the man you should be interviewing. Benny's taking in the senior half of the only father-son combination in Westminster history. Bess is the breeder-owner."

The reporter switched off the mike and ordered the camera man, "Get some footage of the kid with the old dog. I'll try to get it on the 10:00 o'clock news," he promised Nancy before moving on.

Nancy dabbed at her forehead, only half-feigning exhaustion, and turned to Bess. "There's lots of interest in the poodles this year. Fandango's drawing a lot of attention, and everyone's noticed Breaker's credentials, but wait until they see McCreery."

Benny's face lit up like a Broadway marquee. "I told you."

Bess avoided his eyes. Meeting those reporters, listening to Nancy, brought back her misgivings. She was taking a risk exposing the old champion's reputation to that kind of scrutiny.

Nancy misunderstood the doubts playing on Bess' face. She assumed they were about Benny. "If you took in McCreery yourself, you'd be the sentimental favorite. The judge would almost have to make it easy on himself and give you the win."

Benny felt heat rising up through his whole body. Everything he had worked for all these months, gone in a word? He sucked in a deep breath, fingers curled into a fist, and then, remembering himself, sighed it out slowly. He looked Bess in the eye. "Take Breaker. I'm the one who believes in McCreery, not you."

Bess turned to Nancy. "Benny's right. If it weren't for him — and my son David — I wouldn't be here. I know you mean well, but Benny's earned his chance. He'll take in McCreery."

Nancy watched the old woman, the boy, and the old dog stride determinedly toward the Standard Poodle ring. She shook her head and said to herself, "Wait till *Animal Planet* gets a hold of that story."

CHAPTER FIFTY-ONE

Bess found her seat between Holly and Nancy and opened the show catalogue to the section on Standard Poodles. She ran her finger down the pages, studying the dogs' parents and kennels. She peered over the top of her glasses at Nancy. "Have you noticed how many of McCreery's get are entered this year?" She flipped a couple of pages. "In fact, a whole slew of Umpawaug-bred poodles are on the premises."

"Mmm," Holly murmured. She pointed. "Here they come."

Twenty Standard Poodles lined up outside the ring. Fandango was at the head of the line and next came Chicory. Breaker and McCreery were at the end of the line. The judge called the class into the ring and ran everyone around twice before he divided them into two lines.

"McCreery's never looked better, Bess. If you ask me, he's a finer dog now than all those years ago at PCA," Nancy said.

The judge took his time examining each dog carefully. With each passing minute, the little tension knot in Bess' neck grew tighter. The longer he took, the harder it would be for Benny to hold himself together, not to mention the wear and tear on McCreery. The dog was no spring chicken in spite of how well he had gotten himself up for today.

After what seemed a lifetime, the judge joined the two halves together and told them to circle the ring. As the dogs passed by, he checked their numbers against notes he had written on a piece of paper and signaled some of them to one side. Chicory came out, then Fandango, then Breaker. A black dog Bess had sold as a puppy to his handler was next, followed by a silver and two other blacks she didn't know.

"I'm pretty sure Breaker's in the line he's planning to keep," Holly said.

"Don't count chickens," Bess warned, afraid to hope.

The judge studied the two lines carefully one more time. It seemed as though Breaker had made the cut. The judge started to walk away, then, almost as an afterthought, turned and pointed at McCreery.

The people in the grandstands began studying his pedigree in their catalogues. "That's who he is," the woman sitting in back of Bess told her companion.

Bess held her breath. Could Breaker and McCreery both have made the short list? In answer to her silent question, the judge waved the longer line off with a loud, "Thank you, everyone." Eight dogs were left on the short list — Breaker, McCreery, and Chicory among them.

"Do you think the judge recognizes McCreery?" Holly asked.

"How could he?" Nancy said, brushing an imaginary spot off her skirt. "McCreery hasn't been out in public for years. I imagine he's more curious about Benny."

One by one, the judge called out the eight remaining dogs and moved each one down, back and around the ring. Benny was resting McCreery at every opportunity the way Bess had taught him. She sat rigidly on the edge of her seat and reminded herself to breathe.

When the last dog had finished, the judge walked solemnly down the line. He paused when he came to

McCreery, and a few people in the stands began to clap. Apparently indifferent to the crowd, the judge continued his walk and waved Breaker, Chicory and Fandango forward. Jim and Breaker were at the head of the line.

"That's it for McCreery," Bess whispered when the judge ordered the five dogs in McCreery's line to circle the ring one more time. She figured he would wave them all off after this last chance to be seen. But no! As McCreery came around the last turn, the judge motioned him to the head of the line in front of Breaker. With a wave, he dismissed the other four dogs. Bess could hardly believe her eyes. Her two poodles were in the final four and a third was McCreery's get.

Nancy gave a quick look through her field glasses. Flashes were coming from cameras all around them. "At least the judge will be able to keep them all straight: a brown, a white, a black, and a brown in a hunting clip shown by a kid. The photographers love it."

"He's moved those dogs seven times already," Holly shouted over the clapping. "McCreery couldn't look better if you were showing him yourself, Bess."

The judge called out McCreery for another turn around the ring. The drill was the same as before: down and back and once around in a circle.

"Easy, Benny. Easy, son," Bess warned in a whisper, knowing how excited he must be. In a million years, she never thought she would be in this spot. Breaker had the youth and vitality to go the distance, but her heart — and the crowd's — was pulling for McCreery.

"Look at that magnificent animal! It's taken generations to bring the breed up to that level," the announcer stage-whispered into his microphone. It was strictly against tradition, but nobody could do anything about it now.

Next came Breaker. Jim moved him around the ring like they were floating, and then the whole performance was repeated with Chicory and Fandango. "I hope McCreery and Benny can hold out," Bess wished out loud.

Once more around the ring, and then the judge told Fandango and Chicory to step to the side. McCreery and Breaker stood alone in the ring, father and son.

The crowd cheered madly. Everybody knew they were watching the performance of a lifetime. Even the handlers who had been cut earlier clapped as the judge checked and rechecked the two dogs.

"Listen to that crowd. It's like they own stock in those two dogs," the announcer exclaimed with more than professional excitement.

"What a fabulous pair!" Hannah shouted over the din to anyone who could hear. Breaker had all the beauty of youth and generations of breeding behind him, but McCreery had the heart of a true champion and had stolen the affection of everyone in that great auditorium. When the judge moved him around the ring yet again, the announcer discarded the last of his professional composure and shouted, "I've never seen anything like it. Who are those dogs?"

"Either way, you've got a winner, Bess," Holly said. How could she say what everyone was thinking? Let it be McCreery.

Breaker's turn came again. He had never looked better. This was a great game to him, one he would love to win.

The judge called McCreery out again. "Take him down and back one more time," he ordered. Benny was holding himself together, his hunger to win written on his face, but the tightness around his mouth showed the effort he was making.

Holly stamped her foot. "What's the matter with that judge? Why doesn't he give it to McCreery?"

"McCreery's doing it all for you, Bess," Nancy shouted into her ear.

Benny signaled McCreery forward. The dog hesitated.

Benny signaled again. McCreery trotted a few paces, stopped, shook his coat in place, and started again.

From where she sat, Bess could see Benny's mouth moving, speaking encouragements. They trotted a few more yards, and McCreery stopped again. He turned. For a long moment, he studied Breaker thoughtfully. Then he gazed across the ring into the grandstand and stared straight at Bess. He puffed out a sigh and sat.

Benny swung around in front and yanked on the lead, as if he could bring his vanquished hopes back to life. "Come on, boy. You can do it," he pleaded, almost in tears, but McCreery remained immobile with a powerful determination of his own. He looked into Benny's eyes and tapped his paw insistently as though begging him to understand.

Benny nodded. He walked McCreery out of the ring.

"Let's hear it for number 19, Champion Umpawaug McCreery!" the announcer shouted — breaking the rules again by announcing his identity. "Twenty-five hundred of the world's finest dogs entered today, one hundred and twenty-five breeds from every state, and I'm here to tell you, we've seen a dog here today with a heart so big Westminster will never forget him."

Bess rushed from her seat and onto the floor. As soon as he saw her, McCreery's tail began beating slowly. "Rrrrrr," he welcomed softly.

Bess reached around his neck and laid her cheek on top of his head. "Dear, dear, McCreery," she whispered.

He wormed his head under her arm.

The hushed crowd burst into wild applause, and even the serene Nancy Valentine clapped until her hands were red. Over the roar of the crowd, the judge pointed at Breaker and yelled, "First!" but almost no one heard him.

"There are enough photographers on the floor to make a major. Everybody wants a picture of that poodle," Bess heard the announcer say. "First time in Westminster history they've given the runner-up a standing ovation." The man was so beside himself, he almost forgot to tell his listening audience that Breaker had beaten a Picture Perfect Pete daughter for Best of Breed. By the time he remembered, Bess and Benny had led McCreery downstairs and out of the limelight.

Chapter Fifty-Two

Almost as soon as they reached their spot in the grooming area, McCreery fell asleep on a comfortable mat. Benny and Bess sat on low folding chairs on either side of him.

After a few minutes, Benny turned to Bess and said in a hoarse whisper, "McCreery gave up on purpose. I'm sure as anything."

"I know," she said, her voice coarse with emotion. "He's older than the other dogs, but he's healthy. He could have kept going."

Benny cocked his head. "Then why? He wanted to win. I could feel it."

Bess coughed, choking back her feelings. "No, he wanted me to win. Breaker had the better chance, so he yielded to youth. He gave me back the chance at Best in Show I lost the day I retired him early."

A roar so loud it reached downstairs informed them it was time for the Non-Sporting Group. Eighteen different breeds as different from one another as a Bulldog and a Lhasa Apso would be judged against each other. Jim and Breaker would represent Standard Poodles.

Holly came rushing toward them from upstairs with a message from Jim. "You'd better go, Bess. Jim and Breaker are already lined up."

Bess studied the sleeping McCreery, a tangle of emotions written on her face. Part of her knew it would be foolishly sentimental to miss Breaker's big moment, but she was still concerned about McCreery. He had pushed himself hard for a dog his age, and didn't she owe it to him to stay? Still, Breaker's appearance in Group would probably be the closest an Umpawaug poodle would ever come to winning Westminster's top prize. Breaker had pulled off one miracle already tonight, and miracles seldom happened twice — especially to novices.

She waved a dismissive hand. "You go, Benny."

Benny and Holly glanced at each other furtively, as if they shared a secret. "You've waited your whole life for this, Bess," Holly said. "An Umpawaug poodle up for Group winner at Westminster! You've got to be there."

Benny straightened his tie and stuck out his chest. "I'll stay."

"Me, too," Holly added. "If anyone understands what this win means to you, it's McCreery. He's proven that tonight."

Bess still hesitated, like a cat approaching a puddle. As if to settle the matter, McCreery reached out and pawed at Bess in his sleep the way he did when it was time for a walk. She bent and ran her hand over his head. He breathed peacefully, barely stirring. She straightened up, tugging on the points of her shirt collar and pulling her jacket sleeves down over her cuffs.

Benny rocked on his heels and patted his stomach like he had just finished Thanksgiving dinner and winked at Holly. If Bess hadn't been so preoccupied, she might have wondered why.

Time passed slowly, but finally the clamor overhead swelled again. Moments later Bess hurried downstairs. She held her hand to her heart and gulped for breath. She started to speak, but the words wouldn't come.

"I knew it! Breaker's going to be in Best in Show!" Benny shouted, flinging his arms against his sides and bouncing on the balls of his feet.

Nancy Valentine came toward them almost as breathless as Bess. "Bess, they want you back upstairs right away for the official photograph. CNN, Animal Planet and all the foreign networks want to interview you as soon as the show's finished. Benny and McCreery, too. The four of you will end up on the cover of *Time*."

Holly looked embarrassed. "Nobody thought Breaker could beat the Dalmatian. I'm ashamed to say I wasn't sure myself."

"Breaker had the whole stadium in the palm of his hand. There would've been a riot if the judge hadn't picked him," Nancy said.

Holly turned to Bess. "You'd better go. The photographer's waiting, and they'll be calling for Best in Show any minute."

Bess hesitated and then she surprised her friends by saying, "You come, too, Benny. This is your moment as well as mine."

This time he didn't argue.

The photo only took a minute. The judge shook Bess' hand, then Jim's, and faded into the crowd. Overhead, the show steward called the Group winners to line up for Best in Show. Bess reached into Jim's breast pocket and slid out the grooming comb. It was almost like Jim expected it. He nodded silently and handed her the lead. He shook hands with her, then Benny, and slipped away. Now only the two of them, she and the boy, were left with Breaker. The dog stared up at her, still as stone, as if he knew the stakes were too high for foolishness.

She heard Benny clear his throat. He had to be wondering why she had sent Jim away and told him to stay. To her, the answer was obvious. If it hadn't been for Benny, there would be no Westminster.

She pushed her fingers through her bangs and rested the heel of her hand on her forehead as though struggling to hold in a startling thought. Here she was on the verge of the moment she had dreamed of all her life and she was thinking about Benny, not herself or even about winning. She was wondering whether he should be the one to take in Breaker. No longer a naive, clumsy boy barely in charge of himself, he had matured into a first-class handler. He had faced and conquered every challenge she had thrown at him from Housatonic to tonight. Didn't he deserve to be the one at the end of the lead at the most important moment of Breaker's career?

She no sooner permitted the thought than she shoved it away. She had worked her whole life for this moment. Benny was young. He would have other Westminsters ahead of him, wouldn't he? She deserved this one last chance, didn't she? The class wouldn't take long. She could manage.

Benny sensed her discomfort. He stepped closer. "You're wondering who should take in Breaker, aren't you?"

Tears welled in her eyes, and she nodded.

He patted her arm awkwardly. "You should."

She gasped and tried to catch her breath. "Really?"

"Don't you get it? That's what McCreery was telling you when he sat down in the ring. He wanted you to win, even if it meant letting Breaker be the one who did it. That's how much he loves you."

A shudder ran up her spine as her emotions threatened to overwhelm her. Benny reached to steady her, but she stepped back, signaling she was in control again. "You're sure?"

"Sure, I'm sure. I already got what I wanted tonight. I didn't tell you before, but my whole family's here. Together!"

She watched a warm flush appear in his cheeks and

knew he was telling the truth. "I'll do it."

"Good," he said, hitching up his pants. "I learned something from McCreery tonight, too. You don't have to come in first to be a winner. I'm going to find my own dream, like you found Westminster, and be a winner, too."

Bess' face grew dark and she drew herself up to her full five feet. Breaker studied her with anxious eyes, uncertain what it meant. She slipped him a liver treat and returned her attention to Benny. "Listen to me, Benny Neusner. You're a winner already. Other kids may be better at figuring out the area of an isosceles triangle or memorizing the capitals of Europe, but you're a first class handler. No other boy your age has ever done better, and no one can take that from you."

Benny straightened the knot on his tie and stood taller. "I guess you're right. McCreery and I are winners, no matter who took won the trophy." He rubbed his chin, considering, then broke into a smile. "Pretty good, huh? A poodle as jealous as McCreery letting Breaker get all the credit."

Bess looked fondly at the beautiful brown poodle beside her. "Pretty darn good."

She signaled with the lead and started walking toward the entranceway into the great stadium. Benny followed alongside her. She wasn't going to change her mind; it just felt right to be together.

When they reached the spot only the dogs and their handlers could enter, Benny turned to her with a wistful look. "I wanted McCreery to be the one, but I'm not sorry it's Breaker." He squeezed the puppy's muzzle, careful not to mess up his coat. He hesitated, blushed, and leaned in to kiss her cheek. "Good luck, Bess," he said, and hurried off as if on a mission.

Breaker shook his coat into place and pawed the ground like a thoroughbred race horse at the starting gate. "Come on, big fella," she said. She squared her shoulders, drew a deep breath, and headed for her place in line.

The other six Group winners were already lined up and waiting: the Shetland Sheepdog for Herding, the Standard Schnauzer for Working, a Wire Haired Dachshund, the Gordon Setter for Sporting, a Fox Terrier and the Japanese Chin for Toys. Each dog was a champion many times over. Any one deserved to be proclaimed the winner tonight.

The handlers of the Gordon Setter and the Fox Terrier made a space for her between them and everyone, dogs and handlers, faced forward as on command. The buzz of anticipation grew in the packed stadium, and then suddenly Madison Square Garden was plunged into darkness and a deep voice called out to the crowd. "Ladies and gentlemen. I give you the seven Group winners. Go ahead, clap your hearts out for your favorite."

A spotlight zoomed in on the entranceway, and a show official tapped the Shetland Sheepdog's handler on the shoulder and urged him into the ring. The spotlight found him and the crowd erupted. Matching his pace to the dog's, the handler trotted around the ring, the glare of the spotlight tracing their once-in-a-lifetime journey. They came back to their marker, and the Standard Schnauzer began his circle around the ring. The Gordon Setter followed. The dog's whole body was electric with anticipation. At the end of the lead, Breaker was feeling it too. Bess whispered a reassuring word and watched as the Gordon Setter completed his turn. The next moment she felt herself being pushed forward into the big stadium.

At first, the glare from the spotlight was so strong she had trouble taking in her surroundings, but as her eyes adjusted, they were powerfully drawn to the gold and purple medallion in the middle of the dark green carpet with the Westminster logo. WKC was emblazed in purple letters tall enough to read from the uppermost bleachers. This was it! The spot she had aimed for all her life. Her heart was beating as fast as if she had run a marathon. Westminster was everything she had dreamed of and more.

She licked the thin patina of sweat off her upper lip and circled the ring toward the seven gold markers for each of the seven group winners. A bouquet of yellow chrysanthemums stood beside each one. She halted when she came to the one with "Non-Sporting" written in purple letters. The spotlight left her and moved on to the Terrier. She pulled out a comb and began touching up Breaker's coat while they waited.

In no time, the seven group winners were in place beside their markers and once again the spotlight returned to the entranceway. The announcer presented the judge over the P.A., and, probably like all the other handlers, Bess recognized her name. She raised Toy Poodles on the West Coast and had judged PCA in the past, but how would that play out tonight? Like the judges of the earlier classes, she was dressed in formal attire. Two show stewards dressed in tuxedos escorted her on either side like double fathers in a bridal procession. Rosy sequins shimmered every time she moved, and no one could doubt this was a lady with definite tastes. She stopped for a moment at the judge's table, glancing at the huge purple and gold ribbon and the silver cups for the winner. Then peeling off the two stewards, she began her stroll down the line of markers, pausing momentarily before each dog.

The audience fell silent as a church. Even the peddlers hawking their wares grew quiet. Every handler was keenly aware of each flick of her eye, every muscle twitch. The dogs stood at attention, too, ears pricked, coats polished, eyes sparkling, feet ready to spring into motion. The judge's brilliant smile let everyone in Madison Square Garden know that a more perfect group of dogs had never been assembled before in one spot. Then, her silent march over, she swung her hand out over the ring and signaled the dogs to circle once around.

The crowd came alive again with a roar as each of the seven Group winners passed in front of the judge. Bess caught a glimpse of the Gordon Setter trotting along determinedly in front of her, a symphony of health and youth. She vaguely recalled hearing that this same judge had given him Best in Show once before in Tampa. The Fox Terrier was coming up on her heels — a very good specimen of the breed, a dog everybody downstairs was talking about. The others followed in order until finally even the tiny Japanese Chin had found his marker again, and the judge signaled the Old English Sheep Dog to come forward to be inspected.

Disappointed it wasn't his turn, Breaker tugged on his lead, prancing in place. Bess leaned in and whispered. "Be patient. It won't be long now."

A roar of approval erupted from the crowd as the judge finished her hands on inspection and ordered the Old English Sheep Dog down to the end of the ring and back. In spite of its size, the dog could really move! The handler did a wonderful job of presenting him, but the judge must have noticed the dog broke a little coming back down. Tonight even one tiny flaw could make the difference. He came around the ring and took his place again at his marker.

Two more dogs to go, and then Breaker's turn would come. Bess kept her all attention on Breaker, willing him to stay focused on her. She hardly noticed what was happening a few feet away as the Standard Schnauzer and then the Gordon Setter circled the ring.

At last she heard the Non-Sporting winner called out, and she and Breaker stepped forward. The crowd fell into a watchful silence as the judge inspected Breaker from every angle. Jim had put him down perfectly, but so had the handlers of all the other dogs. Bess pushed the thought out of her mind and concentrated on the moment.

"Take him down to the end of the ring and back," the judge ordered, pointing to the route the other group winners had taken.

The entire Madison Square Garden held its collective breath as Bess and Breaker turned to face the far end of the ring. This was their moment of destiny: hers as well as his. "Here we go, big fella," she whispered, flexing her fingers. She took a deep breath and off they went. Even from the end of the lead, she could see he was breathtaking. All she had to do was keep up. He had never shown like this for anyone else — not once! He was giving his all for her, and the crowd knew it.

They reached the far edge of the ring and pivoted to make the return. The crowd fell silent again. Bess would need to push herself a little now so Breaker could reach his full stride. She readied herself, head held high, and signaled him forward. A lightness came over her body as she stretched her legs out, toes hitting the ground delicately and springing back into the air. For a few magical moments, she and Breaker were moving together, in tune as experienced lovers. The wind sang in her ears, and then, suddenly, the music turned to gasps as she fell to the ground, pulling Breaker down with her.

The silence was deafening.

By the time Jim reached her side, Breaker was licking her face anxiously.

"Don't stand there," she snapped. "Help me up."

"Are you all right? Maybe we shouldn't try to move you."

"Don't be ridiculous. My bad knee went out, that's all. Being a damn fool's not fatal."

Jim helped Bess to her feet while everyone in Madison Square Garden, not to mention the millions watching on TV and webcasts all over the world, waited. As she took her first tentative step forward, the crowd clapped politely.

Jim pointed to a folding chair someone had set up on the sidelines. "Here, sit," he ordered, easing her into it. She leaned back and closed her eyes.

Applause rocked stadium, and she jerked into upright awareness. Apparently, she had dozed. She turned in time to see the judge hand the Standard Schnauzer the heavy trophy. Jim was waiting beside her, but Breaker was gone. Presumably someone had taken him back to his crate. She started to ease herself up. "Well, that's it. Time to round everybody up and head for bed."

Jim pushed her back gently. "Absolutely not. You sit here and rest. I'll get the dogs and bring you over to the Waldorf in our car. Benny's staying the night with his dad and stepmother, so you don't have to worry about him."

She was too tired to argue and grateful someone else was taking charge. Her whole body ached with fatigue and all she wanted was sleep. There would be time enough tomorrow for regrets, but not for second guessing. She had lost her chance for Best in Show through her own actions, but she had made the right choice. Umpawaug poodles made great champions because of their love for their owners, as McCreery had proven to the world tonight. She had acknowledged his gift by taking his son in for Best in Show herself, no matter what the cost.

She must have dozed again because she was awakened by a voice blaring over the loudspeaker, summoning the dispersing crowd back to their seats. "Ladies and gentleman, we have a special treat tonight. The Westminster Kennel Club and The Poodle Club of America have joined together to present a special tribute. Dog lovers everywhere, I give you Bess Rutledge — the woman who has done the most to improve one of the most popular breeds in America."

A spotlight zoomed in on her, making dark spots jump in front of her eyes. Holding her hand up like a visor, she followed the spotlight to the far corner of the stadium.

From out of the darkness strode McCreery, tremendously proud of himself, with Benny at the end of his lead. And that was only the beginning. Behind McCreery came two of his Best-in-Show get — Playing It Cool led by Felix and Tender Trap led by Nancy Valentine. Close behind them came Holly and Jim with DandyLady and three more of McCreery's championship off-spring — one in each hand — followed by two each of their champion puppies, and so on and so forth, all the way out to Hannah with Crumpet and Chicory, until, finally, Breaker brought up the rear alone. An Umpawaug pedigree come to life before her eyes. In the places where the dogs' names would be written, stood the living, breathing animals — generations of fathers, mothers, and offspring — fanned out across Madison Square Garden like the family tree in the front of an old Bible.

The roar of the crowd grew to a crescendo as McCreery came to a halt at her feet. "Rrrrrur," he greeted.

"Sit," Benny ordered, but McCreery bounded up on his hind legs and placed his paws on Bess' shoulders. She wrapped her arms around his neck and pressed her nose into his coat. The lavender scent of the shampoo she had washed him with the night before — a lifetime ago — filled her like coming home after a long journey. "You've done well," she whispered. She lingered a moment, the applause reverberating in her ears. Then she lifted McCreery's paws off her shoulders and urged him back down on the ground.

"You didn't have a clue, right?" Benny asked, a grin like a half moon lighting his face.

She looked up at him, his big frame dwarfing hers. For the first time, she noticed a little peach fuzz on his chin. "Not one."

"It was all of us — David, too."

Her eyes followed the spotlight as it moved back out

into the ring where her friends stood waiting. Imagine them keeping a secret like that — especially from Mona. Her twin sister couldn't have known. She would have given the surprise away for sure. Thinking about Mona, she imagined that her sister *was* there, sharing in it, but the feeling flickered away as fast as it came.

"Laaa-dees and gentlemen," the announcer boomed again. "Let's hear it one more time for Bess Rutledge and Umpawaug Kennels."

Benny puffed out his chest and found his place again at the top of the pyramid. McCreery shook his coat back into place, and they were ready to go.

Bess raised her hand in a silent blessing as McCreery stretched to the end of his lead, head held high. In close pursuit, Playing It Cool and Judge Me Perfect led the top half of the pedigree, while Breaker brought the bottom half safely home. Behind them, yards and yards of puppies fanned out across a ring as big as a football field. Sixty-five champion Standard Poodles, all coming down from McCreery.

It was a sight she would never forget, not as long as she lived.

Author's Note

*A*lmost Perfect grew out of my imagination during the dinners I was privileged attend at the home of Dr. Sam and Mary Peacock during the Annual Poodle Club of America shows. This happened back in the 1970s when PCA was an elegant affair held outdoors in the rolling hills of Pennsylvania. In addition to Mary and Sam, other legends of the poodle world included Wendell Sammet, Jackie Hungerland and Rebecca "Beck" Mason. Over dinner, Beck and Jackie Hungerland, encouraged by the others, described their dream of establishing a brilliant line of brown Standard Poodles. Their hopes were never realized in the flesh, but hopefully the traits and beauty of the brown Standards they wished to preserve are captured in McCreery and his offspring Breaker.

Like the Standard Poodles of the fictitious Umpawaug Kennels, all persons and events are the product of my imagination. Any resemblance to any person, living or dead, is purely coincidental. When a real name is used such as Westminster or The Poodle Club of America, the specific events described are fictitious and liberties were taken with details like dates and places to suit a dramatic purpose.

I have tried to be accurate in describing the way dog shows are run and points are won; any errors are unintended and the fault is mine. My apologies if I have offended any of the hardworking and devoted men and women who spend their time, money and love breeding and showing beautiful dogs of all breeds. No disrespect is intended to the real dogs that actually participate in Westminster.

Many people helped in the writing and reviewing of this book. Chris Bulba, who accomplished the challenging feat of winning Obedience at PCA in 1992 gave me early encouragement. My fellow members of The Bluebonnet Poodle Club also were generous with their time and knowledge. Among this group very special thanks goes to Sherri Smith, a skilled writer/editor and leading breeder of miniature poodles, who helped me traverse the technicalities behind the shows depicted. Barbara Skjonsby brought her keen insight and good eye to a final edit.

Many friends read various drafts of the novel including author/illustrator Berthe Amoss, Renee Casbergue, Mylene Dressler, Diane Hammer, M.D., Susan Howard, Holly Guran McAlary, Millicent Neusner, Linda Siemers and Beth Willinger. The Magenta Writer's Group in Ajijic, Mexico provided support: Marci Bowman, Nina Discombe, Margie Keane, Judy Lacy, Rachel McMillan, and Ada Robinson. Special thanks to Carol Gale Myers for her quick wit and enthusiasm. The Algonkian Group that met in Harper's Ferry with Michael Neff, The William Faulkner Pirate's Alley Society's Words and Music Festival, and Aviva Ehrlich, Robert Guinsler, and Eugene Winick all encouraged me when my book was in its early stages. Jeff Chalkley, DVM, provided veterinary expertise. Special thanks, too, to my literary agent Claudia Cross and Michael Sterling of Folio Literary Management.

My own standard poodles over the years, Miranda, Star, Mister, and now Miss-Tee, have taught me that poodles need love, care, space to run and human patience beyond the usual. They are sociable, high maintenance, and frequently naughty. They do not do well being left home alone in the house or apartment all day. They are not ideal pets for everyone who wants a dog.

ALMOST PERFECT
BOOK CLUB GUIDE

1. Benny's father believes dog shows are nothing more than "beauty pageants," more to show off the people than the dogs. In what way do the people and dogs in the book support or refute that opinion?

2. Both Benny and Bess have difficult relationships with their blood relatives. Why are this teenage boy and this seventy year-old woman able to connect with their different ages and backgrounds when their own parent/child relationships are so difficult?

3. Parents' expectations of their children can influence the direction of their children's development. How did Benny's and David's parents' expectations affect them? Steffie's mother and Steffie?

4. Children like Benny and Steffie are described as "special." What unique qualities compensate for their "specialness."

5. Kate tells David that Benny must learn to accept his mother for who she is and not hope to change her. Is that good advice?

6. What explains the strong and immediate connection between David and Benny?

7. Dr. Kate acknowledges she has her own problems in committing to a romantic relationship with David. How does this affect her professional ability to help others, including Benny and Bess?

8. Autistic children are described as being "on the spectrum" suggesting a wide difference in characteristics of children diagnosed with that disorder. The boy in *The Curious Incident of the Dog in the Night*, for example, is described as autistic and yet is different in many ways from Benny. The criteria in the *Diagnostic and Statistical Manual* that Steffie and her mother study closely have recently changed to be more inclusive. Would it have been more helpful for Benny's dad to pay greater attention to his son's diagnosis? What about Steffie's mother?

9. What explains the attraction between Benny and Steffie? How do their respective strengths compensate for each other's weaknesses? They promise to love each other for ever. Is that possible at their ages?

10. The relationship between adult children and their parents can be complicated. How is the relationship between David and Bess typical? Unusual? David disappoints his mother on the most important day of her life and stays with Kate instead. Was that the right choice? What does it say about him?

11. Bess suspects that she and Kate have more in common than meets the eye, maybe even more than she and Mona in some ways. Is she right? David says he knows

better than to discuss his mother with a Freudian. Even though Kate and David are not married, Kate and Bess seem to navigate some of the potential pitfalls for mothers- and daughters-in-law. How do they manage that?

12. The book takes place in the early 1990s. What would be different if the events took place today?

13. Bess and Mona disagree about the smallest things, yet have the profoundest love for one another. Why is Benny an exception, so that both women can agree about him? Does the fact that they are twins make them different from other siblings?

14. David and Bess credit Mona with nurturing David and helping him become the man he is. How unusual is it for a third party, whether relative, teacher or friend, to make a significant impact on a child's development?

15. Steffie appears to have changed without the benefit of a specific therapist's or adult's help. Is the confidence she displays as she heads off to boarding school genuine? Have other "resilient" individuals in literature or life overcome difficult childhoods and even gone on to become super-achievers?

16. How does Bess' friendship with Benny permit her to do what she had wanted to do all her life but failed — make a try for Best in Show at Westminster?

17. At the end of the book, Benny's dad has changed his view of his son. How did that happen? Was Benny's success in the show ring the only reason?

18. Benny and Bess appear to be deeply affected by McCreery's sacrifice at Westminster. Can a dog understand his owner so deeply that he would substitute his judgment for the handler's? Can an animal really alter a human's character?

19. Bess appears to be different at the end of the book, but can people really change at her age?

20. How does Benny's experience with McCreery and Breaker change him? Is the change going to be permanent?

SUGGESTIONS FOR FURTHER READING

Marley and Me by John Grogan
The Curious Incident of the Dog in the Night Time by Mark Haddon
Seabiscuit by Laura Hillenbrand
House Rules by Jodi Picoult
The Art of Racing in the Rain by Garth Stein

Diane Daniels Manning is the co-founder and director of The New School in the Heights, a therapeutic school in Houston, Texas which helps children dealing with socialemotional challenges find succes in school and life. She has a Ph.D. in Education and a post-doctoral M.P.H from Harvard and is a practicing child psyhoanalyst certified by the American Psychoanalytic Association. Formerly, she was the Director of the Reading and Learning Disabilities Clinic at Tufts University, Lecturer and Research Associate in the Department of Behavioral Sciences at Harvard, and Chair of the Department of Education at Tulane University. She learned the inner workings of dog show kennels by writing an authorized oral history of a lifetime President of the Poodle of Club of America. Her writing awards include the Faulkner-Wisdom Novella Prize and the Women in Film and Television Short Script Competition.

When not at The New School, Diane and her writing partners, a Standard Poodle named Misty and a rescue cat named Elvira, convene at the keyboard to share great thoughts and plan the dinner menu.

For further information about the author and to learn how Almost Perfect can become part of the fund-raising plan for your 501c3 charitable organization, please visit www.dianedanielsmanning.com.

Made in the USA
Lexington, KY
23 May 2014